D1631474

THE INN AT SHADOW LAKE

THE INN AT SHADOW LAKE

JANET EDGAR

THORNDIKE
CHIVERS

This Large Print edition is published by Thorndike Press, Waterville, Maine, USA, and by BBC Audiobooks Ltd, Bath, England.
Thorndike Press, a part of Gale, Cengage Learning.
Copyright © 2006 by Janet Edgar.
The moral right of the author has been asserted.

The text of this Large Print edition is unabridged.
Other aspects of the book may vary from the original edition.
Set in 16 pt. Plantin.
Printed on permanent paper.

LIBRARY OF CONGRESS CATALOGING-IN-PUBLICATION DATA

Edgar, Janet.
    The Inn at Shadow Lake / by Janet Edgar.
      p. cm. — (Thorndike Press large print Christian mystery)
    ISBN-13: 978-1-4104-0552-4 (hardcover : alk. paper)
    ISBN-10: 1-4104-0552-4 (hardcover : alk. paper)
    1. Terrorists — Fiction. 2. Large print books. I. Title.
    PS3605.D456I55 2008
    813'.6—dc22   2007047487

BRITISH LIBRARY CATALOGUING-IN-PUBLICATION DATA AVAILABLE

Published in 2008 in the U.S. by arrangement with Harlequin Books S.A.

Published in 2008 in the U.K. by arrangement with Harlequin Enterprises II B.V.

U.K. Hardcover: 978 1 405 64484 6 (Chivers Large Print)
U.K. Softcover: 978 1 405 64485 3 (Camden Large Print)

Printed in the United States of America
1 2 3 4 5 6 7 12 11 10 09 08

Trust in the Lord with all your heart, and lean not on your own understanding. In all your ways, acknowledge Him, and He shall direct your paths.

— *Proverbs* 3:5–6

To Richard,
I dedicate this book to you for all the incredible adventures you have taken me on and for all the adventures we have traveled together. I love you and thank God for our life together.

ACKNOWLEDGMENTS

Thank you to my husband, Richard, for encouraging me to pursue my dream of writing women's fiction. Your unwavering support has and always will mean so much to me. To our children, Sandi and Scott, thank you for always believing in your mom. I love you. And thanks to Mom and Dad and family in New York for your love and encouragement along the way.

To all my writing sisters — what a blessing you have been! There are so many names that come to mind, I can't possibly list you all. You are members of ACFW, FHL, RWA, CRW, HODRW, KOD, NWHRWA, OVRWA, COFW, the AOL Boards, eHarlequin, the Love Inspired Authors loop and the Heart and Soul loop, where we have the best cyberwriting retreats *ever.* You know who you are. You've critiqued my chapters, prayed with and encouraged me when I was about to give up, cheered with me even when we finaled in the same writing contests. I thank God every day for you and for the road He's allowing me to travel as I work toward establishing my writing career.

Thank you to Executive Editor Joan Marlow Golan, who almost made me fall off my chair at an editor appointment in Houston, Texas, when you asked for everything I'd ever written and then told me I should give a workshop on how to pitch a book!

Thanks also to my editor, Diane Dietz, whose voice I heard when I received The Call, and who always encourages me to ask any questions I may have as I learn the process of how a book is published.

A special thank-you also to my agent, Danielle Egan-Miller and everyone at Browne & Miller Literary Associates in Chicago, for believing in me and my works, and cheering me on.

ONE

Zach Marshall instinctively ducked and yanked the steering wheel to the right after a sudden blast of gunfire rippled across his back window. The eerie sound of the bulletproof glass taking the impact of the shots rang through his ears.

In his peripheral vision, he noted a man and woman with guns blazing from the black van coming up fast alongside him. Muttering under his breath, Zach expertly maneuvered his vehicle as another barrage of bullets flew past his 4×4.

His cover was blown.

He aimed the truck into the thick cover of tall western red cedars typical of the Pacific Northwest, cut the lights and did a three-sixty. Zach reached for the subcompact .40 Glock he kept tucked in his shoulder holster. He steered the truck back onto the narrow logging road and positioned it so he was now on the bumper of the black van.

11

Memorizing the license plate number, he floored the gas pedal and lowered the driver's window. Gun in hand, he took quick aim and fired off a few shots, hitting one wheel. Despite the flat tire he caused, the van shot forward with a sudden burst of energy and disappeared into the damp, dark night.

The engine of Zach's 4×4 sputtered, the result of a couple of hits to the gas tank. Thankful it didn't explode, Zach turned the engine off with a twist of the key, and allowed the car to coast.

At least *one* objective had gone according to plan. He'd finally drawn a remnant of the enemy out of their hiding place.

Someone was onto him.

But who?

Three days later

"I'm en route to the inn now." Zach glanced out the driver's window, scanning the dark blur of trees that obscured the edges of the interstate.

Was another shooter hunkered down in the trees, training his scopes on the car? On him? He adjusted the speaker volume of the cell phone mounted to his dashboard. "Any leads on that license plate number I gave you?"

"Just that the van was stolen," Senior Agent in Charge John Castlerock answered. "No surprise there."

"What about prints? Did we find anything?" Zach asked.

"Sorry, Marshall. Clean as a whistle. Wish I had better news for you, buddy."

"Yeah, I figured as much. Those two knew what they were doing." Zach ran a hand through his hair and studied the county road in front of him. "At least the plan is working. I'm drawing them out in the open."

"Right. But a lot sooner than we thought. You want Agent Robbins to meet you at the inn?"

"Not yet." His gaze moved back and forth from the road to the tall trees typical of Washington State. "Let me get a feel for the place first. I'll let you know."

Adrenaline rushed through Zach like wildfire in a wind gust when he thought about the attempt on his life. The protection of the special glass and his quick maneuvering of the unmarked FBI vehicle on the empty logging road had saved his life the other night. That and luck. Or divine intervention. It had been a long time since Zach talked to God. Yet even he recognized God's saving hand.

He didn't want it. Or deserve it.

Placing his life on the line was a daily drill on this assignment. Especially the past couple of years. Drawing all factions of the enemy into one location was exactly what the Bureau had intended. The opposition would be on his tail for the duration. But time was running out. The agency's most recent intelligence reports indicated something big was going down. And soon.

"We're close, John. I can feel it. Let the team know I'll initiate an encounter with Julie before the night is over." With a sense of numb disbelief, Zach's thoughts raced back to the young woman he'd fallen in love with during his last semester of grad school. Disappointment sat heavily in his gut.

Could Julie Anderson, his old college flame, really be one of their prime suspects — a spy, selling national security secrets to terrorist organizations? Hard to believe the girl he'd fallen in love with and the criminal they sought were one and the same person. Maybe it was time they met again, under entirely different circumstances and with a whole new set of rules.

He'd seen the damning evidence of numerous calls placed from an unlisted number somewhere inside Shadow Lake Inn to several internationally known Russian terrorist supporters. "Once I check in, running into Julie will be a snap."

"Good. Your history with her might be just what we need to crack this case. I don't think she'll suspect you, but don't take any chances."

"Yep." Zach understood why the Bureau wanted to take advantage of their past relationship. But he didn't have to like it. "When we split eight years ago, it wasn't exactly on the best of terms."

"You were going to marry her, right?"

"Affirmative." Zach's heart filled with bittersweet memories of the deep love he'd had for Julie. And how she'd refused his proposal. He'd sped away on his Harley so quickly, he'd never heard her explanation. "It didn't work out." He kept an air of indifference in the tone of his voice. No need for the Bureau to figure out how devastated he'd been by her reaction. They already knew too much.

"Don't let any old emotions influence what you have to do. Sweet-talk her, Marshall." John chuckled. "I've seen you in action."

"Right." Zach drew a quick breath. He would take extraordinary measures to protect the lives and freedoms of the American

15

people. All the agents he worked so closely with the past few years would, too. "You know I'll do whatever it takes."

"I'm counting on it. We can't afford slipups. Not with this bunch."

"You don't have to convince me." Zach's resolve hardened. His cover was blown. He needed to be more focused than ever. At their last meeting, John had hinted that Special Agent Richard "Tommy" Tomasino might have gone over to the other side. The last thing the unit needed was having a member turn. Muttering under his breath, Zach recalled the image of the woman firing her semiautomatic weapon from the passenger side of the black van. "Do we have any leads on the identity of the female shooter?"

"Negative. Our sources indicate that Yuri's wife, Katya, was just seen in Moscow the day of your encounter." John drew a quick breath. "She'd be our first guess. We're still checking our sources on that one. I find it hard to believe she wouldn't join her husband here in the States for what they're planning. Too bad you didn't get a better look."

"Not much to see with their faces covered in black ski masks. Except for that piece of gray hair sticking out from her knitted cap."

16

"Don't sweat it. I'm looking over a list of other suspects now," John replied. "We'll handle it from our end."

"Yeah well, keep me posted. I like to know who's trying to kill me."

"Don't blame you. I'll update Robbins. What do you need from her?"

"Detailed background checks on Julie's friends and associates, everything within the past eight years." Zach paused for a moment, his eyes scanning the heavily wooded area along the road. "Check the file we have on her late husband, see if he was a part of this before his death."

"Got it."

Zach blew out a long, deep breath. "I also want a full report on the British woman Julie hired six months ago. She could be the international connection we've been looking for. Maybe even our shooter."

"She's on our short list. I'll get the ball rolling and make contact with you at the resort."

"Where are you, John? What's your cover? When is your ETA?"

"You'll see me soon enough." John's words were followed by an ominous silence. "I need to fill you in on some new circumstances."

"What new circumstances?"

No response. John had already hung up. Great. Just what they needed. More surprises. As if the recent attempt on his life and sudden disappearance of Agent Tomasino weren't enough. Steeling his resolve, Zach let it go for now. He had his own problems. Winning Julie's trust was just one of them.

He planned to use their shared grief — Julie's loss of a husband, his loss of a wife and daughter — to bring them close again. Opening up to her, revealing his sorrow, his unspoken guilt, would be difficult. He hadn't shared that deep inner part of himself with anyone.

Zach muttered a series of curses under his breath and slammed a hand against the wheel. What kind of man had he become to even consider using such coldhearted tactics against a woman he'd once cared for so deeply?

But someone had almost killed him a few days ago and that changed things. He would do anything to gain Julie's confidence, to pump her for as much information as possible, to keep the bad guys from going for the kill again and from pulling off another horrendous crime against innocent Americans.

The truck's powerful engine rumbled

loudly as he continued the drive north to Shadow Lake Inn. Windshield wipers slid vigorously across the waterlogged glass of his replacement vehicle as the heavy rain continued its deluge.

Rain.

Like the sound of a metronome, the rhythmic resonance of the wipers pulled his memory into the past. Zach's mind drifted back four years, to the last time he saw his late wife and daughter. His little girl would be in kindergarten this year if not for that horrible accident.

Images of Ashley's empty crib the night he'd flown back from an intense Special Ops assignment flooded his memory. Visions forever embedded in his mind resurfaced from that stormy, rainy night. Stuffed animals lying on the mattress where she played with them hours before, the tiny pair of bloodstained sneakers she wore when she died.

If only he'd been home instead of on a mission with the SEALs. Maybe he could've persuaded his wife Lisa to stay put, instead of driving in the torrential rainstorm she'd driven in that day. If only he'd been there for them. His gut tightened.

If only God had been there for them.

Zach adjusted the rearview mirror and

checked the roadway behind him. Dark gray clouds loomed low on the horizon. In the distance, lightning flashed. A deep sense of loss burned in his heart. No more looking back.

He needed to keep a cool edge to solve the international case of espionage and terrorism he'd been assigned. If he didn't focus, he wouldn't live to see the results of his hard work. If he were a praying man as he used to be, now would be a good time to start talking to the Man Upstairs.

But it was too late for him and God.

There was no room in Zach's heart for faith.

No place in his life for memories.

Julie Anderson dragged the cardboard box along the dusty floor of the old attic. Ignoring the stuffy surroundings of the dimly lit room, she pulled the carton toward her. Thunder rolled and heavy rain pounded the roof, charging the confined area with electric tension.

Julie set the box down in the muted glare of the small bulb and rubbed her arms in an attempt to warm herself. The image of the dead body she'd stumbled on during her morning walk two weeks ago still burned deeply in her mind's eye. Paul, the groundskeeper of the inn, dead, his body cold, his blood pooling on the grassy spot under the tall spruce trees. Julie shook her head and whispered a prayer she'd uttered many times over the past week.

God, please. Take that memory from my heart and mind.

Angry over the still-unsolved murder, Julie vowed to overcome her dislike of small spaces to find the photographs in the attic. Maybe they held a clue to the identity of the killer.

The homicide detectives had come up with nothing on the brutal slaying. The police, hinting she was a possible suspect, seemed to be at a standstill in their investigation. How could they even *think* of her as the murderer? Using her cell phone, she had reported the crime to them herself.

Once she'd stopped screaming.

Taking a deep breath, Julie opened the dusty flaps of the old box that held all her photo albums. She peered inside. Would five-month-old photos from the inn's employee day provide her with a clue to the murder?

Suddenly heart palpitations squeezed inside her chest. She wasn't sure if the storm, the spooky attic, or the homicide at her beloved lodge caused her trembling. An old board creaked and she turned to look behind her. Why did she feel as if someone was watching her? Another wave of chills ran through her body and she shivered. The musty odor reminded her of the old shed at her grandparents' farm.

Were childhood memories haunting her again?

Julie prayed for God's presence to encircle her. *Lord, help me not to give in to old fears.* Heavy rain beat a relentless rhythm against the roof and a fierce wind whistled through the old wallboards. Wanting to run from the small space, Julie forced herself to stay. She took a deep, calming breath and then pulled an album from the box.

As soon as her fingers touched the soft velveteen cover, she knew the navy blue album in her hands was not the one for which she'd been searching. This one was older. How long had it been since she went through the old college scrapbook?

A brilliant flash of lightning cast eerie shadows on the wooden plank ceiling, revealing clusters of creepy cobwebs. An explosive clap of thunder echoed behind the flash of light, shaking the very floor on which she sat.

Not willing to stay in the confining space any longer, Julie decided to take the carton with her and look for the employee album in the safety of her office.

Making her way toward the ladder, she shut off the light, wondering for the hundredth time why she felt as if someone was watching her. She turned toward the tiny window and the sound of the howling wind, and swallowed hard. Did she really think she could solve a murder investigation on her own? But the detectives had been more secretive than ever the past few days. She couldn't wait any longer.

The next few months would make or break the future of Shadow Lake Inn. She'd worked nonstop to keep the inn running the past few years. Julie wouldn't let anything get in the way of its success. Not even a murder.

Saying a quick, silent prayer and shaking the uneasiness from her heart, Julie stood and promised herself she would solve the investigation on her own.

The floor creaked under her boots when she walked and another loud crash of thunder rumbled against the roof. Luminescent lightning cast a sinister glow across the attic revealing a small, ancient-looking little doorway she had never noticed before. Funny. Why hadn't she seen that tiny entryway until now?

Maybe she'd call Nick and ask him to look at it the next time he paid a visit, or surprised her again with an impromptu trip up from Seattle. He'd been so sweet, helping to fix things around the lodge since Paul's death.

Julie gripped the box in one arm and made her way down the tall ladder that led to and from the old tower room. Another crash of thunder shook the inn. The heel of her designer boot caught on one of the lower wooden rungs. Losing her balance, Julie dropped the box and held on to the wobbly ladder. The cardboard container flipped over and fell, scattering several photos along the old oak flooring of the corridor beneath her. Holding on for dear life, Julie prayed she wouldn't meet the same fate.

"Whoa!" Strong, muscular arms settled around her waist and guided her down the ladder. "You okay? You almost took a nasty tumble." A man's deep voice rumbled gently against the back of her neck, his breath warm on her cheek. Gently turning her around in his arms, his gaze connected with hers. Familiar steel-blue eyes widened in surprised recognition. "Julie?"

Swallowing hard, her gaze flew to the familiar face of her college sweetheart, Zach

24

Marshall. She forgot about the storm thundering overhead, the murder at the inn and the narrow escape of falling from the ladder. Her heart reeled with a sudden rush of sweet memories.

Zach's good looks, tall lean body and mischievous grin had attracted her initially all those years ago. But his honesty and charm had won her heart. One slow smile from Zach and she was over the moon. And when he kissed her . . .

"Julie!" Chuckling lightly, a slow grin lit his face. "Is it really you?"

Julie swallowed and fought to still the dizziness as the passageway began to swirl around her. She blinked and cleared her mind, yet there he was standing before her. "Z-Zach?"

"Yeah," he answered, chuckling again. "I never thought I'd run into anyone I knew . . . way out here." His intense gaze held hers. "Hey, you sure you're all right?" he asked, his voice deep and low. "You're shaking."

"Yes." He stood merely inches away, his strong arms still lightly placed around her waist. Her hands rested on his cotton shirt. His steady heartbeat pulsed against her fingers. "I'm fine," she managed, gazing into his eyes.

He let her down until she stood on solid ground. Slowly lowering her hands from Zach's hard, muscular chest, she pulled her gaze from his and turned toward the loud, clattering sound of approaching footsteps.

"What on earth?" Beatrice, Julie's British lodge manager, stood in the hallway. Placing both hands on her ample hips, she glanced up toward the attic door. "What were you doing up there?" she asked with a nod of her head. "You know it's haunted," she added, fixing a stern look at Julie.

"Don't be ridiculous, Beatrice." Yet Julie wondered. She stole a glance at Zach, half-tempted to touch him again and make sure he wasn't an illusion from her past. She pressed a hand to her lips. He really *was* here. But why?

Beatrice hurried to collect the loose photographs that lay scattered across the floor. "Are you sure you're all right?" she asked over her shoulder.

"Yes, I'm fine. Really," Julie insisted, though she felt as if she might keel over when she noticed the subject of the pictures lying faceup on the floor.

Zach. On his Harley.

"What madness sent you up that ancient ladder anyway dressed up the way you are? And during a storm, no less." Beatrice clucked her tongue in disapproval and placed the pencil she'd been holding into her curly, gray hair.

"I . . . had some things to take care of." Julie smoothed her long, black skirt. She couldn't blurt out she was looking for clues to the murder. Not in front of Zach. Or anyone.

"You should have asked for help," Beatrice admonished. "You could've fallen. We've had enough *accidents* around here lately." As she spoke, she flipped through the photographs in her hand. Eyes wide, she looked back and forth from the old pictures to Zach, then stood, transfixed.

For the first time Julie could remember, Beatrice appeared speechless. Julie's gaze focused on the photographs in Beatrice's hand. She remembered with vivid accuracy the day she took those pictures — Zach on his bike moments before he proposed and then sped away.

Out of her life. Forever.

Until today.

Glancing at Beatrice and placing a finger to her lips, Julie realized that her friend recognized him as the man in the photos. Would she at least have the common sense and decency to keep her mouth shut?

"Let me grab that for you," Zach offered.

27

He reached for the overturned carton on the floor. "It looks heavy."

"No!" Julie and Beatrice exclaimed in unison, exchanging frantic glances.

Zach's eyes narrowed. "You sure?"

"Yes." Julie cleared her throat. "I can manage it." Brushing remnants of cobwebs from her ice-pink cashmere sweater set, Julie gave her friend and coworker a warning look.

Beatrice raised an eyebrow in response. "You should take some time off." She stole another glance at Zach and the pictures she held in her hand. "After all, you *are* the owner. You certainly deserve a break. Especially after everything that's happened around here the past few weeks." She eyeballed Zach again.

"I'm fine . . . really," Julie croaked. She bit her lower lip. "No need to take the day off." Surely, Beatrice knew not to utter a word about the murder or that Zach was the man in the photos. How embarrassing. Didn't she have any sense of privacy?

Though the lodge couldn't afford the extra cost, Julie had insisted on paying a security guard for the safety of the guests. Besides the police, she and Beatrice were the only ones who knew about the crime.

Beatrice just happened to be there when Julie came stumbling into the office in her

28

bloodstained sweats early on that awful morning. Blood on her hands, too, from when she tried to awaken Paul, in vain.

Soon after, the police had discreetly arrived, not wanting to alarm the guests, yet questioning several of them. The detectives said that maintaining a low profile was vital to the ongoing investigation. But keeping the brutal slaying quiet weighed heavily on Julie's nerves. She didn't like it.

Still holding the snapshots in a death grip, Beatrice placed both hands on her hips again. "I shall speak with you later," she added in her very proper British accent. She turned and started down the long corridor.

"Wait!" Catching up with her, Julie gently took the photos of Zach from Beatrice's hands. "I'll take those." Whispering lightly she added, "Not a word!" and marched back to the troublesome box before Zach could get a look at its contents.

"Well then," Beatrice said after a moment. "I guess I'll leave you to your . . . guest." She gave Zach a fleeting glance, turned on her heel and stalked away.

Julie and Zach faced each other. A silent moment that seemed to stretch into eternity. The storm and the murder weren't the only mystifying elements causing her pulse to race. His tall, powerful physique, black leather jacket and well-fitted jeans added several extra beats to her already fluttering heart.

Her mind drifted back eight years. She saw herself riding with him on his motorcycle, her arms tightly wrapped around his waist. Memories of his clean, masculine scent — flashbacks of Zach wearing the very same leather jacket he wore today — filled her senses. Julie felt the distinct memory of his lips against hers. Images of their private picnic spot at Hurricane Ridge filled her mind with thoughts she should have forgotten, even as a chill of awareness prickled her spine.

She'd been so young. Only twenty-one. Yet she'd loved Zach with all her heart. Julie forced herself to breathe. The deserted hallway suddenly seemed much too small, too narrow. Chestnut-brown hair fell across his eyes. His slow, crooked grin released a stream of remembrances to flood her mind — the way his eyes darkened with emotion when he kissed her, his tender touch.

Did he end up in California on his impromptu adventure, the one he had asked her to go on with him the day he proposed? Surely he couldn't have expected her to leave her family and friends on a moment's notice and ride off with him into the sunset.

She'd never even had the chance to tell him about her grandmother's death the night before. He'd always been too adventurous for her. Too impulsive.

She told him "no," yet watching him speed away on his Harley without her left an ache, an emptiness deep in her heart. There had been many sleepless nights when she relied on God's strength, wondering if she'd made a mistake in not going with him.

But she couldn't leave her family. Julie needed time to grieve over the passing of the beloved grandmother who had always made life fun for her and her brother. If only she'd had the chance to tell Zach. She drew a shaky breath. She'd never heard from him again. Until now.

"What were you doing up there alone?" Zach asked, nodding toward the attic. Slowly his gaze drifted down the length of her body. His hands fisted inside the pockets of his leather jacket. His intense gaze returned to meet hers.

"Nothing, really." Zach was the only person she ever told about her claustrophobia. Had he remembered? "What are you doing in this section of the inn, Zach? This corridor isn't open to guests. It needs to be renovated. Didn't you see the sign?"

"Sign?" Zach glanced down the hallway.

"Must've missed it."

"I guess so." Taking a quick breath, she reached for the box and slowly turned it upright being careful not to let the albums or any other photos slip out for Zach to see. She lifted it from the wooden floor. "I'll just put this away." *Far away.*

"I can't let you do that," Zach said grabbing the carton.

"What? Wait, I —"

"It's way too heavy. Good thing I happened to wander by." He easily lifted the cardboard container from her arms. "You might've fallen off that ladder if I hadn't been here." He raised an eyebrow and nodded toward the stairs at the other end of the hall. "Lead the way."

"Fine." Several minutes later, they reached the main floor and Julie opened the door to her private office. *I should've duct-taped that box shut. Permanently.*

"Where do you want this?" he asked, hovering in the doorway.

"Thanks, I can handle it from here." Julie took the box from his arms, walked to the far corner of her office and then lowered it onto the carpet. She turned to face him. "See, it wasn't that heavy."

"If you say so." Zach leaned against the doorjamb, arms crossed over his broad chest. His blue-gray eyes filled with a familiar longing and a lazy smile eased its way across his face. "So, how are you, Julie?"

"I'm fine." She took in a much-needed breath. Zach's sudden presence in her life was taking its toll on her already frazzled nerves. The pleasant aroma of vanilla almond coffee brewing in the Capresso machine in the corner of the room gave her the sense of normalcy she so desperately needed. Beatrice always made her a fresh pot of coffee at this time of day. At least something was going according to plan. Julie curled a loose strand of hair behind her ear. "It's been a while, Zach," she said, leaning one hip against the top of her desk.

"Yeah." Zach scanned the office before his penetrating gaze returned to meet hers. "About eight years, Jewels."

He called her by his old nickname for her. The one she hated. Yet, hearing it now brought forth a rush of precious memories. She forced the sweet thoughts from her heart and mind. "Has it been *that* long?" Though she knew all too well exactly how long ago it had been.

"Yeah. So, what have you been up to?" he asked.

Julie smiled. "Running the lodge, for one thing."

His gaze locked on hers. "You really own this resort?"

"Yes." She nodded and took in another quick breath. It was good to see him. Zach had meant the world to her once. "My husband and I bought it and —"

"Right." His sudden, cool gaze confused her. "You look great. You haven't aged a day." He pushed off the doorway and backed up a step.

"Thanks." Why was he deliberately making her uncomfortable? It wasn't like him. At least not like the Zach she used to know. She lowered her gaze so he wouldn't notice the moisture in her eyes. "I'd . . . better let you go," she said once she composed herself. She lifted her gaze to meet his.

"Yeah, I'm off to do some exploring." He ran a hand through his hair. "You know. Take a drive around the lake, find a couple of places to fish."

Julie ached to do a little exploring of her own and run her fingers across the roughness of his jaw. It was good to hear his deep, familiar voice. She had to get a grip on the overpowering emotions coursing through her. Seeing him again, old feelings resurfaced, stronger than ever.

A strand of hair fell across his forehead and she fought the overwhelming impulse to smooth it back, as she used to. "How long are you staying, Zach?" Surely, he couldn't be their "mystery man," the one who had insisted on main level accommodations with a view of the lake. But the way her day was going . . .

Julie wished she'd made more time to be involved with the lone guest who had mysteriously booked a room for an extended stay. If she'd seen his name, she would've had some warning. "Are you with your family?" she asked, hoping he would say yes.

"No. It's just me." He smiled, but it wasn't real.

Julie studied his face. Something was wrong. He was their "mystery man," all right, in more ways than one. "Is your room okay? We wanted to make sure that you'd be comfortable. You know, for such a long . . . vacation."

"Yeah. It's great." His distant gaze held hers. "You and your husband must love it here."

Julie walked to stand at the open door with him. Through the floor-to-ceiling windows at the far end of the lobby, she surveyed the silvery lake and the tall evergreens of the densely treed property.

Her heart felt as heavy as the thick morning mist that rose from Shadow Lake. The steely gray presence curled up the vast, manicured lawn near the back of the lodge, lingering at the tall windows until it enveloped the building in a translucent cocoon.

Eerie, yet beautiful. Peaceful, but lonely.

Just like her heart.

Dragging in a deep breath, and wondering about her sudden case of melancholy, she turned to face Zach. "My husband . . . Tim —" she blinked and cleared her throat "— he . . . he died suddenly. Three years ago." She still found it hard to discuss Tim's death and the virus that had weakened his heart in a matter of weeks.

Zach reached out and gently lifted her chin so her gaze would meet his. "I'm sorry, Julie." His words, so sincerely spoken, revealed the tender man she remembered. The gentle touch of his long fingers brushing her cheek stirred emotions she'd tried to bury along with their past.

He took her hands in his. His gaze connected to her soul this time and a glimmer of sunshine filtered into the fogginess of her heart. His strong, warm hands felt so good around hers. They stood only inches apart. "You sure you're all right?"

Thoughts of their past raced through her

mind and she wondered what it would be like to kiss him again. Clearing her head, she pushed the thought away. "I'm fine." In Zach's strong arms, she felt like a college girl all over again. Could he feel how her hands trembled in his?

"Okay. I'm off to do some sightseeing." Gently, he released her hands from his.

"Thanks for saving me from an embarrassing fall."

"Yes. Catch you later." Zach chuckled. He winked and for a split second, his teasing gaze held hers.

She'd always loved his sense of humor. In seconds, he was out the door with no plans and probably no map. He hadn't changed at all. But *something* in his life had left the emptiness she saw in his eyes. After all these years, why would God bring Zach back into her life now? Circumstances at the lodge couldn't be worse.

Zach would never admit it, she knew, but he looked as if he could use a friend.

Placing a hand to her heart and reeling from the deep emotions swirling inside, Julie suddenly realized, so could she.

Especially since . . . the murder.

Two

Zach pulled his vehicle into the small parking lot across from Shadow Lake Inn after having spent the last four hours mapping out the perimeter around the lake and meeting with team members on the case.

Senior Agent John Castlerock hadn't been at the rendezvous point as planned, and none of the other agents knew his whereabouts. Zach didn't like the troubling thoughts running through his mind.

Was John keeping something from the team? From *him?*

He'd never worried about John's loyalty before. So why was there a sudden feeling of apprehension creeping its way through his gut? Why *wasn't* John here yet?

He crossed the narrow road to the inn and his thoughts turned to Julie. Zach hadn't expected the sudden rush of affection he felt when he held her in his arms again. He thought he had braced himself for the impact of seeing her when he studied the pictures the Bureau had shown him. Blue eyes, silky blond hair, her killer smile — it was enough to bring a man down. Her slim, well-toned body and feminine curves didn't help matters, either.

Muttering a curse, he mentally repaired the protective wall he'd built around his heart and forced his concentration back where it belonged.

On his assignment.

Julie — the suspect.

He made his way along the hallway leading to the business section of the inn. The door to her office was slightly open giving him a perfect opportunity to sneak a quick look at her books and gather more information on the nosy Brit. Checking to make sure no one saw him, he quietly slipped into the room.

The suspicious box still sat in the corner. Obviously there was something inside that Julie didn't want him to see. Heading toward it, he came to an abrupt halt when he noticed a small figure sitting in the brown leather chair. He could hardly see her over the top of the desk.

"Hello." She jumped from the seat and scooted around the desk to face him. "Are you the misty man?"

Zach swallowed. "Uh, the what?"

"You sure look like the misty man to me." The little girl tilted her head, placed her hands on her hips and gave him a quick once-over.

What in the world was a misty man?

Light blond hair, combed into a neat ponytail, bounced with every move she made. One strap of the denim jumper she wore slipped over her shoulder and the white turtleneck underneath the dress. Tennis shoes, laced in red, had matching frilly things centered in the bows. One of the laces was untied. She could trip and fall.

Without warning, she grabbed Zach by the hand and led him to the leather chair behind the desk. Her warm, small hand wrapped around his fingers as she tugged him toward the desk. "Want to see my picture?"

His heart stopped at her innocent touch. Who *was* this kid and what was she doing in Julie's office? Inwardly, he muttered an unspoken oath. It was too late to hightail it out of there. "Yeah, sure."

"You sit here," she instructed. Smiling up at him, a familiar blue-eyed gaze met his.

His heart almost stopped. There was no denying the uncanny resemblance. Julie had a daughter, a little girl about the same age

40

as Ashley would've been.

Zach almost stopped breathing. Why hadn't this *minor detail* been in the report he'd studied?

Suddenly she was sitting on his knee, showing him the drawing. "See? This is Mommy. And this . . . is Prince Charming." She turned to gaze at him again and her sweet face touched Zach's heart in a way he'd known only once before.

The kid squirmed on his lap. Instinctively, he placed an arm around her so she wouldn't fall. He waited for the heartache, the pain to grip his soul.

"Do you like it?" she asked hopefully. "Hey. He looks just like you!" She turned to study his face. "See?" She touched the image of the man she had drawn then pressed her fingers to Zach's cheek.

Zach sucked in a breath and glanced at the stick figure. "It does kind of look like me, huh." Maybe this kid had the answers he needed.

"And this —" she pointed to the stick figure woman in the picture "— is Mommy. Isn't she pretty?"

"Hmm." Zach lifted the drawing from the desk and held it close so they could both examine it together. He whistled. "She sure is."

She giggled and rested her head on his shoulder. The top of her ponytail brushed his cheek and Zach's eyes grew moist. But this time he didn't feel the usual anguish. This time, his heart filled with something good.

Pure. Sweet.

Was it possible, after all he'd been through and seen, there was anyone truly virtuous still left in the world? He steadied the little girl on his knee. "Uh, your shoelace is undone. Let me tie it for you."

"Okay." She stretched out her leg and lifted her foot.

Fingers trembling with memories of other little shoes, Zach fumbled with the red laces and tied a double bow. "Here you go," he said, his voice breaking.

"Thank you." Her sweet round-eyed gaze reached into the depths of his soul with her little girl innocence and trust.

"You're welcome," he managed, his voice barely above a whisper.

"Emmie," Julie said quietly, standing in the doorway. "Honey, what are you doing?"

The little girl jumped from Zach's knee and ran to her mother. "Mommy, it's the misty man. He's here! See?" She nodded in his direction and smiled.

"Emmie, sweetheart, I don't think that —"

42

"Yep. Here I am. In the flesh." Zach leaned back in the chair and grinned. "Misty Man."

Julie's gaze met his and she smiled. Kneeling, she hugged her daughter. The tender sight, mother and daughter quietly laughing together, overwhelmed Zach. He didn't welcome the unexpected current of emotions he felt charging through his body. He didn't want to think about families and little girls.

Not now. Not ever.

Julie sighed inwardly and rose to her feet. Seeing her daughter sitting so comfortably on Zach's knee had touched her deeply, reminding her how much Emmie needed a father in her life. And how much Julie longed to fall asleep every night in the arms of a man who loved her. Hand in hand, she led Emmie to where Zach sat at her desk. "Zach, this is my daughter, Emmie." She turned to her little girl. "Sweetheart, this is . . . Mr. Marshall."

"I showed him my drawing." She smiled up at Julie, a proud look of accomplishment in her sweet eyes.

"Oh, you did?" Julie glanced at the picture on her desk and turned to Zach. He smiled and Julie's heartbeat quickened. Did she still have feelings for him? That was ridiculous. He was just an old friend. That's all.

"Mommy," Emmie whispered turning to Julie. "He's the misty man."

She really needed to watch what she said around her daughter. Julie turned to Zach and offered a rueful smile. He raised an eyebrow and flashed a slow, crooked grin.

"You of all people should know that, Julie."

She blushed at the hint of intimacy in his words. "Zach, I —"

"Oh, there you are. I've been trying to warn you all day. The myst—" Beatrice marched through the open door into the already crowded office and stopped abruptly to stare at Zach. Placing a hand to her heart, she stammered, "Oh, h-hello, Mr. Marshall. Hmm, quite nice to see you again. Was there something you needed?" A pink blush flooded her cheeks and she drew in a quick, shaky breath. "I . . . trust the room is to your liking?"

"Yeah. It's fine." Zach's eyes narrowed. He rose to his feet. "I'd better get going."

"No need to leave on my account. I only came to ask if Emmie wants to taste test our new chef's chocolate chip cookies," Beatrice added, lifting her chin.

Julie detected the slightest twinkle in her

44

friend's eyes. She was probably trying to warn her that Zach was their "mystery man." It was what they'd come to call him from the time he made his rather mysterious reservations. Apparently, they'd referred to him by that name in front of Emmie too many times.

She knelt down, eye level with her daughter. "Cookies sound good. What do you say, sweetheart?" Julie smiled and affectionately caressed Emmie's pretty face.

"Yummy. Chocolate chip's my favorite." She gave Julie a kiss on the cheek and a quick hug. Running back to the desk, Emmie grabbed the drawing and skipped over to Zach. "You can keep this," she said, proudly smiling up at him.

Zach crouched down beside her and accepted the drawing from her outstretched hand. "Thanks. It's a great drawing, Emmie." He winked and gave her a quick smile.

Slowly, Julie stood. Having witnessed Zach's tenderness with her daughter, her heart unexpectedly filled with longing. If only Emmie could have a good family man to be the father she so desperately needed. A man who would be home every night to tuck her in and read her a bedtime story. Who would share in the wonderful joy of raising her daughter. But now was not the time for silly sentiments. She had a crime to solve. A business to run.

Emmie skipped over to Beatrice and then reached for her outstretched hand. Beatrice gave Julie a knowing glance then closed the door after them. An endless moment ticked by.

"You have a daughter." Zach's eyes filled with tenderness. "She . . . looks just like you."

"Thanks. She's a real blessing, especially after losing my husband."

In an instant, Zach closed the distance between them until he stood only a breath away. Curling his fingers under her chin, he lifted her gaze to meet his. "Can you get a sitter? I'd like you to have dinner with me."

Julie smiled despite how her heart danced recklessly inside her chest. It would be fun to share a meal with someone. With Zach. She would have the chance to ask him all the questions that had her mind spinning. Why was he here?

"Tonight," he whispered, pulling her into a light embrace. "We'll catch up on all the years."

His deep voice and tender touch awakened feelings in her heart from long ago. A wave of awareness pulsed along her spine. The feel of his warm breath against her cheek,

46

the pulse of his strong, steady heartbeat beneath her fingertips — it was all too familiar.

Gazing into his steel-blue eyes, Julie swallowed hard and opened her mouth to say something.

Anything.

Zach dropped his hands from her arms and took a step back. "You already have plans," he stated.

"No, it's all right," Julie managed. "My parents live only a few minutes away. Emmie will love staying over. Tomorrow's Saturday. No school."

One corner of his mouth lifted in a smile. "You want to eat here or go somewhere else?"

"Well, I need to sample the cuisine my new chef has prepared. Do you want to join me, Zach? We'll have a taste testing of our own."

"What time?" he asked, reaching for her hand as if a lifetime hadn't passed since they'd seen each other.

"Seven?"

"Okay, seven it is." Zach gently pulled her to him and encircled her in his arms. "It's good to see you after all this time," he whispered, his breath warm against her cheek. After a moment, he released her and held her at arm's length. "I'll meet you in the lobby."

"Okay." Her knees felt as if they would give out on her. Why was she reacting to him as if they'd never been apart? It didn't make any sense. Julie ran a hand along the spot on her arm still charged with electricity from Zach's tender touch. At twenty-nine, she had no right responding to him like some love-crazed teen. But her body seemed to have a mind of its own where he was concerned.

"See you later." He started to close the door behind him.

"No, wait." Julie curled a strand of hair behind her ear. "Keep it open. I love these late-October afternoons with the sound of the fire popping."

The pleasant aroma of Yule logs burning in the large, brick fireplace made her think of Christmas. That time of year always brought happy childhood memories to mind, chasing away any sign of loneliness.

"Sure thing." He winked.

"Thanks." Julie glanced through the office door into the massive lobby, and smiled at the clerk at the reception desk. The flames in the brick fireplace crackled, providing welcome warmth to another chilly, overcast day in Washington State.

The mantel, a large western red cedar beam placed across the curved top of the brick firebox, highlighted wooden sculptures and candleholders crafted by various Native American tribes of the Olympic rain forest. Several guests brought their coffee with them and sat on the comfortable forest-green sofas grouped near the massive fire-place.

Walking around her desk, Julie collapsed into the chair, still warm from Zach's presence. This was just like him, catching her off guard, pulling her heart in too many directions at once. Even now, after all these years. She couldn't allow history to repeat itself where Zach was concerned. He'd be leaving again. She had Emmie to think about this time. And the lodge.

Her parents would be thrilled to have Emmie over for the night, if they didn't already have plans. What had she been thinking? They were already keeping Emmie tomorrow evening. Maybe two nights in a row would be too much for her parents to handle.

She dialed their phone number and made the babysitting arrangements only after her mom assured her they would love to have Emmie for the weekend.

■ ■ ■ ■

A few hours later, Julie pulled her small white car into the private parking space at the resort. She adjusted the rearview mirror to check her image. At least she'd had time to freshen up and reapply a light touch of makeup. Even in the high humidity of the rain forest, she was having a good hair day.

Thunder rumbled overhead and Julie hurried up the gray slate steps of the lodge, slick from the daily afternoon rainfall. She checked her watch. Five after seven. She was late.

"Are you always in such a rush?"

Julie looked up to find Zach's amused gaze. She laughed. "Only most of the time," she admitted.

"Come on." He opened the door and guided her inside to the dining room.

"We won't have to place an order," Julie said once they sat down. Zach had changed into beige slacks and a black golf shirt. She was acutely aware of his tall, athletic physique. Zach had a powerful maturity about him that hadn't been there eight years ago. And she had a deep faith in God that hadn't been there all those years ago, either. Zach looked good. Too good. She'd need God's

50

strength to keep from falling for him again. "It's the chef's choice tonight based on some of my favorites. I hope that's okay."

"Sure. I'm very impressed. Looks like you're doing a great job running this place. It's got to be a huge responsibility, both emotionally and financially." Zach leaned forward in his chair and studied her. He seemed to be seeing her in a new light. Had she changed that much since they'd last seen each other? "Especially with a daughter to raise on your own," he added.

"I guess I'm used to the busy schedule by now." Julie turned as the new chef approached their table. She didn't want to talk about the personal heartache after losing her husband, or how many long hours she'd worked trying to put the business in the black. The next three months would prove if her efforts were enough to keep the lodge open for good. To close the place or have to sell it would break her heart.

Julie didn't want to think about that or the recent murder of their groundskeeper, a man in his sixties who had become a dear member of the Shadow Lake Inn family.

The police still had no motive for his brutal, untimely death. Shaking the grief from her heart, Julie set her mind to finding out about Zach. A trace of sorrow glimmered in his penetrating gaze. What had happened in his life to cause the well-masked sadness she detected?

"Good evening." The man Julie recently hired as master chef held two leather-bound menus in his hand.

Straightening in his seat, Zach eyed the man and took the booklet from his outstretched hand.

"John Rockwell, I'd like you to meet Zach Marshall." Julie liked the man she'd hired only a few days ago. His long list of qualifications was more than noteworthy. He had trained at the Culinary Institute of America in Napa Valley and his references were impeccable. Shadow Lake Inn was fortunate to have him.

His résumé had come via the fax machine at just the right moment, when she needed to hire someone in a hurry. Just like when she'd received Beatrice's timely résumé.

John was a tall man like Zach. About six foot two, she guessed. About fifteen years older than Zach, and distinguished-looking with brown hair graying at the temples, he'd been divorced for several years. With two teenage children living in Seattle with their mom, he had just relocated from the East Coast to be closer to them.

"Nice to meet you." John extended a hand

to Zach. He smiled as they shook hands. "If there's anything special you'd like prepared, just say the word."

"Thanks." Zach smiled. "I'm sure everything will be fine."

"Wonderful." John left them to their privacy.

"You know, of course," Julie said smiling, "this meal is on the house." She didn't want Zach to think he had to pay for the costly dinner.

"What, don't you think I can handle it?" Zach's amused gaze met hers and a lazy grin eased its way across his face.

"Well, I hope to have the answer to that and more . . . by the time we get to dessert."

Zach laughed. "Oh, you do, huh?"

"Don't worry," Julie teased. "You know you can tell me anything."

"What about you, Julie?" His intense gaze caught her off guard. "Can you tell *me* anything?"

She was surprised at his sudden seriousness. "You already know everything."

"Well, I know some things, but not everything. For example, just what is a 'misty man'? And why does your daughter think I'm him?" Leaning back in his chair, Zach chuckled lightly and raised an eyebrow awaiting her response.

Julie recognized the mischievous twinkle in his eyes. " 'Misty man?' It's silly. Just kids' stuff. Not even worth mentioning, believe me." She cleared her throat. "Tell me, Zach, what brings you back to Washington State? Business?"

A tray-laden waiter brought an array of appetizers — baked Brie with sliced French bread and apple wedges, stuffed clams and oysters on the half shell.

"First things first." Zach's eyes narrowed in amusement. "I'm starving and this looks great." He laughed lightly. "There are benefits to knowing the owner." He held out his glass of sparkling water to hers in a toast. "To old friends."

She gently touched her long-stemmed glass to his. The soft chime of fine crystal rang softly in the dimly lit, cozy dining room.

Old friends. Somehow, the thought disheartened her. Was that all they were? Julie sipped the water and lowered her glass to the elegantly set table. She placed a slice of French bread and a small helping of buttery Brie onto a plate.

A few minutes later, she realized that finding out what Zach had been doing since he'd driven away on his motorcycle was going to be more difficult than she'd thought. They were almost finished with the appetizers and she had no clue about his life at all. "Did you stay in California or go back to the ranch in Montana? You know, that day you left on your Harley. I often wondered about that," Julie admitted.

Zach glanced at the water in his glass. Slowly, he lifted his gaze to meet hers. "I went for a ride." His expression stilled and grew serious. His attention drifted to the flame of the red tapered candle on the table, which flickered as he spoke. His powerful, intensely guarded gaze recaptured hers and his blue eyes darkened with a veil of mystery. He drew a deep breath.

"A . . . long ride."

"Stop worrying." Despite his anger, Viktor Ivanov spoke quietly into the mouthpiece of his cell phone. Annoyed at having to assure Yuri again, he flicked the ashes from his cigar onto the old, wooden table in the tavern and casually glanced around the small lounge.

The man and woman seated in the corner paid him no attention. A second man at the bar was deep in conversation with the barmaid. Even so, he would take the long way home in case he was being followed.

Glancing out the front window, Viktor cursed the steady rain.

"When I have the disc in my hands . . . then I'll stop worrying," Yuri answered. "Perhaps you should be more concerned. FBI operatives must be taken out before they get too close. The next few weeks are crucial to our plans."

"I cover my tracks. No one suspects a thing." Viktor downed the shot of vodka and placed the empty glass on the tabletop.

"Let's hope you are correct," Yuri responded. "For your sake, Viktor."

Viktor recognized a threat when he heard one. He cursed under his breath. Their organization would be better off without the old dinosaur Yuri Kostoff running things. "I've got a woman helping me."

"A woman? How much can you trust this female, old friend?" Yuri asked. "You were betrayed once before."

"That was a long time ago." Viktor's thoughts touched on memories of the girl he had been in love with from childhood . . . until she betrayed him. Having to kill her wasn't easy. But he'd proved himself worthy to the terrorist organization.

Still, seeing her die at his hands had nearly destroyed him. At first. Now, he would get rid of anyone who got in his way. He would never go back to his life of poverty in Russia. When this deal was over, he planned to buy an island someplace where there was plenty of sunshine. Unlike this dreary place. There he would have the kind of life he deserved. A life fit for a king. "We can trust this woman." He chuckled lightly and took a long puff on the Cuban cigar. "Completely." She didn't even know she was helping him.

"I warn you again, Viktor. It will not be easy to keep them off our trail."

"Just get the information to me. I'll take care of smuggling the disc to our friends," Viktor snapped.

But he did worry. She had almost caught him up in her attic. He would have to get rid of her, and soon.

THREE

"Have you stayed in contact with anyone from college?" Zach cut into another delicious piece of porterhouse steak. He wasn't willing to answer any of Julie's questions. Not yet. He enjoyed watching her struggle to get the truth out of him. Dessert wasn't far off and he hadn't told her a thing.

He forgot how much fun he had teasing her. Zach almost laughed aloud at her predicament. Only the seriousness of his assignment prevented it. He had to gather more information.

"I don't know if you remember Tiffany Saccaro, my roommate from college?" Julie asked.

"Sure." Zach gave a quick laugh. "Every guy probably remembers her. We all camped out at Olympic National Park."

"Oh, stop that." Julie straightened the dark green linen napkin in her lap and took a sip of water. She lifted her gaze to meet his. "Tiff and I are still good friends. She lives down in Seattle. We get together a few times a year."

"Oh? How's she doing? Still dating?"

"No." Julie laughed lightly. "Tiff's been happily married for seven years. She and her husband, Ken, adore each other. They have two kids, with another due in about a month."

"Really?"

"Really." She gently placed her glass on the table. "Zach Marshall, you have procrastinated long enough." Resting her elbows on the white linen tablecloth, she clasped her hands together. "You know all about me. Now it's your turn." She lifted her chin.

This time Zach did laugh. He held up a hand in surrender. "Okay, okay. On one condition." Leaning closer across the table, he took her hand in his and fought the temptation to bring her fingers to his lips. If he rushed things, she might get suspicious. "I'm planning a drive down the coast to Ruby Beach tomorrow. Come with me. I'll tell you what you want to know then."

He slowly rubbed her palm with the pad of his thumb. She always liked it when he touched her like this. His mind filled with memories of other touches. Groaning inwardly, he forced his wayward thoughts back to the investigation.

Julie wouldn't be able to get a sitter for the whole day tomorrow, especially with her parents watching Emmie tonight. She'd never agree to go with him. She'd always hated adventures. He would use the time alone to scout out the area where the groundskeeper's body had been found. "You'll never know where we may end up. Oregon. California." He flashed a slow smile of victory.

Her clear blue eyes sparkled in the flickering candlelight. "I'll go around the loop with you tomorrow . . . if you answer all my questions."

"Hey, I never said I'd answer *all* your questions." He leaned back in his chair. She'd surprised him. "What about your daughter?" She wasn't thinking of bringing her along, was she?

Memories of his own little girl hit with a staggering assault. How many agonizing nights had he spent going over all the scenarios that might have prevented her death and the death of his wife?

The paramedics told him that Lisa had died instantly. His sweet daughter, Ashley, still in the car seat, had been thrown from the vehicle. She was gone by the time the ambulance arrived.

Releasing Julie's hand, Zach sucked in a quick breath. Would he ever get over the guilt he felt for not being there when they needed him the most? Or understand how God could let them die so tragically? He was the one who should've been gone by now, considering the line of work he'd chosen. Not them.

"Every so often my parents take Emmie for an overnight trip to Seattle. This is one of those weekends. Dad made the hotel reservations for tomorrow's outing months ago. They'll even take Emmie to Sunday school when they go to church on Sunday. I'm free as a bird." Her playful gaze met his and she smiled.

More beautiful than ever, Julie's long, blond hair cascaded to just below her shoulders. Mediterranean-blue eyes lit with a warm glow from somewhere deep inside.

Their past relationship would come in handy. He hated to use her, but he had no choice. He couldn't allow old emotions to get in the way of his job.

His instincts were usually right, but with Julie as a major suspect, could he trust the gut intuition he had honed over the past few years?

"Free as a bird, huh?" His life and the lives of other agents depended on his skills.

He wouldn't let them down. "Okay, we'll make a day of it. Everything's on me tomorrow. We'll leave early, about six."

"Six! In the morning?" She laughed lightly.

"Sure. We'll stop somewhere for a picnic." His gaze met hers and for a moment, Julie's blue eyes softened.

Did she remember their last *picnic* up on Hurricane Ridge?

Zach's eyes searched hers. She tucked a strand of hair behind her ear and avoided his gaze. He always *could* read the expressions on her face. He gave a slow grin.

She remembered, all right.

How could she forget the magic of that one night they had spent together with friends at Olympic National Park? The fun evening they'd shared had been more than memorable. Much more. Zach wondered if he could find that secluded spot in the park again after all these years.

Knock it off, Marshall.

No more dwelling in the past. What he needed was hope for the future. He'd let the real Zach slip away as he pursued his career with the Bureau. Hard work had been a lifesaver from drowning in the pain and guilt he felt.

Once he solved this case, if he lived

through it, he would spend more time at home. That meant Montana. A life back on the ranch was what he really wanted. He'd known that for the past couple of years. That was why he'd built the huge log house on the ten thousand acre spread. His folks had sold him the property he wanted so he could start a new life. Someday.

Zach straightened in his chair. He'd only spent a month at home over the past year, and had hired a housekeeper to keep things in order. He'd probably live out the rest of his life alone in that big empty house.

That was fine with him. A family was the last thing he wanted. Or needed. What he needed was to end this terrorist investigation. There was no room for faith or a family in those plans.

"Come on, Julie," he coaxed, giving her his best smile. "What do you say?"

"Well, okay. Just don't forget your promise. You'll tell me what you've been doing all this time."

"Right." In reality, she'd be the one spilling her guts. "Pack an overnight bag just in case. You never know what the weather will be like up there this time of year. If there are heavy rains, we might have to spend the night."

"Oh, Zach, I — I don't know —"

"It might take a while to tell you everything." He raised an eyebrow. Would she take the bait?

She sighed in determined resignation. "I'll be ready."

"Good. It'll be an adventure." Zach grinned and leaned forward in his seat.

"A little trip to the park is all I'm interested in. Just a relaxing little drive and finding out about your life for the past eight years. No adventures." She laughed lightly and sampled a small mouthful of the chocolate mousse the waiter had just brought to their table. "Mmm. This is so good."

"That was one of the finest meals I've ever had," Zach agreed. "Your chef is great." He chuckled lightly, enjoying a sip of coffee before leaning back comfortably in his chair. "You mentioned he was new?"

"Yes. I just hired him." Julie took another small mouthful of the chocolate dessert. "After a meal like this, I think it's safe to say I chose the right man for the job."

"You can say that again." If Julie only knew how right she was. Agent Castlerock had expressed an interest in gourmet foods, but a *chef?* That was, obviously, the new circumstance John had mentioned on the phone. The Senior Agent in Charge had established his cover as master chef at the

64

inn. Good. It made sense. But he wanted answers, no more surprises from the SAC.

Zach took in the welcoming sight of Julie sitting across from him. Could she really be the missing link in this case? The evidence connected her directly to one of America's most wanted terrorists. He'd seen with his own eyes the incriminating surveillance photos of Julie with prime suspect Viktor Ivanov. How intimately did Julie know him? Inwardly he cursed.

Time to make a move. "How about going for a walk around the lake?"

"Sure, it's on my way home." Julie smiled. "I have a little cottage overlooking the water."

I know. Zach knew more about Julie than she could ever imagine. But the information he'd received from the Bureau had nothing to do with her as a woman.

That's what really interested him.

For the investigation, of course.

Would she moan softly, like she used to . . . when he kissed her again?

The reflection of the moon lit the lake with an eerie, iridescent glow. Shadows from innumerable, two-hundred-foot-tall evergreen trees cast a disturbing darkness along the misty perimeter of the lake. Julie shook off

65

the sudden chill that crept along her spine. The recent murder was making her imagination work overtime. She had never feared the lakeside before.

"How long have you owned this place?" Zach bent to pick up a pebble along the rain-soaked, gray slate path. Tossing the small stone into the lake, he watched it bounce several times, sending wave after wave of ripples across the water's smooth surface.

"When we first bought the inn, we lived in the main building." She glanced at the everlasting display of tall trees standing regally across the large lake. Julie loved the lush green scenery, the dampness of the earth, the way the air filled with the pleasant scent of cedar. "About a year later, we decided to move into one of the inn's private homes." She lifted her gaze to meet his. "I've lived here for about six years, I guess." It didn't seem possible it had been that long. At a bend in the path, the house came into view. "There it is." Her cottage home reminded him of a popular artist's painting. Cozy and simple. Warm and inviting.

"Your lights are on," Zach observed.

"I had timers installed so when I got home, the place wouldn't be in total darkness." But no one was there to greet her, lights or not.

"Do you always work late, Julie? Is it this dark every night when you walk home?" He turned to her, a hint of concern in his eyes.

"No, not always." It had been a long time since a man had been concerned about her well-being. The knowledge that someone cared touched her. But there was Nick, of course. He'd helped her out several times with repairs on the inn. "There's nothing to worry about out here in the country . . . even in the dark," she said, lowering her gaze and thinking about the brutal killing of the dear old man.

Julie couldn't bring herself to discuss the unsolved murder of the employee who had taken such good care of the grounds around the lodge the past five years. The sadness she carried over his untimely and gruesome death remained buried deep inside and she found it impossible to discuss without breaking into tears. It had only been a couple of weeks since his body had been discovered.

There was so much grief in the world, in her life. Now an innocent man, a friend, was dead. The overwhelming mourning she felt threatened to creep up to the surface. She sighed and cleared her mind. Alone in her house at night, she could let herself give in to sorrow. But never in front of anyone. She had to be strong for everyone at the inn and especially for Emmie.

Before she realized it, they were at her front door. Zach's ruggedly handsome features, illuminated by the soft glow of the light from her front porch, caused Julie's heart to skip a beat. She drew in a quick breath. She was starting to remember the depth of the feelings she felt for Zach. She couldn't allow that to happen. She retrieved the key from her coat pocket. It didn't make sense that her hands trembled at the thought of asking Zach inside. What was wrong with her?

"Let me get that." Zach gently took the key from her hand and unlocked the door. He opened it and moved over to allow her to enter ahead of him.

"Come on in. I'll give you a quick tour." She smiled and shook off thoughts of the murder. "It'll take all of two minutes," Julie teased even as warning bells sounded in her mind. It would be too easy to move into Zach's comforting embrace.

"Sure." Zach followed her in and shut the door behind them. "Hmm . . ."

"What?" Julie asked, her gaze meeting his.

"It's really nice. Bigger than I thought."

"I know. It doesn't look that way from the outside, does it?" She removed her jacket and placed it on the coat rack in the small foyer. "Come on, I'll show you around."

Zach shrugged off his black leather jacket and placed it alongside hers. "Lead the way." He smiled a slow, lazy grin and in a split second Julie's heartbeat tripled. Was he remembering the spark of electricity that had always been there between them? Did he feel the attraction that was there even now?

She cleared her throat. "Um, we'll start with . . . the kitchen."

Zach scanned what he could see of the first floor. The FBI photos didn't do the place justice. Julie had decorated her kitchen in white with honey oak cabinets. Fresh tulips in different shades of yellow, pink and red filled a crystal vase on a round oak table.

A bay area for the table and four chairs faced the view of the inn through lacy white curtains. She had made this cottage into a happy place to live.

In spite of her loss.

Zach's thoughts raced to his large, empty house in Montana. Would he ever find a woman who would bring him happiness and a home filled with warmth, as this one obviously was?

Face it, Marshall, you're not cut out to be a family man.

You never were.

"Zach?" Julie's gentle voice broke into his thoughts.

"What were you saying?" He ran a hand through his hair and silently reminded himself why he was there.

After all he'd seen the past couple of years, Zach had become jaded, skeptical of anyone's innocence. There was no future in his wayward impulse to kiss Julie and hold her in his arms again. He gazed into her eyes and fought to control the undeniable affection he felt for her. It was nothing more than old memories, he reasoned.

He wanted to kiss her for the deed's sake and not for the coldhearted job he had to do. But if Julie's kisses would get him to the bottom of the investigation, so be it. He'd take all she had to offer.

Maybe I should take myself off this case.

But there was no chance of that happening. Not now. He'd been involved in the assignment from the very beginning when he was called up as a special agent in the attack on New York and the Pentagon. He'd known all the details, including the fact that the woman they would be investigating was

70

one he deeply loved long ago, when life was innocent and full of hope.

Zach's heart told him that Julie was unaware of the goings-on from her lodge. His mind told him he needed facts to prove his instincts. Zach could not assume Julie was innocent. He had seen too much in his life to be that naive.

Someone had killed the inn's groundskeeper, an ex-KGB agent trying to make a fresh start. His death had led the Bureau to Shadow Lake Inn. When was Julie planning to tell him about that? Why was she deliberately keeping the cold-blooded murder a secret, covering it up?

Julie turned to him. "I enjoyed having dinner with you tonight, Zach." She sighed softly and smiled.

"Yeah, me, too. It's . . . good to see you again, Julie," he whispered, gently pulling her to him. His fingers automatically intertwined with hers. It was as if his body was reacting on autopilot. Zach's heart filled with happy memories of the two of them together. She felt so right in his arms. It had been a long time since he held a woman this way — and too long since he'd held Julie.

His gaze rested on her moist, parted lips. He wanted to kiss her. He slowly pulled her closer. She felt so warm and soft. He rested his chin on her head. Against his better judgment, he drank in the clean fragrance of her long hair, letting its softness run through his fingers. He would kiss her during this assignment, no doubt about it, but not yet. It was all part of his job — getting close and then zeroing in for the takedown.

Swallowing a groan, he emotionally placed some distance between them, silently cursing the investigation and all it entailed. He could not let himself trust her. No matter what he felt. He needed to seize control of the intense physical and emotional reaction he had to her. *Now,* before he got lost in her arms, in her kisses.

Julie gently squeezed his hand. "Come on, I'll show you the rest of the house."

Taking his arm in hers, she walked him through a wide archway leading directly into the dining room. Antique mahogany furniture came into view as she flipped a wall switch allowing the crystal chandelier to light the room. Zach whistled. The deep dark tones and lines of the furniture were beautiful and classy. Elegant. It suited her.

Just as the photos had indicated, the furniture was expensive. The background check they did showed there was no way she could afford the cost, and there were no records of the purchase. Had she paid for everything in cash? Money earned by selling out her country? "This must have set you back a few bucks," he managed, his voice more gruff than he intended.

"It was my grandmother's. She left it to me when she passed away. The furniture and all the fine crystal and china she loved to use. I never could have afforded all this on my own." She turned to him and smiled. Julie's eyes filled with fondness as she spoke about her grandmother. "After all these years, I still miss her. She used to make me tea and honey." Her gaze met and locked with his. "And homemade lemon cookies."

How could this sweet woman be a spy?

Zach realized there was a lot he didn't know about Julie. He vowed to change that, to solve the case, of course. He would verify the grandmother's inheritance by morning.

"Are you bored yet?" Julie asked after she had shown him the family room. "We can stop anytime." She laughed lightly.

"Upstairs, Jewels." Zach smiled in spite of thoughts of her involvement in the grueling investigation. He wanted to know more about the home she had made for herself — before he locked her up in federal prison.

She led him up the stairway and Zach admired her slim, feminine body. He forced his gaze away in order to memorize every detail about her home that hadn't shown up in the surveillance photos he'd studied. The fourth step creaked under his foot. He made a mental note of it. The information he gathered might prove useful in saving precious seconds that could save lives. Too many agents had already died or disappeared on this assignment.

"This is my room. I recently redecorated and bought new furniture." Julie flipped another wall switch to light the room and walked inside. "I couldn't resist a sale I found at a shop in Seattle. The furniture was just delivered a few days ago."

The bed was new, all right. It hadn't been in the photographs he'd seen. The rich dark wood of the four-poster bed contrasted with the pale green comforter and floral dust ruffle. Several matching overstuffed pillows leaned against the large hand-carved mahogany headboard.

Zach imagined Julie there, her blond hair draped across the pillows. He drew in a quick breath.

He'd never forgotten her. Even after all the years. Even though he'd married and fathered a child.

Zach cleared his throat and forced the unsettling thoughts from his mind. Glancing around the room, memorizing every detail, he noticed a thick pillar candle inside an attractive heavy glass holder. Arranged with green ivy trailing around its base, the candle arrangement complemented the dark wood of her night table. That was why the room held the light, pleasant scent of vanilla. Zach wondered why Julie felt the need for a fancy, scented candle. And such an intimate atmosphere.

Did she *entertain* up here?

He crossed to the huge bay window and brushed the lacy white curtains aside. Through the open blinds, he could see the distant lights in the windows of the lodge, even with the numerous tall trees on the property. He turned to face her. "Nice view."

Nodding, she stood in the doorway and smiled. The pale pink Victorian lamp on the dresser gently lit her face. Zach's heart filled with memories of the tender love they once shared. It felt unnatural not to pull her close and kiss her as he used to.

"It *is* a pretty view, isn't it?" She crossed to where he stood at the window.

"That it is," Zach whispered, his voice suddenly giving out.

Did she enjoy sleeping in such a huge bed alone?

Had any men slept there with her, held

her close afterward? Julie had never been one to sleep around. Maybe she'd changed. Zach realized he would be disappointed if she had. He'd loved her innocence, her sweetness. Was she still the same woman he knew back then?

The Bureau expected him to use his past with Julie to bring closure to this international assignment. His mission was to stick close until she inadvertently led them to leaders of the terrorist group.

For the first time in his professional career, Zach wondered if he was in over his head. Because of his emotional involvement with Julie, was he in danger of losing his edge? If that were true, he was as good as dead.

"Come on, I'll show you Emmie's room," Julie said, interrupting his thoughts. "It's just across the hall."

Emmie's room.

Zach felt as if he'd been kicked in the gut. He should've thought of that possibility before now. Would he be able to face a little girl's bedroom without feeling the heartache of what could have been? Drawing a deep breath, he raked a hand through his hair and swallowed hard. "I'm . . . right behind you."

Julie flipped on the light switch and Emmie's room came alive. No matter how hard Zach braced himself for the impact, a wave of painful emotions washed over him as he stood frozen in place.

He'd dealt with apprehending vicious criminals before with no problem. He'd worked through the horrors at Ground Zero, but all it took was the sight of a little girl's bedroom to freeze him in his tracks.

An oak bed with a matching dresser and mirror filled the small room. Julie had decorated the twin bed with a pastel pink-and-white gingham comforter that matched the dust ruffle and canopy. A pink floral wallpaper border made its way across the top of the cream-colored walls. A vast array of stuffed animals lay peacefully arranged across the pillows.

Stuffed animals.

Zach recalled his daughter's crib. Picturing it clearly in his mind, he could almost reach out and touch the cherrywood railings . . . and Ashley. Taking her little bed apart, saving some toys and giving away the rest, had been the hardest thing he'd ever had to do. No mission had ever compared to the heartache of that task. No mission ever could.

"I did Emmie's room over, also." Julie smiled up at him, a tender look in her eyes when she talked about her little girl. "I asked her to help me choose the fabric and furniture. I was surprised that she had so many opinions on the subject." She laughed lightly. "This is what we agreed on."

"It's nice," Zach managed. Surprised that his feet weren't glued to the floor, he made his way over to a child-sized table under one of the windows. A small, crayon-filled wicker basket rested on a chair. Several of Emmie's drawings lay scattered across the top. Zach stopped to touch one of them. It showed a house, several trees and an animal that appeared to be a horse, but maybe it was a dog. "I see Emmie likes to draw," he said, turning to her.

Julie nodded. Love and obvious pride in her daughter reflected in her eyes. "She doesn't usually give her pictures away. You must have made quite an impression."

Forgetting his job for a brief moment, Zach's heart filled with happiness for Julie. He was glad she had her little girl to love after the loss of her husband. "Has it been hard for you, raising her on your own?" He pulled out one of the little chairs. Sitting as best as he could on the tiny piece of furniture, he flipped through the rest of the drawings.

Julie sat on another small chair next to

him. "Yes, at times it has been difficult, of course." She sighed. "But my family has been so helpful. My mom and dad are always there, never in an overbearing way, but just when I needed them the most." Taking a quick breath, she wiped a tear from the corner of her eye. "Tim . . . was twelve years older than me and had no family to speak of. He was an only child. His parents passed away before we met."

Zach couldn't bear to see her eyes filling with tears. He had to do something to lighten the moment. "What *is* this? A horse? A dog? A . . . dinosaur?" He smiled and tapped a finger on the animal in the drawing.

Julie laughed. "Oh, that." She sighed. "That's Emmie's dream house, as she calls it." Leaning closer Julie touched the image of the animal her daughter had drawn. "This . . . is a horse." Her eyes lit in amusement. "You were right the first time."

The pleasant, light floral fragrance she wore filled his senses. Zach resisted the powerful temptation to reach out and pull her into his arms. He wanted to comfort her, protect her. Tell her everything would be all right.

But how was a guy supposed to comfort a possible *spy?*

"A horse, huh? She hasn't seen any real horses, has she?" Raising an cycbrow, he smiled.

"No, she hasn't. Not yet. Maybe I should do something about that." Julie's gaze met his and she smiled.

"Yeah." And maybe he should do something about the undeniable feelings he had to hold Julie close. Keep her safe from the evil forces surrounding her and the inn.

Clearing the all-too-vivid intimate scenario lingering in his mind, Zach leaned back in the tiny seat. "If you're ever in Montana, I can show her plenty of horses. We breed them."

"Oh! So you went back to the ranch you loved," Julie said, smiling as if she'd won a prize.

Zach laughed. "Well, that's part of the story. Happy now?"

"Not until I know the rest," Julie teased.

How could he share his grief without the pain that always gripped his heart? Somehow, he would have to allow the anguish he'd been hiding to resurface in order to solve the case.

Yet here he was talking with Julie in her daughter's room. Instead of sadness overcoming his soul, he was sitting at a little girl's table, laughing. In place of the usual heaviness settling in his heart, there was a spark of joy.

Zach cleared his head. He had a case to solve. Suspects to track and bring to justice. The Bureau depended on him. If one more agent went down, they were all in danger. He could not let that happen. He needed a keen eye and an analytical mind to apprehend the spies.

Even if one of them was . . . Julie.

They sat so close that their knees touched beneath the small table. If he leaned in a few inches he'd be able to steal a kiss. Slowly, his gaze drifted to her mouth. Soft, full lips like Julie's were meant to be kissed.

Often. By him. Just as he used to.

Abruptly, Zach rose to his feet. "I'd . . . better go. You sure you want to get up so early on a Saturday?"

"No problem. Besides, you're not getting out of this." Smiling, she reached for his hand and led him out of the room. "You're going to tell me everything tomorrow, remember?"

"Right." Nothing could be further from the truth.

After making their way down the stairway, Zach grabbed his jacket from the coatrack. He confirmed no dead bolts on her door. No alarm system, either. The team of agents would have no problem installing the electronic bugs, the pinhole cameras and microphones.

Zach and his unit would be able to hear every word and see every move inside her home once he had a Federal judge approve the wiretap. On an emergency level, he could get the authorization he needed in six hours, maybe even four. His gut knotted with worry realizing that Julie would be here alone tonight in her unsecured house.

Or would she?

Maybe she was seeing someone with Emmie conveniently tucked away at her folks' house, thanks to him. Whoever her date was, he'd investigate the guy from the day he was born.

Zach pulled on his jacket and opened the door. Turning to Julie, he gently ran a finger along her jaw. "Lock the door behind me."

"I will," she whispered softly. Smiling, she surprised him with a quick hug. "See you in the morning."

The door clicked as she shut and locked it behind him. A lot of good that lock would do. He could slide a credit card through and let himself back inside in a heartbeat, or kick the door in just as quickly.

Zach scanned the area along the lake. He took in the pleasant scent of tall Douglas fir trees that cast dark shadows along the narrow pathway that led back to the inn. The wind picked up and the sounds of waves breaking along the shore spread through the otherwise quiet night.

There were too many hiding places in this remote part of the grounds. Too many places for snipers to focus their scopes on unsuspecting souls and special agents who were onto them.

A steady rain fell as Zach jogged back to his room. Senior Agent in Charge John Castlerock, aka John Rockwell the chef, would be waiting for him with the newest evidence concerning this case.

They would be up all night going over the details on several unanswered mysteries — finding Agent Tomasino, who hadn't been heard from in months, determining who could have taken shots at Zach, and figuring out who had killed the groundskeeper.

An uneasy feeling that he was missing something settled in his gut. While Zach was pleased that John had established his cover at the inn, he had the distinct feeling that his boss was holding something back. Besides the fact that Julie had a daughter, what other details had the Bureau hidden from him?

Zach's intuitive nature overwhelmed him

with two unshakable conclusions.

Julie was in grave danger.

And so was he.

He could be falling for her . . . all over again.

FOUR

"What kind of evidence?" Zach sank into a molded steel chair in the industrial-sized kitchen. Glancing around the huge room, he noted the various copper pots and pans hanging from a ceiling fixture and confirmed that he and Agent Castlerock were alone.

"More surveillance photos," John answered scanning the entrance to the room.

"Hand them over."

John unlocked the briefcase he'd secretly stowed inside a cabinet underneath the granite countertop and offered the large manila envelope to Zach. "Take a look for yourself."

Zach slid its contents onto the counter. Several newer incriminating pictures stared back at him. Julie sitting comfortably next to their number one suspect, Viktor Ivanov, laughing and sharing dinner at some fancy dining establishment in Seattle. Another photograph revealed them kissing on her front porch. Inwardly Zach cursed.

"Satisfied?" John slapped him on the back in a gesture of camaraderie.

"For all we know, she was just dating the jerk," Zach answered. But he knew better. The evidence against Julie was piling up.

"I suppose there's a remote chance Julie is only dating him." John frowned. "I'll give you that." He ran a hand over his brow. "There's more news. Agent Robbins spotted Viktor's boss, Yuri, in Seattle last night."

"Yuri?" Zach stood. "So we're close."

John nodded. "She'll work her way into his life. Once we know where he's headquartered, we'll tap the place. Getting to him is just a matter of time. When it's all said and done, we'll see where Julie fits into all of this."

"Right. But we'll have to move fast." At the sound of approaching footsteps, Zach pushed the photos back into the envelope and handed the folder to Agent Castlerock. John slid the evidence into the attaché case, locking and stowing it back in its hiding place seconds before Beatrice entered the kitchen.

"Oh. You're here early, John." She cleared her throat. "So, what kind of breakfast pastries are you baking today?"

"Anything you want, Trixie." Smiling and pouring on the charm, John gave Beatrice a wink.

"That's Beatrice, if you please. No American nicknames for me." She turned to Zach. "What are you doing here so early?"

Zach rested a hand on the dark granite counter. "Julie and I are taking a day trip into Olympic National Park. I was wondering if the lodge could prepare a lunch. I was just asking John what he could rustle up." He flashed his best smile.

"Yeah, he wants to know what kind of baked treats Julie would like," John said, turning to Beatrice. "What's her favorite? You should know, having been here in the States for what, six months now?"

"Seven months, remember? I already told you." She shook her head in mock annoyance and turned to Zach. "Cranberry-orange muffins. Julie loves them."

"I think I can arrange that," John answered.

"I'll prepare the lunch. Picnic basket, too." Beatrice pushed up the sleeves of her dark green sweater. She grabbed a white apron from one of the drawers. "She can certainly use some time off. When are you leaving?" she asked, turning back to Zach.

"I'm picking her up at six."

"What?" She glanced at the clock on the wall. "It's a good thing I got up early. I'll have just enough time."

Time. Did they have the time they needed to solve this case? Turning to glance out the small window, Zach watched the dawn of another drizzly day. Maybe it was *time* he came to his senses about Julie and realize she was not the sweet, young woman he once loved. She might be nothing more than a coldhearted spy.

"I'm being ridiculous." Julie paced the kitchen as she spoke to her best friend, Tiffany, on the phone. Knowing she was usually awake at dawn, Julie had called to fill her in on Zach's unexpected arrival at Shadow Lake Inn.

"Your feelings for Zach run deep." Tiff sighed. "I remember you two back in college. You were so much in love. I was envious, you know."

"You were?"

"Sure. Who wouldn't be? The special way Zach always looked at you, the tender way he treated you? He was so obviously in love, it made me really think about my life. Then, thank goodness, I met Kenny. Oh, hold on a sec." Julie heard the phone being placed onto a countertop. "AJ," Tiff called to her four-year-old son, "don't push your sister." There was a commotion and then Tiff returned to the phone. "You still there?"

"Yes." Julie smiled and checked her watch. It was just a few minutes before six. Zach would be at her door in a few minutes and Julie needed her best friend's practical advice. "Talk some sense into me before I make a fool of myself and . . . kiss him."

"Here's my take on Zach, Julie, whether you want it or not." Tiff laughed. "Kiss him already."

"Not a good idea." Julie paced the room and tucked a strand of hair behind an ear. "Zach and I have nothing in common. He's like a tornado . . . and I'm more like the immovable tree firmly planted in the ground."

"Nonsense. Just one little kiss or two. Seems to me you need to shake up your life. Zach always could do that to you."

"Exactly." Julie knew that any time spent with Zach would be a hair-raising adventure in one way or another. "I don't need to be shaken up. I like things the way they are."

"Julie, you've cocooned yourself up in the lodge for too long. It's time to break out and fly."

"I've been dating." Julie checked the backs of her small gold earrings, the ones her

89

grandmother had given her for her sixteenth birthday. She didn't want to lose them hiking.

"Dating? You mean . . . Nick?" Tiff cleared her throat.

"Yes. We see each other whenever he can get away from work."

There was a long pause. "Hmm."

"What?" Julie asked detecting the obvious restraint in her friend's voice.

"Oh, I don't know. I just wish you would see someone else. That's all. *Anyone* else, actually."

"What? Nick is . . . nice," Julie answered, surprised by Tiff's revelation.

"He just . . . well, what does he do for a living anyway? Something's not right about him, Julie. I've only met him once, but I don't know . . ." Her voice trailed off.

"Now you're being ridiculous."

"Maybe. Maybe not. But, back to Zach. Now *there's* a guy who could bring some excitement into your life," Tiff answered.

"That's the last thing I need." Julie bit her lip and took a quick breath. She couldn't tell Tiff about the murder. There was no one she could tell. A brief, hard knock on the front door startled Julie and she almost dropped the phone. "Oh, that must be him now. He's right on time." *As usual. Some things never change.* "I have to go."

"Okay, but just wait." Tiff paused. "What harm can one little kiss do? Julie, you've single-handedly turned the lodge into a major success. You're raising the sweetest little girl ever, all alone. Well, with God's help, of course. You're one of the strongest women I've ever known. Yet you're afraid of one little kiss from Zach? Once you *do* kiss him, you might find that the spark . . . just isn't there anymore. That would make things safer, wouldn't it? AJ, sweetie, come here. Look, Julie, I'll call you later when the kids are asleep for all the spine-tingling details."

Julie hung up the phone and checked her hair in the mirror hanging in the small foyer. This little trip today was all about Zach and why he was back in Washington State. Where had he been all this time? Maybe Tiff was right and there would be nothing to the kiss. Nothing at all. Julie didn't know whether to feel relieved at the prospect of a meaningless kiss, or deeply disappointed. She made her way to the front door and opened it.

Zach stood with one arm anchored against the doorjamb. A slow, lazy grin crossed his face. "Hi." Silvery morning mist swirled behind him as his gaze met hers.

Broad shoulders filled the supple black leather jacket that fit smoothly over a gray sweatshirt. His worn jeans did little to conceal the firm muscles in his long legs. Fighting the natural instinct to draw near to him and settle into his warm embrace, Julie swallowed and managed to find her voice. "Hello, Zach."

"You ready?" Running a hand along his jaw, his gaze drifted slowly down the length of her body.

"Yes, I'm all set."

"You're wearing hiking boots. Good. I was hoping we'd find some unexplored spots where we can hike."

"I — I'm not much of a hiker, Zach. I don't want to get all muddy, and —"

"Hey, Jewels, where's your sense of adventure? You must have one deep inside . . . somewhere," he teased.

"Don't call me that."

"Oh, right." He smiled. "Sorry." Reaching out, he gently tucked a strand of hair behind her ear. She fought the impulse to tilt her face into his warm, large hand. Slowly, he let his arm drop to his side. "I need you to help me navigate. It's been a while since I've driven along the Pacific Coast Highway. Or up to Hurricane Ridge." He cleared his throat. "Remember?"

His eyes darkened and Julie's heart melted, recalling the time they'd spent together all those years ago. No matter how hard she tried, more memories surfaced. She booted them back into the recesses of her mind. What had he said? Something about helping him navigate? "Then you must've brought a map." She took her jacket from the coatrack and reached for her overnight bag.

"Map?" he queried in mock surprise. "We don't need any maps. We'll wing it. More fun that way." His gaze went to the overnighter. "I'll get that." Zach easily took the heavy bag from her hands. "What do you have in here, anyway?" He frowned and adjusted the soft, floral duffel bag from one hand to the other.

Julie would wing it to get the scoop on him, even if she had to get her boots dirty. Even if they got lost in the mountains of the rain forest. He'd have his escapade and she'd get the answers she wanted. What *had* he been doing all these years? "Let's stop at the lodge first and get a cup of coffee before we leave. I haven't had any yet," she said, locking the door behind them.

"Already taken care of. I have coffee and warm muffins in the truck. Courtesy of John." Zach flashed a smile.

"Oh." He seemed to have everything under control. Maybe back on the ranch he was used to early mornings. Covering a yawn, she smiled. "Good. I really do need my coffee."

Chuckling, Zach placed his hand on her elbow. "I remember."

Julie swallowed. Were they going on a hike or a walk down memory lane?

They made their way toward the inn, eventually crossing the narrow, dirt road in front of the resort. He pressed the keyless entry remote to pop open the back of the vehicle and then placed her luggage in with his. "I've got a thermos filled with your favorite coffee. Vanilla almond, right?" He turned to her. "At least that's what Beatrice says. She's the one who packed the lunch and the muffins you love. Cranberry something." He opened the passenger door for her then hurried over to his side of the truck. When they'd fastened their seat belts, he reached over to the backseat and handed the thermos to her, along with two thermal mugs.

"Thanks." Julie unscrewed the top, savoring the fragrant aroma. She poured the much-needed steaming liquid into her cup and took a slow, savoring sip. "So, you've spoken to Beatrice already this morning?"

What else had they discussed? Surely Beatrice wouldn't have mentioned the photographs . . . would she? Julie took another sip of hot coffee and prayed that her friend had kept her mouth shut.

"Yeah." Zach pulled out of the parking space and headed along the road to the main highway. "Several times. I'm even getting used to her British accent."

Several times? Julie swallowed too quickly and started coughing. "I'm —" she cleared her throat and took in a deep breath "— surprised she's up this early."

"Really? She was wide-awake and quite chatty, as a matter of fact." He nodded at the thermos. "Pour me some?"

"Oh, sure."

Once they were on the main highway and they'd both enjoyed their morning coffee and muffins, Julie decided it was time to hear about Zach's past.

"You know everything about me, Zach, honestly. Well, you know enough, let me put it that way," she added. "Now it's your turn."

He briefly turned his gaze from the road to meet hers. "I suppose you want me to start talking."

"Yes." No matter how she tried to remind herself that they were just good friends, Julie had to fight the need she felt to comfort him, to somehow ease the pain she saw buried deep within his eyes. "We're friends, Zach. Is it so hard to talk to me?"

Reaching for her hand, Zach turned to face her. "You *are* a good friend," he said, his voice low. "Just give me a little time and I'll tell you everything, okay?"

"Okay, Zach, but sometime today would be nice." She smiled.

Meeting her gaze, Zach chuckled. "Today, I promise."

"Okay." Being friends again would give her the closure she needed. She would finally know about his life and then he'd go back to Montana. That would end the mystery. She'd give him some space until he was ready.

An hour later, after much small talk, Zach turned to her. "I'm starved. Want to look for a place where we can pull off the road?"

"And talk?" she encouraged, giving him a smile.

"Yes, and talk."

"I'm hungry, too. You know, I think I remember a picnic area several miles up the road. We could —"

"Hey . . . look!" Zach indicated the sign they approached. "World's Largest Spruce Tree." He slowed the truck and made a

96

sharp right-hand turn. "We can have our lunch there." His gaze met hers. "What do you say?"

"Um, okay."

"Are you sure, Jewels?" he kidded. "I could turn back around. I know you like everything planned out."

Julie glanced out her side window. "Yes, I do. But I've been wondering about that lately," she added, almost as if she were thinking aloud. She felt restless. Unsettled. Was it possible that Zach was as lonely as she was? She sighed. She *was* lonesome. She hadn't realized how much until now. Maybe Tiff was right. Maybe she *did* need to shake up her world a little. But hadn't her world been tossed around enough with the murder?

Zach turned briefly to face her. "We'll play it by ear, okay?"

"Sounds like . . . a plan." Julie gave him a teasing glance.

Chuckling, Zach slowed the car to the twenty-five-mile-an-hour speed limit. They drove on a meandering dirt road that led them deeper into the ancient woodlands. "We're here," Zach said an hour later, pointing at another sign. "There's the trailhead." He pulled the 4×4 over to the embankment.

"What do you think?" he asked, turning to her.

Julie glanced at the professionally made, wooden sign at the beginning of the trail, mentioning the distance to the World's Largest Spruce Tree, and drew a sigh of relief. How bad could it be with a custom-made sign to lead the way? "It looks good," she said, inhaling the pleasant woodsy aroma of the emerald-green rain forest. "Let's get started." They got out of the truck.

Unloading the heavy backpack with their picnic lunches, Zach placed it around his shoulder and handed a navy-blue blanket to Julie, along with the jacket she brought. "You warm enough? It's a lot cooler up here."

"I'll be fine once we get moving." She put on the roomy, lightweight jacket. "Let's go."

As they climbed, the trail grew thicker, denser. Massive trees and branches loomed overhead, blocking out daylight with every uphill step they took. The world outside the path they were on no longer seemed to exist. Every crunch of their boots along the ground, every snapping twig became the only sounds of the seldom-traveled environment they entered. The airborne mosses hanging from branches of oak trees lent a dreamlike image to the landscape. Julie sighed at the beauty of God's creation. A quiet peace settled in her soul and she thanked God for His presence.

Glancing to her right, she saw a round, flattened out patch of ground next to a huge tree trunk. Had they just passed the sleeping place of a brown bear? Just to see the world's largest spruce tree? What if a hungry cougar was hiding somewhere around the next bend? She'd heard cougars had been attacking hikers lately.

"Boo!" Zach's word echoed softly in her ear, his warm breath on her neck.

Julie shrieked and started to run. Zach grabbed her by the backpack to stop her flight. She turned to face him and swallowed hard, her throat too dry to speak.

"You okay?" He chuckled quietly. "You, uh, you looked a little worried." His gray-blue eyes sparkled in amusement and he ran a hand along his jaw to try to cover a smile.

Julie found her voice and placed a hand to her heart. "You scared me, Zach!" He'd been behind her the whole time and must've noticed her cautious glances. "How could you frighten me like that?" She looked around the path, fearing that wild creatures might run toward them, thinking *they* were lunch. Especially since she'd just screamed. Brown bears and cougars inhabited the area. "Don't do that again!" But his contagious grin made her giggle. "Honestly, you are . . . so bad."

"Sorry. Come on, I think we're almost there." He placed an arm around her shoulder. "You okay now?" he asked, the remnant of a smile lingering on his face.

"I'm fine, it's just creepy . . . so dark in the middle of the day." She glanced around again to make sure there weren't any beasts hiding in the bushes.

"This is it. Look." Zach pointed to a clearing just ahead. "There's the sign again. World's Largest Spruce Tree." Zach turned to her and his gaze met hers. "Is this the perfect place for our picnic or what?" His enthusiastic, boyish smile touched her heart. It was the first real smile she'd seen on him since his arrival.

Julie took a sigh of relief and looked heavenward. "That has to be the largest tree *ever.*" She never would've seen this wondrous spot in the midst of the rain forest if Zach hadn't encouraged her to have an adventure. "It's a Sitka spruce." She turned to face him. "It *is* lovely, isn't it?"

Zach's gaze lingered for a hushed moment then drifted to her mouth. "Yeah, it sure is." He cleared his throat. "Hand me the blanket," he added, his voice husky. He quickly spread it out by the huge base of the tree. "Grab a seat, I'll unpack the food."

"Don't forget the part about talking," Julie teased.

Zach gave a quick laugh. "You'd never let me."

Julie stretched out on the thick, soft blanket as Zach knelt down beside her and unpacked their food. Acutely aware of his closeness, she attributed her emotions to old memories and took a long, calming breath. Lying on her back and stretching comfortably on the soft blanket, Julie looked up again at the tall, massive spruce tree. The trunk itself was at least thirty feet wide, and the tree had to reach over three hundred feet high into the morning mist.

Her gaze wandered over to Zach and she noticed the amount of food he was taking from the backpack. "Let me help you with all that." Julie rose to a sitting position on the blanket. "How much did they think we could possibly eat?" She smoothed a loose strand of hair away from her eyes. "I can't believe how much is in there."

"Yeah, it's a bottomless pit," Zach agreed. He pulled out a large portion of a honey-glazed ham, several pieces of fried chicken, a couple of sandwiches and a thermos of hot apple cider. "This is enough for a couple of days."

"That's for sure." She laughed softly. "It does look good, though." After Julie finished a sandwich and a piece of chicken, she helped herself to a hot cup of cider and another muffin.

Zach still hadn't said a word about what he'd been doing the past eight years. The suspense was driving her crazy. How much longer would she be able to contain her curiosity? What was it that made Zach unwilling to share his past with her?

Was there something he was hiding?

FIVE

Zach ran a hand through his hair. *I need to speed up the investigation.* There was no time to spare. He would play his part with Julie for all it was worth.

By tomorrow, he'd be pursuing a couple of new leads full-time. He had to secure as much information as possible by then. He took one more sip of cider and leaned against the trunk of the huge spruce tree.

Julie sat only a few inches away, staring into her mug. She glanced up and her gaze met his. Looking into her eyes, Zach realized that of all the people in the world, Julie would be the one to make this easy on him. "I was . . . married, you know. About a year after we said goodbye."

A shadow of surprise flickered across her soft face, but she encouraged him to continue. "What happened?"

"A friend introduced us and I fell for her, for Lisa."

Julie inched closer and they sat shoulder to shoulder, their backs resting against the huge width of the ancient tree. "I often wondered what happened to you." She turned and her gaze met his. "I'm . . . glad you met someone you loved. And who loved you, Zach," she whispered.

He rested his chin on her head. "Yeah, me, too." Their marriage hadn't been an ideal one, but he and Lisa had come to love each other in their own way. Zach fiddled with the mug in his hands. "We dated for a while and when Lisa realized she was carrying our child . . . we were married." He glanced to Julie, who sat only a breath away. She didn't bat an eyelash.

Zach gazed into Julie's familiar, deep blue eyes and wished he knew the reason she'd said no to his proposal all those years ago. He forced himself to put aside their shared past and concentrate on the investigation. He'd never been able to verbalize what happened to Lisa and his daughter before to anyone, not at this length. "Did you . . . start dating again, after your husband died?" he asked, searching for new information. A possible new lead.

"After a year or so, but we're talking about you, remember?"

"Right." He took in a long, shaky breath.

"My daughter, Ashley . . . wasn't even one yet . . ." he said, his voice trailing off. Inwardly, he swore. Here he was, forced to talk about the past and the guilt he'd kept hidden deep inside, buried within a well-built fortress of stone. "There was a car accident. . . ."

Julie's eyes brimmed with moisture. "Oh, Zach," she whispered. She reached out and smoothed back the hair that had fallen across his forehead. Her fingers lingered for a brief moment.

Her unexpected, tender touch filled Zach's heart with memories of happier times. Simpler times. He took her hand in his and for one precious minute, he allowed himself to forget his assignment — Julie the spy — and concentrate on Julie the woman. He gently pressed his lips to her palm.

"I tried to convince Lisa, over the phone, not to make that trip with Ashley to see her girlfriend that day. I was . . . out of town." *On a mission.* "The weather forecast predicted torrential rains. The phone lines went down and our conversation was disconnected." He cleared his throat. "That was probably the only day in history they were ever right about the weather."

Julie rested her forehead against his.

"Zach," she whispered. "Tell me what happened."

Julie's warm breath brushed his jaw. Zach wrapped his arms around her, drawing her into a light embrace. The clean scent of her soft, thick hair mingled with the balsam fragrance of the rain forest. Julie's inner glow reminded him of the peace he'd had as a Christian. But because of the life he'd led, he didn't think there was a place for him in Heaven. "There was no way *anyone* could've avoided the 18-wheeler that fishtailed off the wet highway and careened right into them." He cleared his throat and drew in a deep breath.

Julie slowly released herself from his arms and lifted her gaze to meet his. "You lost them . . . both?" A lone tear slipped down her cheek. "The . . . the baby, too?"

"Yeah . . . Ashley, too," he whispered, his voice barely audible. Instinctively, he encircled Julie in his arms again. He needed her warmth, her sweetness to surround him. But was she the same innocent woman he knew back then?

"Oh, Zach, I — I'm so sorry. There are no words. . . ." she whispered, her voice trailing off.

"I know." He drew a much-needed breath. "It's okay." Zach brushed away Julie's tear with the pad of his thumb. He looked deeply into her eyes. The soft, blue eyes of . . . a *spy?* "It happened four years ago," he continued. "Ashley would've been as old as Emmie is now . . . if she'd lived."

"Oh, Zach. It must've hurt, seeing Emmie. Reminding you all over again . . . of what could have been." Gently, Julie ran a hand along his jaw. "I'm glad you told me, Zach. I think I would have lost my mind when Tim died . . . if not for Emmie."

Zach took Julie's small hand in his. Their fingers entwined together again, as if they'd never been apart. "After the funeral and you know, all the official paperwork and stuff —"

"Yes. I know how hard that is," Julie admitted between sniffles.

"Well, right after that, I headed back home to Montana. To the ranch I loved. Work, hard work, was just what I needed." He hated the lies. The half lies anyway. Guilt-ridden after his wife and daughter died, he'd quit the SEALs and headed back to Montana, but within a few weeks, the FBI had recruited him. He jumped at the adventurous opportunity. It was just what he needed to work off his grief. His guilt. If only he'd been there for his wife and daughter, maybe they'd be alive today.

Gently, he brought Julie's hand to his chest. Every time he touched her, the sorrow in his heart became more bearable. But he had a job to do. He would kiss her for the sake of the investigation. But the kisses they shared wouldn't be as sweet. The suspicion that stood between them was like a barbed wire fence.

"I know what you mean." Julie sighed deeply. "After Tim died, I threw myself into building up the lodge. The business grew so fast, I hired Beatrice and a few other employees." Julie brushed another tear from her eye. "I even had my parents helping me for a while." She laughed quietly. "They loved it actually."

"Yeah, work helps . . . that's for sure. But it doesn't ease the pain enough, does it?"

"I know." She nodded. "Burying a loved one . . . the finality of it." Julie's voice broke and Zach pulled her close. "Having a deep faith in God was the only thing that got me through."

God? He remembered the faith Julie had back then. Seeing her now, he realized her faith seemed deeper somehow. How did she manage that? Or was this another act?

They remained quiet for a while. Distinctive sounds of the rain forest surrounded them in restful release. Birds singing, leaves rustling in the light breeze, the sound of Julie's soft breathing as he placed his arm around her and drew her close — all this filled Zach's heart with a peace he hadn't felt in years. But he couldn't let himself be lulled into a false sense of safety.

She lifted her gaze to meet his. "What made you come back to Washington State, Zach? Why are you here?"

He chuckled uneasily. His gut knotted with the story he'd have to tell. But he would not blow his cover with her. "Did I ever tell you about my brothers?"

"Your brothers? Um, yes, I think you did. Luke and —"

"Jake. Anyway, according to them, I've been hard to live with, working long hours." He glanced over her shoulder to scan the area. It was a natural instinct by now. Not seeing anything out of the ordinary, Zach reached for the thermos and poured himself another cup of hot cider. "You want a warm-up?" he asked.

"No, I'm fine."

Placing the closed thermos in the backpack, Zach stretched his legs out in front of him. "You, uh, you sure you want to hear all of this?" He turned to her and smiled ruefully.

"Yes, I do." She cuddled closer.

Good. She was right where he wanted her. "My brothers have been trying to fix me up with a variety of women the past couple of years. The way I see it, they figured I'd be easier to live with . . . if I had a steady woman to, uh, to spend time with." He turned to her and winked. "I'm sure you've had your share of blind dates arranged by well-meaning friends. You've probably dated lots of men the past couple of years, someone as pretty as you."

"Blind dates can be difficult, that's for sure. Although I have been seeing someone on and off the past few months." She turned to him and then crossed her arms in front of her. "Wait a minute. You're doing it again."

"What?" he asked innocently. His heart raced with the possibility of a name. Good old Viktor would be using another alias. Or maybe he was still using *Nick?* Zach wanted to confirm the first and last name Viktor was going by these days. The surname was bound to be different from the other names he'd used. Once they had that information, the Bureau could zero in on him. "So who are you dating? Do I know him?"

"This is about *you,* not me." She playfully poked him in the chest.

"Oh, yeah, right." No problem. He'd get

the details he wanted soon enough. "I for-got."

"You, *forget?* Please." She took a sip of cider and returned her gaze to meet his. "Okay, so your brothers were trying to set you up. What happened?"

Maybe she knew him too well. This might not be as easy as he thought. "Well, I told them in no uncertain terms to knock it off. I thought I'd convinced them. Anyway —" he drew in a quick breath "— they insisted I get away for a while. The deal was, they got to send me on a vacation of their choice. They told me not to come back until I was my old self again."

"So they sent you to Shadow Lake Inn," Julie stated.

"Yeah. I didn't know until the day I left, the day they handed me the airline ticket, that I'd be going back to Washington State. When you and I literally ran into each other in the lobby and I learned that you owned the place, I just figured —"

"Wait. You figured I was *in* on it?" Julie asked, a surprised look on her face. "That somehow I was working with them . . . to get you to take your vacation here?" Her wide-eyed expression revealed her disbelief.

"Yep, I sure did."

"How could you think such a thing? So

that's why you —"

"Yeah. That's why I acted like such a jerk. Why I acted so cold." But the real reason for his anger was the disappointment he'd suddenly felt knowing that Julie might be selling secrets to terrorists. "I called home later that night and spoke to Luke. He really had no idea what I was talking about. I finally believed him. I knew then that I needed to apologize to you." Zach turned to her and cleared his throat. "You meant the world to me once, Julie. It really was good to see you again after all these years. And now . . ." He looked into her eyes, and lowered his gaze to her lips.

"And now?" she whispered softly.

Julie tilted her face up to meet his gaze. It had been so long since they'd shared sweet kisses. Too long. "Julie," he managed, his voice barely above a whisper.

Before his lips touched hers, Zach heard the sound of a twig snapping in the distance. Had he been set up? Was someone lurking in the massive woods surrounding them, ready to take him down?

Reaching for the Glock he had resting in his ankle holster, he scanned the horizon somewhere over Julie's right shoulder. A flash of light appeared from the farthest sector of the highly wooded area. Was there a shooter out there ready to take him out? Suddenly, Zach saw the more imminent danger.

"Hey, uh, Julie," he breathed. "Just how fast can you run in those boots?" He slipped the handgun back into its holster, grateful he hadn't drawn it for her to see. He reached for the backpack that held the cider and the rest of the food. Zach handed her his keys. "Get back to the truck. I'll be right behind you. Unlock it and get inside." He lifted her from where she sat and nudged her toward the path they'd taken. "Go!" Zach turned her in the direction they'd taken on the way to the picnic spot. "Now!"

Stunned, Julie turned to see what he'd been staring at. She blinked and tried to move. A huge bear lumbered toward them. The monstrous animal stopped for one frightening moment to stand on its hind legs and roar an unearthly sound that Julie would never forget. Somehow, she got her legs to work and she started to run. Branches and overgrowth pelted her in the face as Julie tried desperately to find the trailhead and the safety of Zach's truck. Was she even on the right path?

"Keep going!" Zach shouted behind her. "Don't stop!"

Julie slipped and fell in a muddy section of the trail.

Oh, God, please . . . don't let me die in a mud pit!

In a horror-filled moment, and what felt like slow motion, she lifted herself up from the ankle-deep muck. Zach caught up with her and without breaking his stride, grabbed her by the waistband of her jeans. In one swift move, he brought her to her feet. "Go! Move it!"

Together they ran toward the truck. Breathless, Julie almost passed out when she finally saw the vehicle. Would they make it in time? The thunderous roar of the bear seemed even louder than before.

"It's right behind us. You still have the keys?" Zach yelled as they continued running and stumbling down the hilly terrain.

Julie had them in a death grip in her right hand. "Yes. I — I've got them," she shouted, thankful she hadn't dropped them in the mud.

"Hit the unlock button. Hit it now, twice . . . and get inside. Hurry!"

In a heartbeat, Julie pressed the button and opened the passenger side of the 4×4. She slammed her door shut and turned to see Zach, backpack slung across his shoulder and the navy-blue blanket waving in the breeze as he sprinted to the truck.

The huge bear was not wasting any time trying to get to him. Zach tossed the entire heavy red backpack at the bear, smacking it squarely in the snout. Stunned, the animal slowed then sniffed to inspect the gourmet contents.

Zach rolled across the hood of the truck. He climbed inside the driver's side and slammed his door shut. Julie had already placed the muddy key in the ignition and started the engine. Zach gunned it and tore down the road. Tires screeched, kicking up the dirt. During one terror-filled moment, Julie prayed they'd get the traction they needed.

"Come on!" Zach shouted, urging the 4×4 into action. Suddenly, the truck lifted onto the highway and sped down the road.

Julie stared as the animal paused to tear at the lunch Zach had thrown to it. Once she knew they'd be okay, she turned to Zach. They were both breathing hard. He glanced at her. A big grin crossed Zach's face and his eyes lit in excitement. He laughed aloud. "You sure can run!" he said, snagging her hand. "Did you see that bear? It was *huge!*"

Julie pulled her trembling hand from his.

"This . . . is not funny. We could have been killed!"

"Yeah, but we weren't." He glanced at her shaky hands as she wiped them on her mud-stained jeans. "Hey, you all right?"

"Am I . . . all right? Of course I'm not all right. We were almost eaten alive by a bear!" She smacked his shoulder with her hand. "Ouch!"

"What? What happened?"

"That . . . hurt." She rubbed her hand and sniffled.

Julie's wide-eyed expression and mud-smeared face was enough to give Zach a reality check. She was frightened. What would she say if she knew there might be someone with an automatic weapon after them? Did she already know? Had she *planned* it that way?

"You think this is . . . funny, don't you?" she asked, her face reflecting disbelief, fear and anger.

"No . . . no, of course not." Zach cleared his throat and ran a hand along his upper lip to hide a smile. She sure was cute, all fired up and feisty. He turned to her again and reached across to trace a smudge of mud that stretched from her right temple to the corner of her full, soft lips. Lips he

116

wanted to kiss before another moment passed. There was no time to waste in this investigation. He was running out of patience and needed to make a move. Now.

Spotting the well-hidden turnoff he'd already mapped out, he pulled the truck over, knowing they'd be safe concealed there for a couple of minutes. Shifting the gear into Park, he left the motor running just to be on the safe side. The bear had spooked him, too, even though he'd enjoyed the excitement of the chase. But he cursed himself for being so flippant about it with Julie. She was obviously scared. Or giving an Oscar-worthy performance.

"Come here." Zach pulled her to him. "You're shaking," he whispered. He wanted to console her. And if he didn't kiss her soon he'd lose his mind. Maybe once he did kiss her, she'd tell him about the guy she was seeing. *Viktor.* "Let me hold you a while. I'm sorry. That encounter with the bear *was* close. Too close. And not the least bit . . . funny." He bit down on the inside of his cheek to stop himself from laughing.

He had no reason for levity with the possible glint of a weapon he'd seen from a distance. But he hadn't had this much fun in what felt like forever. The anticipation of kissing Julie made him feel like a carefree college guy again. He'd forgotten the old Zach Marshall. Was it possible that guy still even existed?

He stroked her silky, blond hair and held her close. She rested her head on his chest as he whispered comforting words to calm her. After a moment, she relaxed and snuggled close.

"Julie, you're more beautiful than ever." He brushed his lips along her soft mouth. His breath caught in his throat.

"Zach, I've . . . missed you," Julie whispered. She sighed and his heart ached at hearing the soft, familiar sound. There was still something special between them. Julie was the only woman he knew who could capture his heart so completely.

Julie, his college sweetheart — and the Bureau's prime suspect in a national security case of espionage — had the power to mesmerize him with nothing more than her gentle touch. Or one sweet kiss.

But they were too vulnerable parked along the roadside, even in the cover of the dense brush surrounding them. This case was escalating at a quicker pace than any of them had realized. He needed to come to his senses about this pretend relationship.

They had no real future together.

Julie was a courageous woman who had

built a wonderful life for herself and her daughter. Did that include spying for the Russians?

Zach pulled her more closely against him. She moaned softly in his arms. The delicious sound nearly drove him nuts and for a moment, he toyed with the idea of lingering and taking things a step further. Breathing hard, he trailed a finger gently along her chin down the length of her soft neck. In a sudden bone-chilling moment of clarity, he wondered . . . was Julie using *him?*

Inwardly, he cursed. Okay, he was up for the part.

He'd get what he needed to solve this case. He'd kiss her senseless and drive himself crazy by spending so much time with the woman he once loved — when life was young and the world was theirs.

Six

Julie closed her eyes and leaned into Zach's embrace. Kissing him was even better than she remembered. Much different, she realized, than when she kissed Nick. "I don't think this . . . is such a good idea," she whispered.

"You . . . really believe that?" he said breathlessly, his lips feathering her neck.

"No," she answered, her voice barely audible.

"Me, either." Running the pad of his thumb along her bottom lip, Zach's intense gaze met hers. "I want to be with you again, Julie."

"Zach, this . . . scares me." Slowly she broke free from his embrace.

"What, you think that bear is still following us?" he kidded, glancing out the window.

"Oh!" *The bear.* She'd almost forgotten about the bear! She turned to look out the back window. "You don't really think it would follow us, do you?"

"No, he's probably still eating the rest of our lunch. Especially the honey-glazed ham."

"Beatrice will have a fit," Julie said, sliding over to the passenger seat and pressing her face to the window to get a better look.

"We need to stop somewhere and wash up." Leaning toward her, he slowly pulled the seat belt over Julie's lap and secured it in place. He turned her to face him. "Did you hurt yourself when you fell?"

"Only a little." She shrugged her shoulders. "I think I was more worried about dropping the keys in the mud. I'm a little shaky, that's all." Julie took a moment to appraise the condition of her muddy clothes. Her long-sleeved shirt had worked its way loose from the waistband of her jeans. Mud covered the front of the soft cotton and streaked down her chest. The top two buttons of her shirt had come undone. "Oh, look at me."

"Yeah, you're covered in mud."

Julie suppressed a giggle. "I'm not the only one."

"What?" Zach examined his image in the rearview mirror and ran a hand along his jaw. "Huh, you're right."

Zach's good looks were only enhanced by

121

his "romp in the woods" appearance. Great. There went the theory that once she kissed him, they could just be friends.

Zach checked his watch. "I'd wanted us to take a drive along the coast, but maybe we should head back. As it is, we'll probably get in late, around ten." He fastened his seat belt and placed the truck into Drive. "We'll stop for dinner at one of the port towns we passed on the way. What do you say?"

Turning to Zach, Julie recognized the unmasked awareness in his blue-gray eyes. "That sounds good. I'm sure we'll be hungry by then. I didn't have a chance to finish my food," she admitted. "But the bear had a really good lunch."

Zach laughed. "Yeah, but I think he would've preferred *us*." He glanced down at her legs. "Your jeans are ripped. You sure you're all right?" Reaching over, he gently touched the exposed skin around her knee. "You've got a nasty cut."

"Oh." Julie examined her jeans. There was a large tear below her knee on one leg and several rips on the other. The pain she'd felt on her leg turned out to be a bad scrape. She was surprised to see a trickle of blood and a large bruise peeking through another jagged opening of her jeans. "I didn't notice these." She ran a hand over her knee. "Guess I was too busy running."

Zach reached over and gently traced a finger along her jaw. He curled his fingers under her chin and lifted her gaze to meet his. "At least you didn't scratch your face," he said, examining her closely. "How bad is your knee?"

"Um, not too bad."

Zach drew a deep breath and turned his head away, muttering a string of curses under his breath. "I'm sorry, Julie."

She placed a hand on his arm and said, "It's not your fault."

"Yeah, it is." He turned to face her. "You didn't want to go up that trail in the first place and now . . . you're hurt."

"It's nothing, really." She smiled, thinking about the bear chasing them, the beauty of the world's largest spruce tree and the deep, personal emotions they'd shared. The honesty of that special moment would always be a precious memory for her.

Another memory.

Was their relationship destined to be nothing more than a series of reflections leading nowhere? Thinking about their narrow escape, Julie couldn't help but smile. Despite the danger, in her mind's eye she pictured Zach running from the bear. She tried to squelch the deep laughter bubbling up inside. Wiping away a tear with the back of her hand, she took a deep breath only to start laughing aloud.

"What's so funny?" Zach asked, his eyes fixed on the road ahead.

"That bear . . . running after us," she managed between fits of giggling. "Eating our specially prepared *gourmet* lunch."

"You thought that was funny?" Turning his eyes from the road to glance at her, he raised an eyebrow.

She nodded her head. "You, running with the blanket and the backpack . . . with Beatrice's special lunch inside. And then —"

"What?"

"You hit it right in the snout." She laughed aloud again, realizing she hadn't had this much fun in years.

"What did you expect me to do? You sure you're okay?" he teased. "It didn't seem so *entertaining* at the time." Zach gave her an incredulous look. "I could feel his breath on my back!"

Julie wiped away another tear. "Really? Oh. But Zach, it was just so . . . funny. It was like something out of a movie!" She giggled again. Sometimes being up ten thousand feet in the mountains made her giddy.

"Are you saying you actually *enjoyed* this adventure?"

His teasing voice and twinkling eyes made her smile. She'd been so scared when they had to run for their lives from that huge animal. She thought her life was over when she'd fallen flat on her face into a grimy pit of mud. Yet here she was, filled with excitement and happiness.

If she had to do it again, she would. Maybe God had brought them together again as friends, so Zach could find the laughter in his heart and she could enjoy breaking out of her orderly life. Maybe Tiff was right. Maybe it was time to get out of her cocoon of comfort . . . and fly.

"Yes, I guess I am," she answered. "It was fun."

"Then you'll come with me again when I plan another trip?"

Turning to him, she studied his handsome profile. Julie wanted to share more *adventures* with Zach. But just what kinds of adventures did he have in mind?

If they were anything like the thoughts running through her mind, then she was in big trouble.

"We can't tell Beatrice or John what happened to their fancy lunch," Julie whispered as they trudged into the deserted lobby of Shadow Lake Inn later that evening.

"I'm thinking their reactions would be worth the loss. Don't you?" Zach smiled.

Laughing, Julie agreed. "Hmm, maybe you're right. We could have a lot of fun with it, couldn't we?"

"Definitely." Zach winked and placed a hand on the small of her back as they crossed the reception area. The scent of burning wood made him think of snowy winter nights in Montana. He pictured Julie seated in front of the huge stone fireplace in the great room. He'd never been able to imagine any other woman there. Why did Julie's image seem so clear, so right?

Stay sharp, Marshall.

Zach scanned the lobby. "Do you always keep the fire burning this late?" He checked his watch. "It's almost midnight."

"No, we don't." Julie glanced at the massive fireplace and frowned. "That's strange."

"Come on, let's check out the kitchen." Zach took her hand and led her through the large lobby. "I see a light on."

"Oh." Julie nodded. "You're right."

They still needed to confirm Viktor's alias and get the newest last name he was using. So far, the investigation had come up with nothing more than Nick. It had been a week since the information that Viktor was in Washington had made its way to the Bureau. Julie and the murder at the inn seemed to be the closest connection to him.

Vivid images of surveillance photos of Julie kissing Viktor appeared in Zach's mind like a recurring nightmare. Until he could prove otherwise, he'd be wise to cool off and remember she was a suspect — nothing more.

"You scared me to death!" Beatrice's distinctive British accent filled the entryway to the large industrial-sized kitchen.

"Me? I almost decked you. What are you doing up at midnight anyway, wandering around like a ghost?" Castlerock sounded agitated. Had Beatrice caught him? Was his cover blown?

"I couldn't sleep, so . . . I thought I'd check on supplies here in the kitchen. Then I noticed the fire going. I thought . . . oh, never mind. I can't tell you what I thought."

"What? Why not?" Castlerock managed to chuckle. "In the short time we've know each other, you haven't had a problem speaking your mind."

Still holding her hand, Zach led Julie quietly into the kitchen. He made eye contact with Castlerock and stood silently behind an agitated Beatrice.

"I didn't expect you or anyone in the kitchen at midnight," she answered, waving a wooden spoon in her hand. "I almost hit you with this." She pointedly held the large utensil up for him to see, and then glanced around at the bowls of flour, sugar and eggs all over the granite counters. "What are you doing, anyway? I've never seen the kitchen in such a mess. And I've never seen scones prepared this way," she said, still waving the large spoon in the air as she spoke.

Castlerock held his hands up in the air and wore a huge grin. "Woman, be careful where you shake that thing." He folded his hands in front of him and shook his head. "You're attempting to swat a Master Chef . . . with a spoon!" He laughed aloud. "Remember, I *am* a graduate of the CIA."

Zach ran a hand along his jaw and his gaze met John's. His partner was getting a little too close to the truth for comfort.

"What?" Beatrice pressed a hand to her heart, the spoon dangling from her fingers. "You — you're with the Central Intelligence Agency?" She swallowed and her face paled.

"The Culinary Institute of America. Surely you've heard of them," Julie stated. "You know . . . C-I-A. Not *the* CIA."

Startled, Beatrice yelped and turned to face them. "Good grief! I didn't hear you two come in. Are you trying to give me a heart attack?"

John chuckled. "Behave yourself, Trixie. Now put that weapon down before you hurt someone." He gave Zach a quick nod of assurance. Apparently, John had also noticed Beatrice's nervous reaction to the CIA reference.

"That's Beatrice if you please. No American nicknames for me." Straightening her navy-blue sweater over beige slacks, she placed the spoon on the counter and turned to Julie and Zach. "You're finally back." She cleared her throat. "We've been worried."

"Funny, you don't look worried to me," Zach answered. He exchanged an amused glance with Julie.

"What are you arguing about?" Julie walked over to the counter and looked at the tray of freshly baked scones. "These smell delicious."

"Trixie and I were just —"

"Beatrice, my name is Beatrice."

John crossed his arms in front of him and drew in a deep breath. "We're having a difference of opinion on the proper procedure for making scones." He turned to Zach. Leaning against the counter, he continued, "I have the perfect solution, now that you two are here."

"What do you have in mind, exactly?" Zach pulled up a stool and sat at the counter. His partner must have also been an actor in his pre-FBI days. John Castlerock wore that white chef's apron as if he was born into the profession. Zach knew better. John was among the best agents in the Bureau. What was he up to now? Did they have some new evidence on the Englishwoman?

"We'll prepare the scones both ways. You two decide which is best. If I win, I get to call you Trixie." Glancing at Beatrice, John smiled. "If you win, I'll name the scone after you." He laughed heartily. "What do you say, old girl?"

"What? Of all the nerve!" She folded her arms across her chest.

Julie laughed in spite of Beatrice's look of outrage. Or maybe because of it. She enjoyed watching someone get the best of Beatrice for a change, the way John did.

"We'll call it 'Trixie's English Scones.' I'll place them on the morning menu. Sunday brunch, too," John offered, an amused look on his face.

Beatrice paused to think for a moment. "Okay. But we'll call it 'Beatrice's Traditional English Scones.' "

"Nah, too stuffy." John laughed good-naturedly. "The menu is my responsibility and 'Trixie's English Scones' is final." He glanced to Zach. "All this talk has made me hungry. There are some hors d'oeuvres I've already prepared in the refrigerator. What do you say to a midnight snack?" He looked to the three of them. "I don't do this often. Speak now or forever hold your peace."

"Wait a minute." Julie laughed lightly. "You mean *now?*"

"I *am* kind of hungry," Zach said. "Starved, actually." Apparently, John wanted to study the relationship between the two women. This charade would give them that opportunity. Working closely with John the past several years, they were able to communicate with no more than a glance. Maybe they could at least get the two women to admit there had been a murder on the property. The longer that detail was kept from them, the more guilty they appeared in the eyes of the Bureau.

"You're *hungry?*" Beatrice looked at them in disbelief and placed both hands on her hips. "After that huge lunch we prepared? That was enough food for a week."

"Well, yes." Julie cleared her throat and tried not to laugh. After a brief, knowing glance at Zach, she turned to John. "How long will this take?"

"About twenty minutes. Everything's already prepared. I just need to get it in the oven." John reached out to open the industrial-sized refrigerator. "Then we'll make both batches of scones."

Beatrice walked over to the refrigerator and took out a bottle of Pellegrino. "Here, you two enjoy some chilled water while we wait on the appetizers." She handed the bottle to Zach and two long-stemmed crystal glasses to Julie. "How was the lunch, by the way?"

Zach exchanged a quick glance with Julie. "Well, I can honestly tell you that it was thoroughly enjoyed." He gave Julie a wink. "There's nothing left." He cleared his throat. "At all."

Julie fought to keep her laughter from erupting.

"How was the honey-glazed ham?" Beatrice asked.

"Did you enjoy the ham, Julie?" Zach raised an eyebrow and she poked him in the ribs.

Distracted, Beatrice rolled up the sleeves of her sweater and tied a white apron around her waist. She turned back to the open refrigerator. "I'll bring out some cheese and crackers so you can nibble while you wait by the fire."

With the chilled bottle in one hand, Zach led Julie into the lobby. He didn't trust Beatrice. She had started her employment at the lodge at the same time the sensitive information started to exchange hands.

He'd get the answers to his questions soon enough. In the meantime, he'd watch the interplay between the two women. He needed answers and there was no time to waste.

After the long day they'd spent outdoors, the warm glow of the fire felt good. Julie curled up on the sofa, her shapely legs tucked beneath her. Her bruised knee peeked through the hole in her jeans.

He was relieved they'd stopped to clean and bandage her bruises before sitting down. Zach sat next to Julie, and filled their glasses. He placed the bottle on the coffee table across from them.

Comfortable with Julie at his side, Zach needed to get a handle on his emotions. Where were they coming from? Past memories? A change of scenery? Gazing into her eyes, Zach suddenly knew that being with Julie was the reason for the spark of joy in his heart. Not the change of scenery or anything else.

He wanted to be with her now more than ever. More than he'd ever wanted to be with any other woman. This time the feelings he had for her were stronger, more mature. He could see her clearly with him at the Marshall ranch. Sharing a life with him. A couple of kids. Zach shook off the unwelcome images blazing through his mind. They only complicated his life, not to mention his assignment.

After a few minutes of casual conversation, he refilled Julie's glass and poured a little more for himself. "You must love owning and living at the inn. It's nice."

"Yes, it is." Inching closer to him, Julie made herself comfortable on the sofa. "We've built up a good reputation for our fine dining, too." Her mellow gaze met his and she sighed contentedly. "Tell me about Montana and your ranch, Zach. What's it like?"

Drawing a deep breath, he placed his glass on the table. Was she making small talk or did she really want to know? "My parents started the ranch when they were first married. With lots of hardwork, they built it into a successful business."

"Horses, right?"

"Yeah. Since I went back, I purchased five hundred acres from my folks to start a horse ranch of my own, diversifying the business a little with various breeds. It proved to be a good financial move." His gaze met hers and he fought the urge to pull her into his arms. "Living and working on the ranch is something I want to do for the rest of my life." That much was true.

With every assignment, he'd placed his life on the line, especially on this case. Julie was still a suspect in the eyes of the FBI and in his eyes, too. He couldn't let himself forget that. As soon as this investigation was over, he could get back to Montana and pursue what he really wanted to do: work the ranch as a cover for the Bureau. That's where he would find peace, doing the two things he loved most.

Julie smiled and encouraged him to continue. "What's it like in Montana? I've never been there." Her blue eyes softened and all Zach wanted to do was fall asleep with Julie tucked safely in his arms.

He shook off the thought before it had time to take hold. "It's beautiful. Wide-open spaces, horses running wild. Mountains. Trees. Big sky. You'd love it." He gently ran a hand through her long, disheveled hair. Touching her, feeling the silkiness of her hair, was not helping him focus on the case. He needed to start asking questions.

"What about before then?" she asked, placing her hand on his.

"Before then?" he asked.

"Yes." Julie blinked and her thick lashes fluttered. It had been a long day and she was tired. Vulnerable. He hated taking advantage of her, but he had a job to do.

"What did you do before Montana?"

He drew a quick breath. Sweet Julie was zeroing in for the kill. Those fluttering lashes were not the result of being tired. She wanted to know about California. He couldn't help but smile. She'd probably make a great agent, he realized, almost laughing aloud. Understanding that she could very well be working for the other side, he sobered quickly. Her mellow mood was, most likely, an act. Adrenaline surged through him, jolting his senses into high alert. He cursed silently. He'd almost fallen for it.

"Why did you go to California before you went back to Montana, Zach?" Sighing deeply, she seemed sad.

Was it possible she hadn't wanted him to leave without her? It hurt so much when she'd said "no" to his proposal. He'd never heard her explanation as he gunned the engine of his Harley and sped away. He never realized that he might've hurt *her* when he left. All these years later, he still wondered why. Why had she said no?

Gently, he traced a finger across her cheek. Heart racing, Zach took the glass from her hand and placed it alongside his on the table. He drew her close, knowing that she was still a suspect no matter what his gut told him. Forcing his eyes away from the sweetness of her tempting lips, he met her gaze.

Her blue eyes filled with emotion and there was only one thing he wanted to do. Any practical thoughts he had about the investigation faded into the background, even though a warning signal shot off in his cold, analytical FBI mind. It was a warning he ignored. Zach found himself tortured between his overwhelming feelings for Julie and his practical need to investigate her.

Encircling Julie in his arms, all common sense disappeared as his lips met hers. Zach almost stopped breathing at the pure joy of holding Julie in his arms again. He would think about the investigation tomorrow.

For now, he was desperate for her kisses. Her enthusiasm. Her love.

Julie was a light for his soul, overpowering the darkness and emptiness that had lived there for so long.

And the loneliness.

Was it possible that he'd never stopped loving her?

SEVEN

"Your jeans are ripped!" Beatrice stomped into the large fireplace room of the inn and stared wide-eyed at Julie's bandaged knee. "I can't believe I didn't notice it before. What have you two been doing all day?"

"Um . . . I don't know where to start." Julie sat up and laughed self-consciously. "Short story is . . . we went hiking and I slipped and fell in the mud." She turned to Zach and smiled.

"Are you all right?" Beatrice placed the platter of hors d'oeuvres and cheese, and four sets of silverware on the coffee table then shook her head in apparent disapproval. "Those pants are ruined."

"I'll make them into cutoffs. For the summer."

"Oh, well that's a good idea." She cleared her throat. "But how did you cut yourself falling in the *mud?*"

"It's a long story," Julie answered.

John joined them, carrying four small plates of scones in one hand and two more glasses in the other. He set the plates on the table and sat on the sofa next to Beatrice.

Taking the glass of sparkling water that John offered her, Beatrice turned to Zach. "Where did you go anyway?"

Zach controlled the anger boiling inside at the woman's nosy line of questioning. Why did she have the need to know where Julie was every minute? "We were going to take a ride along the Pacific Coast," he answered quickly. "Never made it to Ruby Beach." Turning to Julie, Zach placed a finger on one of the larger rips in her jeans revealing the Band-Aid they'd placed over the cut. "Maybe next time, right, Julie?"

"It would be nice to see Ruby Beach again." Her gaze met his and she smiled.

Zach recalled the late afternoons they'd spent walking hand in hand along the shore watching the sunset over the Pacific Ocean. Reluctantly he pulled his gaze away from Julie and turned to the manager of the lodge. "We got sidetracked." In his peripheral vision, Zach saw that he had Agent Castlerock's full attention, though John remained casual in his demeanor.

"What happened?" John asked nonchalantly.

"How can I put this?" Zach turned to Beatrice. "Your gourmet lunch was the hit of the rain forest. But we didn't get to finish it."

"What?" Beatrice's fingers tightened around the stem of her glass.

"I'm sorry, Beatrice," Julie replied. "It's a shame, really. Everything looked so good. It's just that we were chased by a bear. If it hadn't been for Zach's quick thinking and your huge, delicious lunch —"

"What did my lunch have to do with it?"

"I had to throw the backpack — with your lunch in it — at the bear." Zach eyed Beatrice to monitor her reaction. If it hadn't been for that bear, the shooter he'd seen might've made an attempt on his life. But maybe Beatrice already knew that. Maybe she really *was* surprised to see them walk into the lodge. "It was a close call."

"My word!" Beatrice dramatically placed a hand over her heart. "My gourmet lunch! Eaten by a bear? Are you sure you're all right?"

His instincts told him she was playing the concerned friend and coworker bit for all it was worth. Maybe they should *all* go into show business. Was anyone here telling the truth?

"We're fine. It was scary, but kind of fun."

Julie turned to Zach and flashed a thousand-kilowatt smile. It was good to see that smile again. Taking two more appetizers from the tray, and one of the warm scones, she turned to Beatrice. "I'll tell you all about it tomorrow. I'm too tired and hungry to talk about it now." She took a bite of the English treat. "These are delicious."

An hour later, they arrived at a decision. "It's a tie," John said after the votes were in. "We'll place both recipes on the menu. What do you say?" he asked, turning to Beatrice.

She nodded in agreement. "It's only fair."

"Now I get to call you *Trixie.*" John laughed heartily.

Beatrice rolled her eyes. "Peachy."

"It's late." John started to clear the plates from the coffee table. "I'll clean up the kitchen."

"Here, let me help you." Beatrice assisted John and followed him to the kitchen. Stopping abruptly on her way, she turned to face Julie. "I want to know the details about that bear. I'll talk to you in the morning."

"Yes, in the morning."

"Come on, I'll walk you home," Zach offered, placing Julie's jacket around her shoulders. "It's dark along that lakeside path."

"I had a good time today," Julie admitted when they reached her house. Turning to face him, the lights from the porch projected a warm glow over her face, casting an angelic aura over her long, blond hair. Looking into the depths of her blue eyes, Zach tried in vain to find the deceitful spirit of a spy.

The only evidence he saw was the heart and soul of a sweet woman, a vulnerable woman. She was no spy. His gut instincts had never been wrong before. Could he trust them now when it counted the most?

Reaching into her purse, Julie fumbled for the keys.

"I'll get them." Zach took the keys from her hand then stopped. The hairs on the back of his neck bristled and he forced himself not to reach for the weapon he had tucked in his ankle holster. He couldn't blow his cover in front of Julie, but something was definitely *wrong.*

They were being watched.

He'd swear his life on it.

Moving Julie from the light, he leaned close and spoke softly. "Your door's open. You locked it before we left this morning, right?"

Wide-eyed, Julie nodded her head. "Yes. I did." She glanced at the opened door. "Oh,

Zach," she whispered, "I do remember locking it."

"Come on. Let's take a quick look inside." The light from the porch spilled into the front rooms. Zach slowly nudged the wooden door open with his foot, revealing the foyer and family room. The coffee table was overturned. Drawers had been emptied. The bookshelf, too.

Scanning the first floor, he saw that a window in the kitchen was open. A cold breeze whipped the lacy white curtain. He placed an arm around Julie's shoulder. "Let's get back to the lodge and call the police from there."

"Who would do this? Oh, my grand-mother's things! I have to see if they got to them —"

"What? Julie, don't!"

Before he could stop her, she bolted away from him into the dining room. Zach muttered a curse, knowing there could still be someone hiding inside. He reached for his Glock and stowed it in the outside pocket of his leather jacket where he could reach it faster.

In a few strides, he quickly caught up with her. She held two long-stemmed crystal glasses in her hands — the only ones that hadn't been shattered. Watching her as she stood on the broken pieces of crystal glass in her mud-spattered boots and ripped jeans, Zach's heart ached to hold her close and comfort her. But he was a Special Agent with the Bureau and she was his suspect. That would always be between them, even when he did try to console her.

"At least they left the china." She looked up at him, her eyes brimming with tears.

"I want you out of here. *Now.*"

"But Zach —"

"You can come back after the police have checked the place out." He firmly placed an arm around her waist and guided her out the back door until they were inside the relative safety of the lodge.

They must've surprised whoever had broken into her house. He or she had probably crawled out the kitchen window. It could be the work of the woman who'd taken shots at him. Or the same person who had killed the groundskeeper.

Whoever it was, someone had been looking for something. But what? Did it have anything to do with that old cardboard box Julie had brought down from the attic?

Clutching her grandmother's long-stemmed crystal glasses, Julie sat on a sofa by the fireplace inside the lodge. The fire was still going strong. Sitting next to her, Zach took the heirloom glasses from her hands and gently placed them on the coffee table. Curling his fingers under her chin, he lifted her gaze to meet his. "You okay?"

"Yes, I just feel so helpless. And angry. Someone was in my house." She wiped a tear from her eye. "I hate that."

"Do you have any idea who would do this?" he asked, wondering again why she hadn't told him about the murder on the property yet. Why would she hold that back, unless she *was* involved?

Every time he thought Julie was an innocent victim in the intrigue surrounding Shadow Lake Inn, something happened to make him doubt her again. She might have made enemies with someone within the terrorist cell group. In retaliation, they might have ransacked her house and taken something she was keeping from them.

"No. I have no idea who would do this." Julie shook her head and leaned into his embrace. "I have nothing of value except the things my grandmother left me. Zach," she said turning to him, "I can't let Emmie see our home like that. I have to clean it up." She moved to stand but Zach firmly placed an arm around her waist, preventing her from bolting away from him again.

"Whoa. Hold on, Julie. We'll straighten it out later together, okay?" He pulled her close and kissed the top of her forehead. "At least you and Emmie weren't there when they broke in. Come on," he said, brushing a loose strand of hair away from her face. "Let's call the authorities from your office and settle you in a room." He'd have a couple of agents arrive at the lodge in police uniforms within the hour. "You're not staying at your place alone tonight."

He would search her office and her home for that elusive box . . . if someone else hadn't already taken it. He should've checked its contents sooner. There had to be something of vital importance to national security in that old cardboard carton.

Julie tossed and turned in bed. Her suite at the inn was just across the hall from Zach's. She was half-tempted to take him up on his offer to wake him if she couldn't sleep. But she needed the time alone to think. She couldn't call her parents and ask to speak to Emmie although she wanted nothing more than to be with her daughter. But that wouldn't be the best thing for her little girl, waking her in the middle of the night.

She wouldn't mention the burglary to her parents. There was no way she would cause them to worry needlessly. Julie was sure they would have a wonderful time in Seattle with Emmie. She wouldn't ruin the special weekend for them, especially since there was nothing they could do to help. She'd have to keep it to herself, just like the murder.

Julie swallowed. Chills ran along her spine and she pulled the warm comforter up to her chin. Did the break-in have a connection to the brutal crime?

Dear God. What's going on?

Taking a moment to pray, Julie thanked God for watching over Emmie and for the unusual circumstance of neither of them being home at the time of the break-in. She asked for His continued protection.

Her peaceful retreat in the rain forest was turning into something sinister. How long could she keep the events of the past couple of months from her guests? If they knew about the murder, reservations would dwindle down to nothing.

At first, Julie didn't think it would hurt to keep the information secret. But now, after this latest incident, she worried. Not only for the guests, but for Emmie, too.

Julie's first instinct had been to get her daughter and hug her, hold her close. But she couldn't let her little girl see the house in such a shambles. Julie had finally agreed with Zach and the police sergeant who had arrived on the scene, to hire a cleaning crew to take care of the mess in the morning. And another undercover security guard.

It had been nerve-racking to keep the information she shared with the police from Zach. Thankfully, the officers hadn't discussed the murder. Julie smoothed the down-filled comforter and sighed. For the first time ever, she had serious doubts about owning and running Shadow Lake Inn. *Lord, is that really what You want me to do with the rest of my life?*

She turned in the bed and scrunched up two pillows, trying to find a comfortable sleeping position. She'd almost told Zach about the murder today. But what could he possibly do? He'd already helped with the police and in arranging for a well-known alarm company to install a complete home security system first thing in the morning.

As soon as she knew Emmie would be awake, she'd give her parents a call on their cell phone so she could hear the sound of her daughter's voice.

Thank You, Heavenly Father, for keeping Emmie safe and away from what happened tonight.

Fluffing another pillow, she sighed. At least the second story of her home hadn't been touched. Emmie's room was just as she left it.

With Zach by her side, after the police left, Julie had hurriedly packed some personal belongings for their trip to the mountains the next day, thankful that the attempted robbery hadn't been worse. She and Emmie might have been home. If it hadn't been for Zach, who knows what might have happened.

Zach.

In only a few days, he'd started occupying a place in her life again — a place in her heart. Tomorrow while the security company was inside her house, she'd show him her favorite places to visit in Olympia, Washington.

She wouldn't cancel their time together and worry about the break-in. If she did, the burglars would *win.* Julie refused to allow that to happen. She and Zach both needed a pleasant diversion. Tiff was right. She did need to shake up her life.

Help me, Lord, it's time for me to "fly."

She would enjoy the day off. She wouldn't feel guilty.

"She's innocent, John. I'm sure of it." Zach remembered the feel of Julie as she trembled in his arms after the burglary. He wanted to

149

protect her from whoever had broken into her house and locate what they'd been after.

"You're already in harm's way, Marshall."

"I just don't see Julie fitting into this. Not knowingly. She's got to be unaware of the danger she's in or what's already gone down from her lodge."

"We can't afford to take any chances."

"I don't want Julie or her daughter anywhere around here when this plays out."

"She may have brought this on herself." John paced the small area in Zach's suite at the inn. "This burglary could be a setup to throw us off track. If Julie *is* working with Viktor, you can be sure he'll double-cross her when the going gets tough." He stopped pacing and turned to Zach. "We need to find what they were looking for."

"Yeah," Zach agreed. "Yuri won't take any slack from Viktor. That's for sure. I need to find that box."

"You think that's the key? That they were looking for the box?"

"Could be. Both Julie and Beatrice nearly passed out when I offered to carry it for them. They didn't want me near it." Zach drew a quick breath. Glancing at his watch, he noted it was almost dawn. Julie had trusted him enough to give him the extra key to her room. The irony didn't escape him. "We're taking advantage of her house being empty tonight. I have a couple of agents inside and out, going through everything they can lay their hands on. Maybe they'll find something."

"Good. Do we have a team ready for tomorrow?"

"Yeah, they're all set. As soon as we leave in the morning they'll get started."

"They'll have to move quickly."

"Right. While I'm with Julie on our day trip, they'll install the regular system along with the wiretaps and camera hookups. It'll look like the real thing in case Beatrice or someone else comes snooping."

John stood and paused before opening the door. "I have to get back to playing chef. Make sure everything's set up before you get back. We still have too many loose ends," he muttered.

Studying him for a moment, Zach noted the weariness around his eyes. "Something else is bothering you. What is it?"

John ran a hand along his jaw. "We have conflicting reports on the whereabouts of some high-ranking suspects. No one knows for sure where Yuri is. We need to assume he's here somewhere. Yuri would want to handle things himself. But what really worries me is Agent Tomasino. His disappearance concerns me."

Agent Tomasino hadn't been heard from in months. Either he was dead or he'd turned traitor. Zach found it impossible to believe that Tommy would turn. They'd gone through training together. He'd never known a better man, or so he'd thought. "No word from him yet?"

"Nothing." John paused, his hand gripping the doorknob. "Not a peep."

"You think he's turned?" Zach's quiet words echoed ominously in the dimly lit room.

"My instincts have been shot to pieces in this ongoing investigation, Marshall. Anything could happen in this case and it wouldn't surprise me. Watch your back tomorrow. After the incidents over the past few days, we all need to be on high alert."

"Yeah. I know." Zach turned to John and met his weary gaze. "You think Julie set me up, at the picnic?"

John's steady gaze met his. "If what you saw was the reflection of a high-powered rifle, it's possible she had someone follow you. Has she mentioned anything about the murder of her groundskeeper yet?"

"No, nothing."

"Wonder why she's holding back."

"Yeah. Me, too. Especially after the

break-in tonight." Zach drew a deep breath. "I thought for sure she'd fill me in on the murder. I'll get her to spill what she knows tomorrow."

"We have no time to waste."

"Right."

"Get her to talk. We need answers." Checking the hallway before he left, John quietly closed the door behind him.

Running a hand along the back of his neck, an uneasy feeling settled in Zach's gut. His finely honed instincts were trying to tell him something.

But what?

For a brief second or two, he considered praying. But God hadn't listened to his prayers before, so why should he bother? Then he remembered a Bible verse he'd learned as a child, a lifetime ago.

As far as the east is from the west, so far hath He removed our transgressions from us.

Funny. He hadn't remembered those words from the Book of Psalms in all these years. Why was it as clear as crystal in his mind now, just when he needed to concentrate? Was it possible God would forgive him for not being there for his wife when he was overseas?

Could there be forgiveness for the anger hiding under the surface of his heart every waking moment? Zach acknowledged his deep-rooted anger at God for not saving his wife and little girl.

It was hard to believe even God could be that forgiving.

Julie looked across the street to the small parking lot. A patch of morning mist parted to reveal the lush green foliage of the rain forest — and Zach.

Hands tucked into the pockets of his black leather jacket, he stood leaning against his silver truck. A strand of brown hair fell across his forehead. A rush of affection ran through Julie as Zach met her and placed a comforting arm around her shoulder.

"Morning. I have a hot cup of coffee waiting for you. It's cold out this morning." He opened the door of his vehicle for her. Once she'd settled in the seat, he crossed in front of the 4×4 and climbed inside. "Did you get much sleep?"

"Only a couple of hours." She noticed the hair at the nape of his neck touched the soft leather collar of the jacket he wore.

"You going to be okay?" A hint of concern flashed in his eyes.

"Yes." She sighed. "I called Emmie on my parents' cell phone, and I feel better now that I talked to her." She drew a deep breath. "I want to be certain that the alarm system will be installed today. Are you sure they can do it so quickly?"

"Absolutely. I already spoke with them again this morning. The owner gave me his number so I can check in with him throughout the day. He assured me it'll be done by the time we get home." He reached into a pocket and pulled out a business card. "Here's the name and number of the alarm company. You can call them for yourself."

"Thanks for handling things, Zach. I don't normally let anyone do so much for me. I don't want Emmie to know about the break-in. It's hard enough for me to handle the sense of violation. I can't allow her to go through that. She's too young, it'll only frighten her."

"Yeah, I agree." His gaze met and held hers. "You're a good mother, Julie." He reached over to take her hand in his.

"Thanks." An overwhelming sense of safety settled in Julie's soul. But, she couldn't allow herself to depend on his strength. He'd be leaving soon enough.

Giving his hand an affectionate squeeze, she glanced outside at the brilliant array of autumn colors on the hardwood trees. Contrasting with the tall evergreens, the sight touched her heart with the beauty God created. Inspired by the view, she was determined to dwell on more pleasant matters. Julie took a deep calming breath. "I can't believe Thanksgiving is only a week away." Her favorite time of year, besides Christmas.

"Yeah." Zach drew in a quick breath. "I know."

"What are your plans for the holiday?"

He pulled out of the parking space and turned to her. "Unfortunately, I won't be home for the Thanksgiving dinner my parents are having. It's too bad. Mom makes a killer apple pie." He flashed the slow smile she loved.

"What about your brothers?" Julie imagined his parents would miss having Zach home for the holiday. If Luke and Jake were there, it might be easier on them. "Will they be home?"

"Yeah, they'll be there. Dad, Luke, Jake and I usually watch a slew of football after dinner with some of the others who join us." He seemed to be deep in thought. "There's quite a gathering at my folks' place every Thanksgiving."

"We have dinner at my parents' place every year. My brother and his wife come up from Oregon. Why don't you join us?"

Zach turned from the road to face her. Ju-

156

lie felt the loneliness reflected in his gray-blue eyes as his gaze met hers. "I'd like that. Your folks have room for one more?"

Julie laughed lightly. "Absolutely. They love having a full house." She knew how excited her mom would be that she'd asked a friend to dinner. She couldn't deny the happiness she felt, despite the events of last night. God had taken the break-in and turned it into something good — time with Zach.

The anticipation of spending another unpredictable day with Zach filled her with an excitement she couldn't understand. But she didn't want to analyze her feelings anymore. She just wanted to enjoy the time she had left with Zach.

Once they were on their way down the narrow country road, Julie pulled a map from her purse. Surely he'd appreciate the necessity of using one.

"What's that?" Zach teased, glancing at the road map in her hands.

"This . . . is a map." She waved it in the air and smiled.

"Sounds boring." He winked.

Julie laughed and placed her coffee in the cup holder. "I know you like spur-of-the-moment trips, but I need to take a look at this. I want to make sure we can find the right road to a quaint bakery and restaurant I heard about. So we can have one of their famous breakfasts."

"Okay, lead the way."

Once they'd made a left turn onto the paved road indicated on the map, Julie took a leisurely sip of coffee. Half an hour later, they were lost.

"Let me see that map." Zach pulled the car to the side of the road and placed the gear in Park. He reached for the map she had fully opened and spread out in front of her. "Hand it over." He held out his hand and wiggled his fingers. "Come on."

The morning mist hadn't made navigating very easy. Julie found it difficult to recognize the country road in the thick fog surrounding the lush trees and evergreens. Every dirt road looked the same to her in this cloudlike environment. She fidgeted in her seat. She'd forgotten to bring her reading glasses and didn't want to let on that she couldn't see the detailed map clearly without them. Reluctantly, she handed the wrinkled map to him.

"We're going in the wrong direction!" Zach glanced at her in astonishment. Folding the map to a smaller, more manageable size he turned to her, his eyes twinkling with amusement. "Look, we're here," he said, tapping his finger at a crossroads on the map. The beginning of a smile tipped the corners of his mouth. "Just where is this place you want to take me to for breakfast? Canada?"

"Very funny." Julie leaned over to find the town on the map. She focused her eyes and cleared her throat. "You, um, need to unfold it a little more."

"I was afraid of that," he mumbled. Zach opened the map to its full size. The paper crackled and crinkled against the steering wheel. "Are you sure it's in Washington State and not in Oregon or Idaho or something?"

"Here it is, way over there." She looked up to find him smiling at her. "You think this is funny, don't you?"

Zach laughed. "Just proves my point."

"What?"

"You have no idea where you're going." He folded the map back to its original shape, placing it under the sun visor of the driver's window. "Doesn't matter. I know how to get there now," he said before she could come to her own defense. "It'll take another hour of driving, though. Maybe they serve lunch, too." He chuckled and placed the truck in Drive.

"But the map, you aren't even looking at

it." She reached over to take it from the vi-sor.

"We don't need it." Turning to her, his eyes narrowed. Shifting gears, he put the truck back in Park. He unfastened his seat belt and leaned across the seat to face her. "I haven't kissed you good morning yet," he whispered, his breath warm against her cheek, then he slanted his mouth over hers.

He was right.

She *didn't* know where she was going. In more ways than one.

With Zach she was as lost as she could possibly be. For them, there was no real destination. No road map at all.

With one easy move, he unfastened her seat belt and pulled her close. The electric-ity of Zach's tender touch sent a shiver of desire and a wave of deep affection for him through Julie's heart.

She couldn't let herself fall for him again. As soon as they stopped kissing, she'd tell him they shouldn't see each other again.

As soon as they stopped kissing . . .

Zach deepened the kiss, and his control wavered. He wanted to be with her. But not just for the job. Zach wanted Julie in his life, living with him as his wife on the ranch.

There were some dreams that could never

come true. A future with Julie was one of them.

Zach reluctantly ended the kiss. He cared deeply for Julie. Always would. The revelation wreaked havoc on his analytical mind. Would she even think about leaving her home and family to spend a life with him in Montana if he asked her?

If she was innocent.

If she'd ever forgive him for the lies and the wiretaps.

Holding Julie in his arms for a long moment, Zach wished he could move the relationship forward. "What are we going to do?" he asked, running a hand through her silky hair. Her gaze met his and Zach's heart filled with tenderness and love for Julie. "I . . . still have feelings for you. It's like we've never been apart," he whispered, his voice thick with emotion.

"I know," she said, tracing a finger along his jaw. "But there are too many things for us to consider." She sighed and rested her head against his chest. "We have to take this slow. I can't be hurt again when you leave. And I have Emmie to think about. I can't let her get attached to you."

He swallowed a curse. She *had* been hurt. *I never should've left her.* He'd been a fool to ride out of her life the way he had. He'd have to hurt her again when he finally revealed the truth about why he was really here. Zach was in a no-win situation at Julie's expense and he hated it. But there was something else he wanted and needed to know before any more time went by.

"You're right. I'll be heading back to Montana. You have the lodge and your family here in Washington State." He cleared his throat and asked the question that had been on his mind for years. "Why did you say no . . . when I asked you to marry me?"

Her eyes moistened and Zach waited for the answer. Had she been seeing someone else? Her husband?

"Zach, it was my grandmother. She went into the hospital the day before you came back from your week-long hike with your friends." Julie swallowed and cleared her throat. "I'd just come back from the hospital when you showed up on your Harley."

He nodded, urging her to continue.

"It was the last time I saw her. She passed away while we were all gathered together in the room with her. My parents, my brother and me. She just smiled a peaceful, tired smile and . . . took her last breath. I've never seen anything like it before. Gran had a deep faith. Because of her, I do, too. I know in my spirit, she's in Heaven with my grandfather. With Jesus. I — I couldn't leave my family and ride off with you."

"I'm . . . sorry." Zach felt as if he'd been sucker punched in the gut. "I should've listened." He remembered now, that she'd looked upset. Why hadn't he put his arms around her? Let her talk? He'd been a fool. "I never even gave you a chance to tell me."

"I tried, but you kept gunning the engine."

"I remember."

"It was obvious that you wanted to leave and have your adventure. So . . . I let you go." A lone tear fell along her cheek and Zach brushed it away with his finger. "It was one of the saddest days of my life." Julie ran a hand along his jaw and sighed. *Two people I loved left me in one day.*

"I'm sorry." How many lives had he messed up?

"Zach, don't blame yourself. We were young," she whispered, leaning her head against his chest. "It's okay."

"*You were* young. I should've known better." He held her for a few moments and wondered about her deep faith. Zach thought about his childhood beliefs in God from what seemed like a lifetime ago. Could he ever get back the faith he'd had as a boy? Or was it too late for him?

After a few minutes, he kissed the top of

her forehead. "Let's just have breakfast and not think about how many mistakes I made or how far away we'll be from each other when I leave."

"Okay." Julie nodded and gave him a quick hug.

Once they were back on the road, Zach settled his thoughts on the investigation. He needed more information. More names. One name in particular. His boss had already told him to get a handle on his emotions. John Castlerock hadn't stayed alive all these years because he'd been careless. John was right. Zach had to keep his feelings for Julie in check and get more details on Viktor. Maybe if he was lucky, she might even know Yuri's whereabouts or his wife Katya's location.

Was the evil monster of a woman really still in Moscow as the Bureau's numerous reports had indicated? Or had the female scientist who formulated biochemical weapons of mass destruction given them the slip? It wouldn't be the first time.

Zach raked a hand through his hair. He needed to think things through without the temptation of holding Julie in his arms.

It would be better if he didn't see Julie for a while. Once he confirmed the alias that Viktor had surely given her, once he listened to her taped phone conversations and read her e-mails, he'd be out of her life. They'd both be better off. Zach wondered what would've happened if he hadn't left Julie standing in the dust when he rode away on his Harley.

Would they have been married by now?

Would she still be a suspected terrorist spy?

EIGHT

"Hi, Emmie." Julie smiled and placed the phone closer to her ear. "How are you, sweetheart?" Julie's heart filled with joy at the sound of her daughter's voice. "Did you have fun?"

"Uh-huh. I bought a present. For you."

"You did?" Julie settled a plate into the top rack of the dishwasher. "I can't wait to see it, and you, too!"

Emmie giggled. "It's a surprise."

"I love surprises." Smiling again, Julie closed the dishwasher door with her hip. She leaned against the counter.

"Want to know what it is?" Emmie asked in earnest.

"You mean the surprise?" Julie laughed. "You can show it to me when I see you in just a little while . . . when I come over to pick you up, okay?"

"Okey doke."

"Okay then. I'll see you at Grandma and

Grandpa's house for dinner in a little while, all right?"

"Okay, Mommy. I love you."

"I love you, too, Emmie."

Julie replaced the phone in its cradle then rushed to take a shower. She reflected on the time she'd spent yesterday with Zach. They'd enjoyed a late breakfast after finally locating the little restaurant she loved in Port Townsend.

Strolling along Main Street, they'd found an old-fashioned Wild West photography studio. Zach had persuaded Julie to have sepia-toned photos taken of them together.

Julie closed her eyes and let the hot water flow over her face. Her thoughts drifted to Zach and how he looked wearing the black Stetson he'd chosen from the vast array of Western apparel at the studio.

He seemed totally at ease with his hand wrapped around the barrel of the long, heavy rifle he held for the photograph. She'd never thought of Zach as a cowboy before. Did he wear a Stetson on the ranch?

When he'd kissed her under the brim of that hat, any thoughts she had about just being friends evaporated into thin air. Much to Julie's embarrassment and delight, the photographer had snapped a picture of them kissing, in addition to the other poses.

Zach had ordered and paid for the photographs, arranging for the package to be sent to Julie at the lodge. They shared a wonderful, carefree day together, a day where worries had seemed very far away. Julie found herself telling Zach all about her life the past several years. She'd always found it easy to talk to him.

She pulled on her jeans and the soft, black sweatshirt with the small colorful flowers embroidered along the collar Zach bought for her. Julie smiled, thinking about the saloon girl outfit she'd chosen to wear for the photo shoot. She'd also worn a frilly hot pink and black hat, and a black feather boa. She'd never done anything like that before, but had always wanted to.

Another adventure.

She was beginning to enjoy them. She was a different person now than the girl she'd been at twenty-one. Her faith was stronger than ever, though she didn't understand what God was thinking lately with everything going on in her life. She was more independent now. She hadn't recognized the change in herself until Zach pointed out what a good job she was doing with the lodge.

Owning and running the quaint resort *was* a huge responsibility. She enjoyed her work and the beauty of historic Shadow Lake Inn. When she first had to take over the business on her own, she wasn't sure if she could make it profitable. If she had a little more time, she'd be able to turn the business around after some difficult months.

Julie sighed. What she really wanted was a family of her own, with a house in a real neighborhood. She longed for a Christian husband who would love her forever, a man who believed in God and the power of prayer. She wondered about Zach and his faith.

I need to pray for him. He's hurting.

Staring at her reflection in the mirror, Julie closed her eyes and prayed for Zach.

Lord, protect him. Heal his heart. Show Zach Your eternal love. Make Your presence real to him. In Jesus' name. Amen.

She applied a light touch of make up before blow-drying her hair. Though she had strong feelings for Zach, it would never work out for them. He still wasn't ready for a commitment.

God, when are You going to send me the man I'm going to marry? How much longer am I going to play this dating game? I'm getting too old for dating.

And the list of single men was dwindling down to a handful. Or less. She had been seeing Nick Davidson, owner of an export business in Seattle. Julie purchased many of the items for her gift shop from Nick's warehouse. They'd been casually dating for months. Nick was good-looking and pleasant company. But marriage? Julie didn't trust him completely — no one was *that* perfect.

Lord, show me what I need to know about Nick.

Sighing inwardly, Julie checked the house, making sure things were arranged so that Emmie and her parents wouldn't notice anything out of the ordinary. She'd called in an order for replacement wineglasses from one of the finer department stores and hoped they'd arrive before her parents stopped by in a few days. Reaching for her purse on the counter, Julie gave the first floor one last check.

Everything was back to normal inside the house. Her life, however, was another matter.

Agent Sarah Robbins scanned the vast underground passageway beneath the hotels and businesses of downtown Seattle.

I lost him.

The massive corridor of walkways was a perfect place to hide. Yuri Kostoff, head bad

170

guy and partner-in-crime to suspect Viktor Ivanov, had given her the slip.

She was close. Seeing Yuri confirmed it. Had he realized she'd been tracking him? Was it just a coincidence that she lost him in the lunchtime crowd?

No such thing as coincidence.

The words of her boss, Senior Agent John Castlerock, sounded in Sarah's mind and her heart tightened with a surge of fear. It was no coincidence. Was she being set up? Had they already tagged her as an agent?

Sarah headed up the stairs that led to the street level of the city. She had to find Yuri again. She pulled the Bureau-issued cell phone from her purse and hit a speed dial key. "Hey, I've got a hot new lead for you, cowboy." Sarah smiled, knowing Zach never minded when she kidded him about his ranching dreams. She'd been encouraging him to go back to the ranch he loved in Montana. Hearing him talk about it, the place sounded like paradise. She could do with a little of that herself. Actually, a *lot* of that.

"I knew we could depend on you, Robbins," Zach said, chuckling. "You always get your man."

Touché. Let him think the rumors about her were true. Despite the buzz in the

Bureau, she'd never had to hop into bed with a felon to slap the cuffs around his wrists. It was her FBI training and analytical mind that had given her so much success as an agent.

Zach's tone grew serious. "What've you got, Sarah?"

"I spotted Yuri here in Seattle. Lost him in the underground walkway, though."

She heard Zach take in a quick breath. "We're getting close."

"My thoughts exactly."

"Too close. I don't want you out there alone. I'll head down to join up with you."

"Aw, Zach. How sweet," she kidded. She climbed up the steep stairway leading to the street and scanned the crowds.

"Knock it off. You staying in the same place? Up in the cabin?"

"Yes, I'm at the safe house, though I don't stay there much. Too busy." The mass of people on the packed sidewalk prevented her from locating Yuri again and she slowed her pace. "I've lost him."

"Was he with anyone?" Zach asked.

"Affirmative. A man I didn't recognize. I only saw them for a couple of seconds." There had been something familiar about the other man. She couldn't put her finger on it.

"Listen, give John a call right away so he can fill in the team ASAP. I'll catch up with you first chance I get. Don't do anything stupid, at least, not until I get there, okay?"

Sarah chuckled. "Sure." Snapping her mobile phone shut, she drew a deep breath. She'd grab a bite to eat first, then give John a call and resume her search.

Funny how the male population of agents seemed to think she needed their protection. She'd come to their rescue more times than they knew. Yet there was a sense of family in their team. They went the extra mile for one another, putting their own lives on the line.

Missing her friends and family, Sarah welcomed the camaraderie of big brothers like Agents Marshall and Castlerock. She was just "one of the guys" with them.

No one in the Bureau would ever suspect her secret dreams — to fall in love, get married, live in a house with a white picket fence, and have a couple of sweet babies to hold in her arms. And her own little yarn and quilt shop somewhere along Main Street, U.S.A.

But where?

And when?

Time was ticking and Sarah wanted her new life before she turned thirty, which gave her only two years. *Two years.*

Could she stay alive that long?

Finding a small restaurant, she slid into a red vinyl booth and picked up a menu. She was more tired than she cared to admit, even to herself. If she didn't get some rest, if she didn't watch her back on this case, her dreams would never come true.

Maybe it was time she turned back to God. Fully recommitted her life to Him. Her mother had always told Sarah He had a plan for her life. She swallowed hard and blinked away the tears that moistened her eyes. If God did have a plan for her life, when was He planning to fill her in on it?

"Sit still and let me dry your hair." Julie started the blow-dryer and brushed her daughter's long, blond tresses. Emmie danced around in place until her hair was finally dry. "We had room servants . . . in the hotel," she said, hopping on one foot.

"Room servants?" Helping Emmie into freshly laundered, warm-from-the-dryer pajamas, Julie hugged her close. Two days had been much too long to be away from her daughter.

"Uh-huh. They brought me a hamburger. On a big, shiny dish." Emmie stretched out her hands. "It was . . . this big! And ice cream, too!" Her eyes widened.

Room service. Julie smiled. "Ice cream, too?"

"Uh-huh. Grandpa said it was because I was such a good girl."

"You *are* a good girl." She gave Emmie another hug. This was the time of day Julie loved the most — her pajama-clad daughter's hugs after a warm bath. "Thank you for being so good for Granni and Grandpa. I'm glad you had such a nice time. Now, there's school in the morning. You've had a busy weekend, sweetheart. Time for bed."

"No." Emmie's blue eyes darkened with a stubborn streak. "I don't want to go to school." She stomped her foot.

"Now, Emmie, no whining . . . remember?"

Emmie folded her arms in front of her and frowned. Julie almost laughed aloud at her daughter's expression, but caught herself just in time.

"It's almost nine o'clock. Way past your bedtime. You *will* go to school tomorrow. Now, scoot into bed."

"No."

"Emmie," Julie warned.

Reluctantly her daughter climbed into the bed and pulled the covers up to her chin. "Where's my dolly?"

"Here it is, right on the pillow, you silly." Julie smiled and handed Emmie her favorite soft doll. The worn little toy had been her favorite since she'd received it the first Christmas without her daddy.

Emmie hugged it close to her heart. "Read to me, Mommy?"

"What do we say?" Julie raised an eyebrow.

Emmie smiled. "*Please* read to me, Mommy?"

"Good. Thank you." Julie smiled. "*Cinderella*?"

Emmie nodded. "Yes, yes!" Julie hoped Emmie would've been exhausted by her busy weekend. Instead, she was overly tired. They both were. She opened her daughter's favorite book.

"Once upon a time . . ." Emmie prompted, sitting up in bed.

"Once upon a time," Julie began.

The sound of the doorbell interrupted the reading. The noise of the loud, new chime shot a surge of adrenaline through Julie. She wasn't expecting anyone. Still spooked from yesterday's break-in, she hid her shakiness from Emmie and took a deep breath.

The alarm system was set. And what kind of burglar rang the doorbell? Feeling foolish, and reminding herself to explain the system to Emmie in the next few days, Julie took a sigh of relief. "Let me get the door. You look at the pictures and Mommy will be right back, okay?"

Emmie nodded and began to flip through the pages. She yawned. "Okay, Mommy, but you promised."

"I'll read to you, don't worry." Julie hurried down the stairs and pressed in the security code to turn off the alarm system. Upon opening the front door, she found Zach holding a packed duffel bag.

The thought that he might be leaving now, this very moment, filled her with overwhelming sadness. The feeling was so strong she felt as if she would keel over from the impact. Why hadn't he told her?

"Hi, Zach." She fiddled with the gold chain she wore around her neck. "Come in."

He walked inside and dropped his gear on the floor by the coatrack. The navy T-shirt he wore under his black leather jacket revealed the taut muscles of his broad chest. Worn jeans emphasized his trim waist. Julie closed the heavy wooden door behind him and leaned against it to cover the sudden weakness she felt in her knees. "Are you going somewhere?" she asked, trying to keep her voice light and carefree.

"Yeah, I wanted to talk to you first." His gaze met hers then drifted lower to her mouth. Drawing a deep breath, he held his arms out for her. "Come here."

Releasing the death grip she had on the doorknob, Julie made her way over to him. "Where are you going? I —"

Gently placing a finger to her lips, he silenced her. "It's been a couple of hours since I've seen you." Tenderly he ran a hand along her jaw, then he gently tugged her close, lowering his lips to hers.

But before their lips met, Zach shifted his gaze to the stairway behind her. Julie turned to follow his stare. She found her daughter padding down the stairs in her floral blue pajamas, holding the *Cinderella* book in one hand.

"Hello, Misty Man." Emmie giggled and waved her free hand at Zach.

"Hello, Emmie." Reluctantly, he released Julie from his embrace. "I, uh, I thought she'd be in bed by now."

"Well, she's *supposed* to be in bed." Julie smiled and gave her daughter a glance. "Right, Emmie?"

"You promised to read to me." She held the book out for Julie to see.

"I know. I —"

"Can *he* read it?" Jumping up and down, Emmie pointed to Zach.

"Mr. Marshall?" Julie turned to Zach and

smiled. He looked at her as if to say, "don't do this to me."

"Uh-huh. Misty Man. *He* can read my bedtime story." Emmie bounced down the remaining stairs and took Zach's hand in hers. "Okay?" she asked hopefully, lifting her head to meet his gaze.

Zach cleared his throat and tried to find his voice. He'd never really read to a kid before. The few times he'd been home, Ashley had been too little to understand when he'd read the comics in the newspaper to her. But she always smiled.

He knelt down beside Emmie so she wouldn't have to strain her neck looking up at him. Why did the sweet touch of this little girl's hand in his turn him into a pile of mush?

Maybe if he did read to her, he'd get her to explain the *misty man* thing she had going. After all, her mom apparently had no intention of filling him in on that. He glanced to Julie, who wore a big grin. She obviously thought this scenario was funny.

"Okay," Zach answered, gently cupping his hand under Emmie's chin. "Go on." He nodded toward the stairs. "I'll be up in a minute to check on you and read that story, okay?"

Emmie nodded and ran upstairs.

"Be careful, Emmie," Julie said. "Those wooden steps can be slippery."

After she was out of sight, Zach turned to Julie. "I don't know how you do it. Aren't you exhausted at the end of the day?" He took her hand in his.

"Sometimes." Her eyes drifted to his duffel bag.

Zach pulled her close and rested his chin on the top of her head. Closing his eyes, he realized how much he would miss her.

In just a few days, she'd become an important part of his life again. But she was still a suspect. And his heart was being ripped apart because of it.

It was a good thing he was leaving to stake out the lead Sarah had for them. He'd have to be wired every day now and carrying his Glock in a shoulder harness. He wouldn't be able to hide that from Julie, not with the unquenchable urge he had to hold her in his arms every time he saw her. "Listen, after I read to Emmie, let's talk, okay?"

"Um, sure." Julie's gaze met his. She had this uncanny ability to reach into his soul with those baby blues. There was a bond, a chemistry between them that was undeniable. "Let me get her settled in first." Taking his hand in hers, she led him upstairs.

Entering Emmie's room together, Julie's gaze locked with his and she teased him with a smile. "She's all yours." She turned to her daughter. "Sweetheart, I'll be right back. Mr. Marshall is going to read to you while I get the rest of the laundry out of the dryer." She turned to leave.

Zach ran a hand along his jaw. He had no idea how or where to start. He pulled one of the little chairs away from the table and placed it beside Emmie's bed, noting how the seat creaked under his weight when he sat.

He gingerly took the book from the sweet child in the blue flannel pajamas. With every little girl look she gave him, Emmie lifted another small measure of pain and guilt from Zach's heart. In its place an over-whelming peace settled over him. He felt its presence like a warm light healing his soul and was amazed to realize he still had one.

Scooting to the edge of the bed, she leaned closer and prompted him to start. "Once upon a time . . ."

Zach cleared his throat and turned to the first page of *Cinderella*. "Once upon a time . . ."

Julie stood in the doorway of her daughter's room holding a basket of laundry still warm from the dryer. Leaning against the door-jamb, she listened as Zach continued to read to her little girl.

"The clock struck twelve," he read.

"Don't worry, Cindi Rella," Emmie called out earnestly when Zach got to the part about her running away from the ball. "The prince will find you. Won't he?" She turned to Zach for an answer.

"Uh, yeah, I think he *does* find her."

"Let me see the picture." Emmie sat up on her knees.

"Oh, right, I forgot." He turned the book so she could see the illustrations. "See? The glass slipper came off her foot." He paused for a moment and smiled. "She probably runs as fast as your mommy, so the slipper *flew right off!*"

"As fast as . . . Mommy?"

"Yep."

A fit of giggles overtook Emmie. Julie pressed a hand to her lips to stifle a giggle of her own.

"What's so funny?" Zach raised an eyebrow and smiled at the unexpected silliness.

"Mommy's a slowpoke. She can't run fast!" Emmie laughed again and covered her face with the comforter.

"Oh, yes she can," Zach said, a lazy grin crossing his face. "I've *seen* her run, you know." He tapped the top of her head through the comforter.

Emmie peeked out from under the blanket, her eyes wide. "You did?"

"Yep, just the other day. She runs fast with a bear behind her." He chuckled.

Emmie tilted her head. "You're so silly! Please read me some more."

Zach read until the end of the book. "And they lived happily ever after."

"That's my favorite part." Emmie sighed dramatically.

"What is?" Zach asked, a puzzled look on his face.

"The happy ever after part, silly."

"Oh, *that.*"

"Uh-huh." She held her arms out to Zach. "Aren't you going to hug me good-night?"

"Uh, sure." Zach placed the book on the night table and leaned over to Emmie. She gently wrapped her little arms around his neck and gave him a hug. Her soft hair brushed his cheek. Taking a deep, shaky breath, Zach gave her a quick hug. She smelled clean like . . . baby shampoo. A scent he'd long forgotten until now. His heart broke inside him. He couldn't allow himself to love this little girl.

Clearing his throat, he pulled the covers up to her waist. Gently he brushed his hand over Emmie's hair and stood. "Good night, Cindi Rella," he whispered, his voice thick with emotion.

"Good night, Prince Charming," Emmie answered, her eyelids heavy with exhaustion.

Tears came unbidden to Julie's eyes. She blinked and quickly wiped them away. Zach's tenderness with her little girl touched her in a way she couldn't explain. How would they fill the emptiness of not having Zach around when he left?

Julie remembered too well how empty a home could be without a father around. She'd never forgotten that one summer when her dad had gone oversees on a business trip. She'd worried the whole time that he wouldn't return. She'd been miserable the entire summer, no matter how her mother had tried to assure her. But happily, her father had come home. Emmie's dad never would. And now, Zach was leaving.

"I know you're the misty man," Emmie said softly, yawning and placing her little hand on his. She sighed deeply and smiled. "But you're *really* the prince, aren't you? And Mommy and me are going to live . . . happy . . . ever after."

Zach smiled. "Just how do you know I'm the misty man anyway? I've been meaning to ask you about that —"

"Did you enjoy the story, Emmie?" Julie asked quietly as she entered the bedroom. She wanted to keep the special atmosphere that permeated the room without having to explain the nickname her daughter had adopted for Zach. Having to tell him about the photo album and the mystery surrounding his reservations would be too . . . embarrassing.

"Uh-huh." Emmie nodded her head and rubbed her eyes. "I want my dolly."

"It's right here under the covers." She handed the soft pink doll to her daughter and tucked her in. "Time for your prayers." Julie glanced at Zach. Leaning against the doorjamb, he gave her a wink.

"Dear God," Emmie began, her eyes squeezed tightly shut. She pressed her hands together in the classic prayer position. "Please bless Mommy. Tell my daddy hello, and that I'm five years old now. Tell him I'm being a good girl . . . most of the time." Peeking through one open eye, she shut them both tightly again. "Bless Granni and Grandpa. And thank You so much for sending Prince Charming for Mommy. Just like I asked You to. Amen."

"Amen," Julie whispered. She gave Emmie a good-night kiss, and turned off the lamp. As usual, the night-light automatically came to life. "Pleasant dreams. See you in the morning, sweetheart." Quickly wiping another tear from the corner of her eye, Julie sighed. She'd never known that her little girl had been praying for a prince.

" 'Night, Mommy."

Julie partially closed the door and looked up to find Zach in the hallway, gazing at her. Had he heard Emmie's prayer? Was *he* the prince Emmie had been praying for? "Thanks for reading to her, Zach. I hope it wasn't . . . what I mean is, I hope it didn't make you sad, remembering."

"That's just it," he whispered, his voice barely audible. He reached over and pulled her gently into his arms. "Instead of sadness, you and your little girl have brought happiness back into my life." His lips brushed against hers as he spoke. A sense of homecoming surrounded her. Julie's heart filled with joy but in the next instant crashed to the depths of despair.

Zach was leaving. He couldn't and wouldn't stay. She needed to encourage him to go back to the ranch he loved. That was where his heart would heal and where he would find the happiness he deserved. She wouldn't take that from him. There was no hope for a real future with Zach. So then why did she hope there could be?

She kissed Zach again, not wanting to give him up yet. For the first time that she could remember, Julie wished she'd never had an accountant's practicality. Did she always have to be so levelheaded and sensible?

Was that really the way she wanted to live her life?

NINE

"We have to talk." Living with a broken heart when Zach went back to Montana was one thing, but allowing her daughter to be hurt when he left was another thing altogether. Emmie had already lost her father, although she had only been eighteen months old at the time and sadly, didn't remember him. However, Emmie *would* remember Zach. How could she explain *his* leaving?

Resting her hands on Zach's chest, she placed some distance between them. "Let's go downstairs and have a cup of coffee before you go." Taking Zach by the hand, Julie led the way to the kitchen and started to brew a small pot of decaffeinated French vanilla coffee.

Zach sat and watched her every move. "What's on your mind?"

"You." Her heart ached knowing how much she would miss him. But she knew she was doing the right thing for all of them.

"Me?" he asked, giving her a smile.

"Yes." Turning to him, she leaned back against the granite counter and sighed. "You're leaving."

"You knew I would be," he said softly.

"I know." Julie wished that the dream world she was in with Zach could last forever, but wishing for and living in paradise were two very different things. Having Zach around again even for a short time, she wanted to reach out for the adventures a lifetime together with him would offer. Julie wouldn't let that false ray of hope filter into her soul.

"What is it?"

"I think maybe it's a good thing . . . that you're leaving." Julie dragged in a quick breath, deciding to get the conversation over with before Zach's tender touch robbed her of any logical thought. "We both know that things are moving too quickly. And this time," she said, tracing a finger along his strong, square jaw. "This time, I have Emmie to think about." And an unsolved murder to worry about.

Zach brought her palm to his lips. Gazing into her eyes, he brought her hand to rest on his chest. "You and I know better than most people how short life is. I know things have been moving quickly. The truth is . . .

we still have feelings for each other. There's something special between us, Julie. Always was."

Realizing the profound truth in his statement, she shifted her gaze away from his. How could she tell him they shouldn't see each other again?

Looking into his eyes, Julie realized she'd never stopped loving him. There was a special place in her heart that belonged to Zach, only to Zach, especially now that she was falling for the man he'd become. "I've missed you," she admitted, her voice barely above a whisper. "I realize that now more than ever. But it's important that you go back home, to Montana. You'll find your peace there. I know you will."

"Wait a minute. Is that what you thought?" He shook his head. "I'm not going home. Not yet."

"You're not?" She tried to deny the rush of relief filling her senses.

"I'm just heading out of town for a couple of days on business and maybe a few days of camping or something." He smiled. "I'm supposed to be on a vacation, remember?"

"Oh, that's right," was all she could manage. She didn't trust her voice to say anything more.

"It'll be lonely without you." The sound

of Zach's laughter washed over Julie with a familiar warmth, its resonance filling the cold emptiness that had settled in her heart. "You won't be there to help me run from the bears or any other wild animals. Or to insist that I use a map," he whispered, his breath warm against her skin.

She smiled. "You really *will* be lost without me."

Zach laughed. "This is true."

Julie reached over to touch her hand to his face. "You need this time alone, Zach. I know you do." She ran her fingers through his thick hair. *I miss you already.* Was it possible they could work something out, some kind of long-distance relationship?

Pulling her close, Zach held her for a long moment. "I'll miss you, too." He loosened his embrace and gazed into her eyes. "You know I will. But you're right. I do need this time alone."

She swallowed hard. He really *was* leaving. Again. And she'd just encouraged him to go. *Would* he be back in a few days? Or would he disappear from her life? Just like the last time?

"Anyway, you probably have a ton of guys lined up waiting to date you, Jewels." He ran a finger along her cheek. "You're the most beautiful woman I've ever known," he whispered, his voice deep and low. "I wish I *could* stay."

Then why are you leaving?

He smiled ruefully. "One last kiss?" His breath was warm and welcome against her cheek. Zach's lips gently brushed hers and Julie's resolve weakened at the impact his touch had on her. Deepening the kiss, Zach drew her to him.

Because she cared for him, she had to let him go. Zach needed this time by himself to find closure with his past — so he could live again. Much like she had recently done.

Zach ended the kiss. He held her close and rested his chin on her forehead. "I'll see you in a few days." Slowly, he eased her from his embrace and stood. He made his way to the coatrack. He grabbed his jacket then reached for his bag on the floor. His intense gaze met hers. "I'll be in touch." He shut the door quietly behind him, and was gone.

A piercing silence filled the little house on the lake and echoed loudly in Julie's lonely heart. The only things she would ever have were photographs and memories when it came to Zach Marshall.

Nothing else. Julie almost groaned aloud.

Had she just made the biggest mistake of her life?

Again?

"I e-mailed you over a week ago and you haven't answered me yet. What's going on?" Tiff asked, sounding concerned.

"Sorry." Julie sighed softly into the phone. "But wait, is everything all right with *you?*" She should have called Tiff to make sure she was doing okay so close to her due date.

"Yes, I'm fine as can be for a pregnant *whale.*"

"You're not a whale." Julie had deliberately avoided contact with anyone over the past few days. She needed some quiet time to think things through. "I should've called you. You're not in labor now, are you?"

"No. The doctor says only a couple more days." Tiff drew in a long breath. "That's not why I called. What's going on with you and Zach?"

"Nothing, really. I just haven't been online since I sent that e-mail." Julie recalled the long message she'd written to Tiff about her feelings for Zach one night when she couldn't sleep. "Things have been hectic."

"I noticed from the subject header on the message that it was the middle of the night, when you sent the e-mail. What's going on? I'm worried about you. And . . . I'm in desperate need of some adult, female con-

193

versation. So start talking."

Julie told Tiff about the days she'd spent with Zach. "I can't let myself fall for him again. He's leaving. He loves the ranch he has in Montana. I won't stop him from going home where he belongs. And I have . . . the inn. We're over sixteen hours away from each other."

"If you love him, if he loves you —"

"Tiff, it's complicated. Emmie adores him. I'm worried about having to explain it to her when he's not around. I won't do that to her. And . . . no one has said anything about love."

"He's spent time with Emmie?"

"She calls him Prince Charming. It's sweet really —"

"Prince Charming?"

"Yes, he read her *Cinderella* the other night —"

"Wait, he actually read to her?"

"Tiff. Stop interrupting me." Julie laughed.

"Well, if you had e-mailed me back with all this juicy information I wouldn't be interrupting. Wow."

"I know. It was just too much to type in an e-mail."

"Okay, what else?"

Julie sighed. "He was married."

"He was? What happened?" Tiff asked quietly.

"Zach lost his wife and one-year-old daughter . . . in a car accident. About four years ago."

"What?" A moment slipped by. "Oh, Julie, how awful. I don't know what to say. I'm sorry."

Julie drew a deep breath. "I know."

"How is he?"

"He's okay, but I understand the heartache he still feels. I can't imagine what I would've done, how I would have made it if I'd lost Emmie, too."

"I can't even think about how he must feel." Tiff sighed deeply. "Seriously now, tell me about the two of you. You always made such a sweet couple. It made no sense when you each went your own way. But that was in the past. What are your feelings for him *now,* Julie? And don't you dare hold anything back."

A day after Zach's departure, Nick Davidson called to ask Julie to Seattle for dinner. They made plans to meet at his company's downtown headquarters so she could order the handcrafted Christmas items she wanted for her gift shop directly from his warehouse.

Julie was uncertain about spending another night away from Emmie, especially since the police investigation hadn't turned up any leads. But maybe a little time away, a change of scenery, was just what she needed. Even her mom thought it was a good idea. But her mother didn't know about the murder. And Julie still needed to search through the employee picnic photos.

After some persistent prodding from Beatrice, who also persuaded her to go, Julie decided to give herself a night and day in Seattle to do some early Christmas shopping. Thanksgiving was only a few days away and the gifts had to be delivered to the lodge in time for the holiday season.

Nick was always so nice, letting her have one or two items to keep for herself as a bonus. She felt somewhat uncomfortable with that arrangement, but when she mentioned it to him he'd assured her he did the same for all his good customers.

Julie loved the quality of the alpaca sweaters and clay pottery the artists in the area created, along with the beautiful natural honeycomb candles and balsam wreaths they crafted.

According to the marketing surveys she took, the guests looked forward to purchasing the authentic Pacific Northwest items placed inside the inn, especially during the holidays. They often bought them right off the walls. She'd learned to purchase extras of everything for the overwhelming percent of return visitors to Shadow Lake Inn.

Decorating the lodge was the task she loved the most as owner of the rustic resort. Next to meeting and keeping in touch with the guests. As a result, Julie had friends all across the country. Many e-mails had been sent from time to time, checking on people she cared about, and who cared for her, as well. Being in touch with good people across the nation gave Julie a sense of connection to the rest of the country, a connection she cherished.

She packed her bag for the trip and her thoughts turned to Zach, as they did a thousand times a day. Where was he? It had been almost a week since they'd last seen each other, and she hadn't heard from him yet.

On an impulse, Julie took a newly purchased item from her dresser and hesitantly placed it into her overnight bag for the trip down to Seattle. She tossed the never-worn, silk pink nightgown into the suitcase. She would wear it for herself, as she always did. Wearing silky things made her feel pretty.

Nick's upscale import-export company

had put her up in the most prestigious hotel in the city and provided a limo to pick her up at the inn. Julie preferred not to make the five-hour trip so late at night by herself, so taking the limousine that Nick offered and staying over at a hotel was the practical thing to do. At least, that's what she told herself.

Her parents would pick Emmie up from school this afternoon. Julie had personally handed the note giving her okay to the school's secretary yesterday. She sighed with relief knowing Emmie would be fine.

Checking her image in the full-length mirror after seeing the limo parked in front of the lodge, Julie admitted it felt good to wear a business suit and heels for a change. She hurriedly walked from her house to the inn, pulling her heavy overnighter behind her on the graveled path.

The limo was waiting in front of the main entry. After the driver opened the door, Julie settled into the comfortable backseat and took a deep breath. Certainly, this trip would lift her spirits.

But no matter how hard she tried to concentrate, her mind drifted to Zach. The ache in her heart would not go away the entire time she rode in Nick's limo. If Zach wasn't back from camping by the time she returned to the lodge, she'd take a look in his room for some kind of clue, since his room was still reserved. There had to be more to his appearance at the lodge than just a conversation with his brothers. It didn't make sense. How could he leave the ranch for such a long time?

The limo pulled into the back driveway of the warehouse, and Nick greeted her. "You look gorgeous as usual," he said, taking her hand in his. The dark gray designer suit he wore complemented his blond hair and hazel eyes.

"Hi, Nick." She smiled up at him, hoping he wouldn't take this visit in the wrong way. She had no intention of getting serious with him. But she did crave something different in her life.

A little excitement, maybe?

An adventure? The theme song from a popular action-adventure movie ran through her mind.

Memories of Zach's slow crooked grin and mischievous blue eyes filled her heart, along with the heart-stopping image of him in the black Stetson. She forced her mind to concentrate on Nick.

For three hours, Julie toured the warehouse and chose a vast array of gifts and decorations for the lodge. Nick glanced at his watch. "It's almost six. Let's head out for dinner now."

"Sure. I am hungry." She smiled. "I'm taking this one, Nick, as my gift, okay?" Julie nodded in the direction of the lovely piece of Christmas china she'd chosen as the complimentary piece Nick had insisted she choose. The charming two-handled vase would look perfect on the dresser in her bedroom. She'd place a small poinsettia plant in it for the holidays.

Nick's cell phone rang and he reached in his pocket to get it. "Sure," he answered hurriedly as he left the room to take the call in private.

Lifting the surprisingly heavy vase and handing it to the clerk in the shipping office, Julie arranged to have it packaged and sent to the inn along with the other items she'd purchased.

The restaurant Nick had chosen was a five-star establishment and a very fashionable one in the Seattle area. The limo driver had them there in only fifteen minutes. The lounge area, overlooking Puget Sound, displayed a lovely after-sunset view when the twinkling lights across the water lit the horizon.

Turning to Nick, Julie smiled. "This is

perfect. I'm glad you suggested it."

He smiled, placed an arm around her shoulders and drew her to him. "I'm glad you're finally here."

"Me, too." She smiled and realized it was true. After the past couple of weeks, she needed to unwind. It was time to have a little fun.

They ordered their drinks and sampled small appetizers. After a half hour of casual conversation, Nick placed an arm around her waist. "Looks like we'll have a long wait for our table."

Julie turned to look at the full dining room. "I think you're right." In the brief time since they'd arrived, the bar had completely filled. Julie couldn't see the end of the long marble countertop with all the people crowded at the bar. There were people standing in rows at least two deep behind them. If only she could get some of these people up to the Olympic National Park and her inn. She made a mental note to produce a new brochure she could market in Seattle. Maybe she could run a contest in a local coffeehouse.

The persistent warning that something was wrong continued to pull at her heart. There was a degree of discomfort in having Nick make her hotel arrangements. She didn't know him that well. They'd only dated a few times. Their relationship had been more like friends than anything else. She took a sip of her Pellegrino sparkling water and offered a quick prayer.

Okay, Lord, what is it You're trying to tell me? I want to hear Your still, small voice. Why am I feeling so apprehensive?

"Affirmative. I'm walking into the place now."

The uniformed doorman opened the beveled glass door of the swanky restaurant, nodding almost imperceptibly to Zach. *Good.* Team members, including the agent posing as the doorman, were already in place as per the latest plans. Walking inside, Zach "spoke" into a cell phone, which disguised his communication with John that was picked up by the sophisticated microphone hidden in his tie clip. "Robbins here yet?"

"Affirmative. She's wearing a red dress," John informed him. "Says she's making a move on Yuri now."

"Good." Zach scanned the large area of the bar.

"Our team is in place but watch your back," John added.

"Right. I'll check in again at the scheduled time."

"Make sure you do. Don't want to lose any more agents."

"Got it." Zach scanned the area again. "I'll keep Sarah out of trouble."

"It's not Sarah I'm worried about . . . not right now, anyway," John admitted.

"Relax, John. I'm cool. Is there a problem?"

"Just a hunch, that's all."

Great. John's hunches were more accurate than some best laid plans. Drawing in a deep breath, Zach checked out the bar. That's where Agent Sarah Robbins would be waiting to attract the likes of one Yuri Kostoff. If anyone could lead them to Viktor, Yuri would. With the help of Agent Robbins, of course.

Zach strode over to the crowded bar. The classy watering hole was packed. After a few minutes, he made his way to a recently vacated bar stool and ordered a club soda. He loosened his tie when the bartender produced his drink. Taking a swallow, his gaze drifted across the room as he automatically checked out the female population. Where was Sarah?

His heart almost stopped when he saw her. She wore a sleek black suit with a short skirt and a silky, cream-colored blouse. Long, honey-blond hair was worn up in some kind of appealing twist. He'd never seen her looking so gorgeous. Zach swallowed hard.

Julie.

What are you doing in Seattle?

Cursing under his breath, he took another quick swallow of the drink. Forcing his gaze from Julie, Zach searched the crowd for the agent in a red dress. He finally spotted Sarah, her hair dark brown as part of her cover in this case, at the other end of the bar. Raising her glass in a toast to him from the bar stool beside Yuri, she directed her gaze to Julie.

What was she trying to tell him, that Julie was on a date? He could see that. But there was more to Sarah's subtle look. Zach leaned forward to get a better view of the man seated next to Julie. The jerk had his arm possessively around her waist as he leaned closer. Too close. Zach's heart rate doubled when the guy turned around and he got a better look.

Viktor Ivanov. Aka Nick.

Julie was with him. Again. Pulling his gaze from them, he glanced over to Sarah. Arm in arm with Yuri, they made their way to Julie and her date.

"You there, John?" Zach muttered into his tie clip.

"Affirmative," John responded over Zach's earpiece. "Did you find Agent Robbins?"

"Yeah, Sarah's here."

"Is Yuri with her?" John's voice crackled over Zach's earpiece.

"Affirmative." Zach cleared his throat. "We got 'em both."

"Say again?"

"We hit pay dirt." The excitement Zach felt knowing they were close to apprehending two major suspects was tempered with his concern for Julie's safety. Even if she was guilty.

"Confirm that last message, Marshall."

"Both men are here." He couldn't risk saying their names, even under his breath.

Zach heard John's sharp intake of breath. "Okay, stick with Viktor. Tail him until we know where he's holed up. Our team is ready. Let us know where he ends up tonight."

"Right." Zach drew a deep breath. "He's . . . with someone."

"Viktor's with someone?" There was a pause. "Anyone we know?"

"Yeah, we know her all right," Zach answered, his voice barely audible.

"It's Julie, isn't it," John stated.

"Yeah." Zach's pulse raced as adrenaline surged through every cell in his body. Usually that rush was what he counted on in a mission. This time, the adrenaline was more like a Molotov cocktail exploding in his gut.

"Stay on Julie and Viktor," John said, breaking into his thoughts. "Sarah will stick with Yuri. Okay, you know the drill."

"I'm on it." Scanning the area, Zach was confident no one noticed his apparently one-sided conversation. He'd perfected the art years ago. He'd had to.

"I expect to hear from you every couple of hours."

"You will."

"I'm in contact with Robbins. She knows her assignment. Any questions?"

"No. You know I'll do whatever it takes."

"Good. A lot of people are counting on you."

"Right." Zach glanced over to see Viktor whisper something in Julie's ear. He was practically nuzzling her neck. This guy had only one thing on his mind tonight and it had nothing to do with selling military secrets to the Russians or supporting terrorists' causes.

Zach's heart kicked into high gear knowing Viktor had more than just a mean streak. He'd murdered innocent people all along the way — he'd even used chemical gas on his own people. Viktor would stop at nothing to complete his dirty work. Was Julie a willing partner or an innocent victim?

Zach felt his chest tighten. Whatever the scenario, she was in harm's way. He covertly turned to watch them. A smile lit Julie's soft features but a hint of worry worked its way across her brow. She was obviously uncomfortable.

Cursing under his breath Zach downed the rest of his soda and kept himself hidden from her view.

Julie . . . do you know who you're with?

TEN

Julie pressed a trembling hand to the lobby level button inside the elevator. She looked down at her new silk blouse. Tucking it more neatly into the wrinkled black skirt, Julie prayed for her hands to stop shaking. She brought a hand to her throat in an effort to calm the palpitations she felt. Thinking about what might have happened, Julie forced herself to breathe.

Nick had booked her in the same room in which he was staying. Ignoring her protests, he'd locked the door behind him, and pushed her onto the bed. In the ensuing struggle, her blouse had ripped open.

If not for that niggling sense from God warning her to be careful, she would've been caught completely off guard. For a split second, when she'd looked into Nick's angry eyes, she had feared for her life. Her years of taking self-defense lessons with Tiff had finally paid off.

After several tense minutes, Nick was left rolling in agony as Julie bolted from the room, grabbing her bag as she fled. All she wanted to do was go home. Her instincts about Nick had been right. If only she'd listened to God's quiet voice of warning a little sooner. Feeling dizzy in the small confines of the elevator, Julie struggled for a deep breath.

The door finally opened into the plush lobby. At this late hour even if she did find a cab, she wouldn't get home until five in the morning. But it didn't matter. Home was where she wanted to be. She would be safe there, especially with the new alarm system installed.

Julie picked up her heavy overnight bag and adjusted the wide strap over her shoulder. Drawing a deep breath, she hurried to the concierge's desk on the opposite side of the stately atrium. Maybe one of the hotel employees could find her a cab for the long ride home.

"You always in such a hurry?"

A deep familiar voice stopped Julie in her tracks. The weighty bag slipped from her arm. She knew who it was even before she turned around to face him.

Zach.

Dressed in a dark three-piece suit, crisp

white shirt, designer tie and tiepin, he stood before her frowning. She'd never seen him in a suit before. He looked like a powerful business magnate, and she forced herself not to dwell on the effect he was having on her. She drew a quick, much-needed breath. Suit or Stetson, the man set her heart racing. "What are you doing in Seattle? I . . . thought you went camping," she managed.

"There's a horse breeders' convention in town." Zach's gaze narrowed as he quickly appraised her disheveled appearance. A muscle in his jaw clenched and his eyes darkened in anger. "I had some ranching business to attend to."

"Oh." He hadn't mentioned that to her before he'd left. Julie reached down for the strap of her bag.

"Where are you headed in such a hurry?" Zach raised an eyebrow and easily lifted the overnighter from the marble floor. "You don't know how to pack light, do you," he stated briskly, his gaze roaming the length of her body.

After a long silent moment, he fingered the lapel of her suit jacket, exposing the front of her almost buttonless blouse. "What happened to your shirt?"

"It's nothing." Mortified, she blinked back the tears that threatened to fill her eyes and pushed his hand away. "I was just going to get a cab and go home." She adjusted the blazer to completely cover the silk shirt. Turning on her heels, she headed for the concierge's desk.

Zach caught up to her in one long stride. "At this hour?" he asked, placing a hand around her upper arm. Gently he turned her around to face him. "Isn't that guy you were with going to take you home?"

"Wh-what?"

He placed his free hand on the small of her back and guided her out the front door. "Or at least let you use . . . the limo?"

She turned to face him again. "How do you know —"

"I saw you. In the restaurant."

"You were there? Why didn't you say something?" Julie looked to him for an answer. Her patience with men had just run out.

"I didn't want to interrupt anything. It looked like the two of you were having a good time together. You know, a few laughs?" His eyes narrowed as his gaze met hers. "That jerk's not your boyfriend, is he? You know, the one you've been seeing?" Zach handed a generous tip to the valet, who'd returned his truck to the front of the hotel.

"That's none of your business."

"Yeah, well, I'm making it my business. Someone has to look out for you." He indicated his vehicle with a nod of his head. "Get in."

"I'll grab a cab." Julie reached for her overnight bag but Zach beat her to it.

He stowed the luggage in the back. "Get in the truck, Julie." He opened the passenger door and drew a deep breath. "It's been a long day. I don't have time to stand here and argue."

It *had* been a long day. Julie didn't see one taxi in the area. "Fine," she said, stepping up into the vehicle.

Zach got in, fastened his seat belt and turned to face her. "So, *was* that your boyfriend . . . or just maybe a one-night stand?" Pressing his foot on the gas pedal, he abruptly drove the truck from the curved driveway of the lavish hotel.

"How can you even *think* that? If that's what you really believe, then you don't know me. You don't know me at all." Folding her arms in front of her, Julie glared at him. "Where are we going?"

Zach turned to face her. His gaze shifted down to her legs and the short skirt she wore. Stormy, lightning-blue eyes met hers. "I haven't decided yet. But you're not taking a cab all the way home, alone, dressed like that, that's for sure," he growled.

"What? What's wrong with the way I'm dressed? I was there on business, if you must know."

"Didn't look that way to me."

"How would you know?" Julie recalled the advances Nick had made at the bar and even during dinner. Mortified, she almost groaned aloud at the memory. Surely if Zach had seen her, he'd seen Nick's moves. What must he think of her?

"How would *I* know?" Zach stopped at a red traffic light and his angry gaze met hers. "Because at a business meeting, the guy, if he were even half a moron, would never place his arm around a woman and touch her the way that snake did."

Julie instinctively knew his deep, quiet voice was controlled, belying his anger.

His intense stare dared her to deny what he'd obviously seen. Leaning to her, he gently fingered the collar of her blouse. "What happened to the buttons, Julie?"

Again, she pushed his hand away. Zach's gaze held hers and Julie realized that he was right. She'd been a fool. The traffic light turned green and she glanced out the side window again, her eyes filling with tears. How did she ever get into such a mess?

So much for breaking out of my cocoon.

"Fasten your seat belt." Zach's heart filled with conflicting emotions of raging anger and genuine concern. He'd been staking out the hotel room when he heard the struggle going on inside the room Julie was sharing with Viktor.

He'd been tempted to blow his cover and kick in the door. Thankfully, he'd heard Ivanov's cursing and the sound of the door opening seconds before he could carry out his plan.

Zach had pretended to open a door diagonally across the hallway as if he were just another hotel guest going into his room. Out of the corner of his eye, he'd watched a very upset Julie emerge, moving almost as quickly as she had when they'd escaped the bear.

After a quick talk with John Castlerock through the infrared earpiece and tiepin as he made his way down the stairs, Zach decided he would stick with Julie and take her to a safe house for the night.

Zach analyzed Julie's emotional state as she sat across from him. What had the jerk done to her? How far had his advances gone? His eyes went to her black suit, disheveled blouse, and then back up to the loose tendrils of blond hair falling from the fancy hairdo.

Julie wasn't the kind of woman who would be intimate without being married. Zach's instincts to protect her from the evil man she was with had been overwhelming. It took every ounce of courage to walk out of that hotel without blowing his cover and taking the guy down.

Shifting in his seat, Zach couldn't stand the thought of another man kissing her. Especially a lowlife like Viktor. He glanced over to find her staring out the side window, her arms folded protectively across her chest. Was she hurt? Bruised? He wanted answers.

Time was running out. The Bureau needed a name — the most current name Viktor was using. Julie was their only lead. Zach turned north on the highway and headed to the safe house he'd been staying in the past few days. He reached over to take her hand in his and his heart broke when he felt her trembling. Her fingers were as cold as ice. "We need to talk."

She continued to stare out the side window. "Fine."

Great. Zach hated when any woman said the word "fine" in that tone. It meant the furthest thing from things were just hunky-dory than any other word in the English language.

Noticing they were quickly approaching an exit ramp, he headed the car off the highway and pulled into a small all-night grocery store parking lot.

Zach shut off the motor and unfastened his seat belt. After scanning the surroundings, he turned to face her. "Tell me about the guy who did this to you." He drew a quick breath. "You never were the kind of woman to get into one-night stands. I'm sorry I even implied that." He carefully lifted her gaze to meet his. "Forgive me?"

Julie turned to stare into the blue eyes that had become more than familiar to her. The ache inside her heart, the longing for a good Christian man, brought fresh tears to her eyes. Zach could be that man. She quickly blinked them away. "Okay, *fine* . . . I forgive you."

The beginning of a smile tipped the corners of his mouth. "Thanks." He ran a finger along her cheek and his countenance took on a more serious look. "Julie, did he hurt you?" he whispered, his voice thick with emotion.

She glanced away for a moment. If the pain was any indication, there *was* a bruise.

Julie turned to Zach. "I . . . should have known better."

Zach muttered several curses under his breath. "You sure you're all right? You're still shaking. He didn't —"

"No." She shook her head. "It's okay. Nothing happened."

Zach undid her seat belt and pulled her to him.

Julie welcomed his embrace and quietly let the tears fall. Fear, anger and the knowledge of how close she'd come to date rape overwhelmed her.

Holding her gently, Zach caressed her face and whispered words of comfort. "It's okay. It's over." He drew a long, deep breath. "Stay with me tonight. I'll keep you safe."

"I don't know, Zach." She brushed away a tear with her hand and noticed the wet stains on his tie. "Oh, I — I've ruined your tie. I'm sorry." She ran her hand along the smooth, silky fabric and in the process, her fingers rested on the unusual tiepin.

"No problem." Zach gently held her wrist with one hand before she could examine the interesting tiepin. "You can trust me, especially after what you've been through." He tenderly ran his thumb back and forth across the underside of her wrist. "I don't want you to be alone tonight, that's all."

Julie realized he was right. She didn't want to be alone tonight. Her instincts about Nick had been right. She silently thanked God she'd been able to walk away from what could have been a disaster.

Turning to Zach, taking in his handsome face, square jaw and silver-blue eyes, she felt comforted by his friendship, his honesty. He'd been nothing but upright with her since he showed up at the lodge.

"You're right. I don't want to be alone tonight. But please understand —"

"No problem. We're good friends, remember?"

"Right." She nodded her head. "Good friends."

"Here's the deal. I'm staying at a buddy's cabin." He smiled. "Two bedrooms. We'll talk all night if you like."

"I don't want you to get the wrong idea." If he only knew how she longed for them to be together, completely. But there was no way she could let that happen. Premarital sex went against all her beliefs. As it was, her heart was already breaking knowing he would leave.

"I know."

Zach started the engine and pulled out of the parking lot. After a few minutes, he glanced over at her. "How are you doing?

Better?"

"Yes. I'm not used to life in the fast lane and tonight, well, like I said, I should have known better." Drawing in a quick breath, she continued. "I was so vulnerable up in that room with Nick. All he'd told me was that his company had put me up in the hotel. I didn't know it was *his* room. He didn't let me in on *that* until after I was inside."

Are you getting this, John?

"Get the last name, Marshall." Even through the tiny earpiece, Zach recognized the excitement in Agent John Castlerock's voice.

Zach gripped the steering wheel until his knuckles turned white. "Nick, huh. Nick who?" His heart raced with the need for Viktor's latest last name. He stared at the road ahead.

An eternity passed in silence.

"Nick Davidson," Julie finally answered in disgust. "He owns an import-export business over by the Public Market downtown. I buy some of the craft items for my gift shop from him. Or I used to. I never want to see him again."

"I don't blame you."

"Got it, Zach. Stay with Julie. Consider it

protective custody. Don't let on that you're with the Bureau. Not yet. I'll get back to you. If she *is* innocent . . . she's still in danger." Zach's earpiece, hidden from Julie's view since he wore it in his left ear, buzzed with the sound of John Castlerock's hurried response. "I'll start the ball rolling at this end. Watch your back. This could all be nothing more than an act."

Zach's heart filled with conflicting emotions of caution and relief that they were one inch closer to zeroing in on Ivanov and Kostoff — and proving Julie's innocence.

But John was right. This *could* be nothing more than a ruse. He turned his eyes briefly from the road to face her. "Do you need to call your family, let them know where you are? You can use my cell phone if you'd like."

"I'll talk to Mom and Dad in the morning, when I'm not so shaky. I don't want to upset them. They can get in touch with me anytime on my cell phone if there's a problem with Emmie." She turned a weary gaze to Zach. "How far is this cabin?"

"Not too much longer. Only about half an hour. It's a small, old place tucked away in the woods."

Driving in companionable silence for the rest of the trip, Zach pulled into the long graveled driveway a few minutes ahead of schedule. The newly built cabin, bathed in the glow of a full moon, came into view as they made a right turn into the narrow drive. "Here we are."

Julie gasped. "Oh. This is not what I expected." She smiled and turned to Zach. "You had me thinking it was some broken-down old cabin."

He gave her a wink. "Not bad, huh?"

"That's an understatement." Julie's laugh sounded relieved. "I was actually expecting a shack."

"A shack? Would I do that to you?"

"Yes."

Zach laughed. "Come on, I'll get our bags out of the truck. It's late and you look tired." Once they were out of the vehicle, he grabbed his duffel bag and Julie's heavy overnighter.

He'd find out exactly what had happened with Viktor in Julie's hotel room. Zach was more determined than ever to put Ivanov away for good.

They walked the short distance to the front door. Zach unlocked it and let Julie in ahead of him. After settling in, Zach insisted Julie take the master bedroom. Removing his suit jacket and loosening his tie, he lit the logs in the fireplace and turned to face her. "There's some food and soft drinks in the fridge. You want to talk?"

"All right." Julie smiled. "But I'd like to shower first and change into something more comfortable. I'll join you in a few minutes."

"Sure."

Using the wireless phone in the cabin, Zach dialed John's number as soon as Julie closed the door to her bedroom. He filled him in on what almost happened at the hotel and where he and Julie were now. "Did we apprehend Viktor?"

"Not yet. They lost him."

"What?"

"Seems that Ivanov, aka Nick Davidson, slipped through the crowd. We confirmed the business he owns in Seattle. I just found his company's file tucked away in Beatrice's desk. Either she hid it from us or we missed it in our search. He's been doing business with Julie for almost a year."

"Where does Julie stand now?"

"Julie's a valuable witness, Zach." John drew a long breath. "I'm convinced, like you, that she's innocent. He's been using her and the lodge somehow. But we'll need proof. I could be wrong."

Zach sat on the sofa across from the fireplace and removed the tiepin and earpiece, placing them in the pocket of his suit jacket. Pulling off his tie, he tossed it onto the back of the couch. "She'll need protection. Her daughter, too." There was no way Zach would leave Julie's side until the investigation ended. "I'm the only man for the job, John. You have to know that."

"Relax. You're the only agent I want with Julie. We still can't let her know anything about the investigation, though. Not yet. If my instincts are right, Ivanov will be seeing her again. After his stunt in the hotel, I don't think it'll be a pleasant meeting for Julie. The less she knows . . . the better off she'll be."

"We're staying here tonight, at the Bureau's cabin." Zach looked down the darkened hallway to the closed bedroom door. "Maybe tomorrow night, too."

"Sarah's on her way there now."

"I thought she was with Yuri."

"She was until they said good-night at the restaurant. We have other agents tracking him now," John stated.

Zach thought for a minute. "Tell her she's going to be my sister-in-law as her cover when she gets here."

"Right."

"This is *her* place. I've referred to it as my buddy's cabin."

"Affirmative."

"What about Beatrice?" Zach asked. "Has the overseas report on her come in yet?"

"I'm still waiting for a couple more details."

Zach muttered a curse under his breath. "I want to know the results as soon as we get them. Listen, Julie's daughter is with her grandparents."

"Yeah, Beatrice mentioned that."

"Are we watching their house, too?" Zach asked. "If Beatrice is working for Ivanov's team, Emmie isn't safe, either."

"I put a couple of agents on it an hour ago. It's covered."

"Good." Zach raked a hand through his hair. "I'm taking off my wire. I can be reached on my cell. It's been a rough night."

"Got it. Watch your back. They might've followed you. If it's a setup, Julie might've placed a bug somewhere so they could trace your location."

"Understood." Zach shut off the phone and replaced it in its cradle on one of the end tables. He watched as flames kicked in around the logs in the fireplace. The golden light filled the room with a warm glow. The crackling of the burning wood brought visions to mind of his own fireplace at home in Montana — and of Julie spending a lifetime there with him.

He turned at the sound of the bedroom door opening. Julie appeared in black stretch pants and the black sweatshirt he'd bought for her in Port Townsend. Long blond hair cascaded down past her shoulders. He let his gaze drift down from her soft hair, blue eyes and shapely body until it settled on her pink painted toenails. He swallowed a groan.

Zach would mask the undeniable feelings of love he felt for Julie. He would not let his guard down. He would be there for Julie and her daughter. Even if being this close to her was torture. She needed him, and he would protect her with his life.

"Tell me more about your family." Julie settled next to Zach on the dark green sofa and propped one of the soft plaid pillows behind her.

"You sure you want to hear this?" he asked, chuckling.

Julie smiled. "Sure. For starters, tell me about your brothers." She tucked her legs beneath her. "And that new house you built."

"Ah, the house." He drew in a long breath and poured some warm apple cider into two glass mugs. "Well, it's kind of big, I guess." Zach handed a glass to her. He took a sip then placed the mug on the end table. "Who knows, maybe I'll have a family again . . . someday."

Julie took several sips and cupped the mug in her hands. "I'm glad, Zach. I wondered if the thought of a family of your own would be too painful."

"It was, for a long time. Still is. My folks encouraged me to build the house. I decided that maybe I did have a life to look forward to in the distant future." Pulling her close, he gently touched his hand to her face, stroking her cheek with his finger. "After seeing you again, I'm wondering if the future is closer than I thought. I can see you there, Julie. At the ranch with me," he whispered.

"I'd love to see it someday." She sighed. "What's it like?"

"It's a two-story log home. Lots of windows with mountain views. I have my office there along with four bedrooms, a large kitchen and family room. Dining room, too." He reached over and wound his fingers through her long hair. She should always wear it like this. Loose and free. "There's a newly built barn on the property, too, top-of-the-line, for the horses."

"Sounds beautiful." Julie placed her mug on the end table. Taking another deep breath, she sat closer to him and put her head on his shoulder.

Zach smiled. "Emmie would love it." He chuckled lightly. "We'd probably have to drag her away from the horses."

"I think you're right." Breathing deeply, Julie cleared her throat and placed some distance between them because the images of what could never be filled her mind. "Tell me about your brothers."

"Jake and Luke." Zach stretched his legs out in front of him, crossing them at his ankles.

"Are they married?"

Zach placed an arm around her shoulder. "Luke came close once. He's a doctor and has his home and office on Marshall property. Still works the ranch, too."

"He's older?"

"Yeah, Luke's almost three years older than me."

"What about your other brother? Is he married?"

Zach gave a quick laugh. "No, Jake's only twenty-four. He's having a good time playing the field." He traced his thumb along her lower lip. "He's older than you were when we fell in love."

"We *were* kind of young, weren't we?"

"You were, anyway." Gently he curved his

fingers under her chin. "Only twenty-one."

"I never forgot the time we spent together, Zach."

"Me, either." His gaze searched hers. "I thought about you a lot since that day . . . when I left."

"You did?"

"Yeah."

"Me, too," she whispered.

"I hurt you when I left. I'm sorry. I never meant to."

"We can't hold on to the past anymore." She rested her and on his. "What good would it do anyway?"

"You're right." How would she react when she knew the truth about him? She was his assignment. Julie had become much more than that, but she'd never believe him.

"Do you have any sisters?" she asked.

He turned to meet her questioning gaze. "No, it's just us three boys." He smiled. Julie looked like a teenager with her clear blue eyes, soft smooth skin and long, blond hair. She never looked more beautiful. Her gaze met his and she grinned. Zach raised an eyebrow. "What's so funny?"

She smiled and waved her hand lightly. "It's . . . nothing."

"Come on, Julie," he coaxed. "What is it?"

"I'm picturing you as a mischievous little

boy. How did your parents ever live through having *three* sons?"

Zach laughed. "I think they're amazing. They'd have to be, with the three of us running around the ranch. We were a handful." For the next few minutes, Zach told her about growing up on the ranch with his practical-joking brothers.

"You miss them, don't you?" she observed.

"Yeah, I miss them." He rested his head against hers. "You tired?" he asked, pulling her closer.

She nodded. "Yes. It's . . . been a long day."

Zach pressed his lips to her temple. "I care about you, Jewels. A lot."

"I feel the same way," she said, leaning into his embrace.

"How are we going to make this work?"

"I don't know. It seems impossible. You in Montana. Me in Washington."

"Not impossible." Gently he held her face in his hands. "We'll work something out. I promise. Let's not talk about it tonight. You need rest after the day you've had." Zach ran his hand through her hair. "Are you sure you're all right?"

Julie nodded.

"He hurt you," he stated, gazing into her misty blue eyes. Rage brewed dangerously inside Zach's heart. The pleasure of payback time grew sweeter with every passing minute.

"Yes, he did." Julie sighed and rested her head against his chest. "Thanks for being there for me tonight, Zach," she whispered. "And for understanding."

"Anytime." He hugged her to him. "You want to talk about it?"

Julie looked into his eyes and drew a shaky breath. "I don't really know Nick that well." She reached for her cup of hot apple cider and took another sip. "He's been asking me to see his renovated warehouse in Seattle for months."

"What else?" Zach curled a strand of hair behind her ear.

"That's it, really. I finally agreed and, well, here I am."

"How'd you get him to stop, Julie? Tonight I mean."

Julie returned the mug to the table and lowered her gaze. "I kneed him in a delicate area." Glancing down at her hands, she shook her head from side to side.

Zach cupped her face so their gazes met. "Good for you." Holding Julie in his arms, he longed for the moment when he'd know for sure that she was innocent.

Would that day ever come?

His thoughts were interrupted at the sound of someone trying their key in the front door. Zach gave Julie a quick glance, then made his way to the door. *Sarah?* He held his hand on the doorknob to prevent it from opening.

"Is someone in there?" Sarah asked from the other side of the door. "What's going on? Open the door. Who's in there?"

"Sarah? It's me, Zach. Your . . . brother-in-law."

"Well, let me in, cowboy!" Sarah's surprised laughter could be heard through the door. "Do you intend to keep me standing out here all night?"

"Hold on." He opened the door.

"Howdy." Sarah gave him a teasing smile. She peeked beyond him to acknowledge Julie. "Hi," she said, waving hello.

Sarah's darker hair was a different look for the female agent on the team. She looked younger. Sweeter. Dressed in gray sweats, with her long hair tied up in a ponytail, wearing a dark pink shade of lipstick, no one would guess she was a "guns blazing, ask questions later" FBI agent.

Closing the door behind her, Zach turned to watch Julie as Sarah walked over to her.

"Hi, I'm Sarah, Zach's sister-in-law. He was . . . well, he was married to my sister."

"Hi. I'm Julie." She stood. "It's good to meet you. Is this your place?"

"Yes. I live in California and keep this place as a much-needed getaway. I told Zach he could stay here anytime he wanted. I even gave him the key." She turned to Zach and mouthed, "This is our spy?" She wiggled her eyebrows and mouthed, "hubba hubba."

Zach nodded and bit back a laugh. Sarah had seen Julie's photos but Julie was even more beautiful in person. "Yeah, I guess I should've phoned you, but staying here tonight was a last-minute decision. Julie and I are friends." He turned to give Julie a wink. "We needed a place to crash."

Julie took a step toward them. "I hope it's all right, I —"

"Of course." Sarah turned to Julie and smiled. "I'd love the company, actually. It's nice to have someone here already when I open the door."

"Thanks, Sarah." Julie drew a quick breath and glanced around the interior of the house. "It's a lovely cabin."

"I'll put Julie up in the guest room." Zach took Sarah's bag and made his way into the main bedroom. "It'll just take a second to grab her overnighter and —"

"No, Zach. Please, don't be silly. I'm sure

Julie's already settled in. I'll take the guest room. I insist."

"You got it. I'll take the sofa." Zach brought Sarah's duffel bag into the guest room. He stood just inside the door to observe the two women who were talking and laughing as if they'd been friends for years.

Julie must feel at ease talking to another woman. She'd probably get a full night's rest, too. Good. She needed it.

Zach would sleep better, too, with a third person in the cabin tonight.

That was for sure. . . .

ELEVEN

Zach woke to the sound of Julie's scream.

Was someone inside? *In* her room? He reached for the Glock hidden under his pillow and bolted toward her bedroom. Gripping the weapon in both hands, he edged the door open with his foot.

Wide-eyed, Julie swallowed and gathered the green flannel sheet up to her chin. Her sleepy gaze met his. "Wh-what are you doing?" She blinked and stared at him. "You have a gun?"

"Yeah." He cleared his throat. "Sarah always keeps a loaded gun in the cabin." He put the safety on the Glock and stowed it in the back waistband of his jeans. Willing his heart rate to return to normal, he ran a hand through his hair. "In case of bears." Muttering under his breath, he made his way to the window. Peeking through the wooden blinds, he surveyed the area outside the house. "I heard you scream. Did you see a bear?" He turned to face her. "You all right?"

"I . . . guess I had a nightmare. Nick again," she answered, her voice breaking. "The jerk." Pushing the covers away, she stormed out of the bed and headed toward the bathroom.

"Julie?" Pulling his gaze from her, Zach scanned the hallway to the front door and swallowed hard. "Where are you going?"

"I need to splash some cold water on my face," she explained, her voice muffled behind the closed bathroom door. "And brush my teeth. I need to . . . wake up."

That makes two of us.

Zach glanced at his watch. Three o'clock. There was no way he'd get any sleep now. Not the way his adrenaline had kicked in at Julie's screams. Or how she looked. More beautiful than he remembered. And he'd remembered a lot.

Coffee. That's what he needed to wake up and get a grip on the situation. Zach made his way into the dark kitchen. Knowing that Ivanov was more than capable of having them tracked and eliminated, he wouldn't make it easier for him by turning on the light. The moonlight was bad enough.

He blew out a long breath and concentrated on the details of the planned raid

235

they'd prepared for, once Ivanov was in sight. He reached into the cabinet and placed the coffee tin on the counter.

"What are you doing in the dark?" Julie asked quietly, standing in the doorway. Without warning, she flipped the wall switch and the kitchen filled with blinding illumination.

Rushing to where she stood, Zach placed his hands on the wall next to her and gazed into her sleepy, blue eyes. Swiftly and silently flipping the switch, he killed the light.

"Don't you want to see what you're doing?" she whispered breathlessly. "It's . . . dark in here."

Was she deliberately setting him up for a shooter's scope? Zach wanted to shake her. What was she doing involving herself with Ivanov? How'd she get herself into this mess?

"You sure you're all right?" The moon cast a perfect light for him to admire Julie's natural beauty.

She nodded and gave him a slight smile. "I'm fine."

"Julie," he whispered, pulling her to him. "You're beautiful." Lowering his mouth to hers, he kissed her.

She reached around his waist in a light

embrace and her hand brushed against the cold steel weapon tucked into the back waistband of his jeans.

"Oh," she whispered, breaking their kiss. "The gun."

Zach's breath caught in his throat. He tightened his hand around her wrist and brought her hand to his chest. He'd never made the mistake of letting anyone get that close to his gun before. What was he thinking? Slowly, he dragged in a shaky breath. If he lost his edge in this investigation, he was as good as dead. And so was Julie.

"Yeah, the gun." Reluctantly releasing her, he drew a deep, ragged breath. "I'll finish making the coffee. In the dark."

"Whatever you say, Zach." Julie swallowed and pressed a hand to her heart.

Good. It's still beating.

How could she have jumped out of bed dressed only in her nightgown? On second thought, no wonder she'd run from the bed. She'd almost stopped breathing at the sight of Zach, bare-chested, wearing only a pair of worn jeans. She had to do *something* to get her heart going again.

Zach had held the gun and aimed it at her as if he'd been born with one in his hand. She'd had the distinct impression that he would shoot to kill. A chill went through Julie like a warm knife through softened butter. "Who *are* you, Zach?"

"What?" He gave a quick laugh. "What do you mean?" He crossed his arms over his broad chest and leaned back casually against the counter. Moonlight drifted in from the skylight above. His eyes glistened with unmasked desire. "You know who I am," he answered, his voice deep and low. "More than anyone."

"The way you held that gun . . . like it was second nature."

"Yeah, well, I have to shoot wild animals out by the ranch every once in a while," he answered quickly.

Julie swallowed hard. Zach Marshall *was* a mystery man.

Suddenly, fighting the natural impulse to be with Zach again, the man she'd never stopped loving, seemed impossible. Meeting his hooded gaze, her heart filled with the knowledge that she was falling in love with Zach again. She'd always loved him, but these feelings were newer, stronger.

"Are we having a party?" Sarah's cheerful voice broke into Julie's thoughts. Making her way into the kitchen, Sarah gave a nod to Zach, who nodded back. Why did Julie suddenly feel like the odd man out? Was there more than a brother-in-law-sister-in-law relationship where Sarah and Zach were concerned?

"Sarah, I'm sorry I woke you. I . . . had a nightmare. I feel so foolish." She didn't want to give Sarah the wrong impression.

While Zach made the coffee, she briefly explained what had happened at the hotel. Sarah listened intently while she poured Julie a fresh cup of coffee. Julie found it easy to talk to Zach's *buddy*. She wondered if Zach's wife had been anything like her sister. Beautiful, smart, generous and kind. No wonder he'd fallen in love with Lisa.

A few days later, Julie planned the annual Thanksgiving preparations at the inn. The resort was fully booked through New Year's Day. Taking a sigh of relief that the inn just might make it after all, Julie leaned back in the brown leather chair.

Since their return from Seattle, Zach had hardly left her side. She tried not to think about Nick and what had happened at the hotel, but the uneasy feeling she had the night she had dinner with him was back. This time, Julie would listen for God's still, small voice, for His direction a little more closely.

Lord, am I being overly concerned or are

You trying to tell me something?

Beatrice barged into the office, banging the door into the wall. "Oh, so sorry." She eased the door shut behind her.

"You scared me half to death!" Julie bent to pick up several sharpened pencils and a small nail file that she'd knocked to the floor. "What's the matter?"

"It's been quite a day." Seating herself in the chair across from Julie's desk, Beatrice's weary gaze met hers. "Besides my scaring you just now . . . are you okay?" she asked, straightening the stack of paperwork she held.

"Yes." Julie placed the filled pencil holder back onto the desk. She curled a strand of hair behind her ear and met her friend's concerned look. "Why?"

"I don't know, you just don't seem yourself lately. Is Emmie all right?" Beatrice sat back in the chair.

"Emmie seems much better since I took her to the doctor's. It's just a cold."

"Good, but something's wrong, Julie." Beatrice folded her arms, holding the paperwork to her. "Are you worried about . . . the murder?"

"Not any more than usual." Julie sighed and turned to the window to watch the rain.

"Then what is it?"

"Nothing, really." Maybe she should share a little of what had happened with Nick. At least Beatrice would know why they were no longer doing business with him. Turning back to Beatrice, she offered a rueful smile.

"What do you mean 'nothing *really*'?" Beatrice persisted.

Julie took a deep breath. "Over the weekend, Nick made a pass while we were in Seattle." That was putting it mildly. "He's . . . not the man I thought he was."

"Oh, dear. I'm sorry. What happened?" Beatrice straightened in the chair. "I never did like that man."

"You didn't?"

"He made me . . . nervous. Fidgety."

"I wish you'd shared that feeling with me," Julie said.

"Sorry, it just seemed silly," Beatrice admitted.

"I know what you mean. By the way, we need to find another supplier for our gift shop and look into broadening what we order from other vendors. I don't ever want to see him again."

"Maybe you should report it —"

"No, it's over. I made that very clear." She sighed. "I don't want to think about it. I want to look forward to the holidays."

"Good." Beatrice nodded. "I can't believe

we're decorating for Christmas already." She smiled and drew a deep breath. "It's going to be even more hectic than usual around here."

"It's always this way." Julie smiled. She was glad she'd hired Beatrice to manage the inn. It gave Julie time to be with her family and not worry about the lodge so much. "You remember you're invited to Thanksgiving dinner tomorrow, right? Mom keeps asking about you." Julie smiled. "It'll be your first Thanksgiving in the States."

"I know. But I need to be here at the inn for the buffet. I'll give your mother a call this afternoon and apologize. But I promise to make it over for dessert, if that's okay. I wouldn't miss seeing you and Zach together for your American holiday," she said with a smile.

"I'm glad he could make it. His family is in Montana, so he's alone."

"Oh, I see."

"They have a ranch. With horses."

"Really?" Beatrice wrapped her arms around the stack of papers she held. "No motorbikes?" She smiled.

Julie laughed. "He may just have an old Harley hanging around somewhere, I suppose."

Beatrice smiled. "I'll have to ask him

about it —"

"Don't you dare! Do *not* mention the photographs, either. Understand?" Julie sat up in her chair.

Beatrice raised an eyebrow, looking innocent. "Who, me?"

"I mean it."

"Don't worry." Beatrice lifted her hand in a gesture of compliance. "I'm sworn to secrecy."

"Good." Julie sighed.

"Your secret is safe with me." Beatrice crossed her heart. "Dining here at the inn will be quite lovely, actually. John and I are having dinner together in the dining room with the guests."

"You are?" Julie smiled. She thought there had been something developing between those two. "Interesting."

"Well, it makes perfect sense." Beatrice brushed a strand of curly gray hair from her face. "Don't go making anything out of it. It's strictly business. John has put together the most exquisite holiday dinner."

Julie smiled. "We'll look forward to seeing you for dessert then." Beatrice and John made a nice couple. Together, the two of them could probably manage the lodge on their own, if Julie ever moved away.

TWELVE

At home the next night, Julie hurried down the stairs to the sound of a knock at the front door. Seeing it was Zach, she opened it for him. He'd taken off his tie and loosened his collar. "Hi. Come on in. I just put Emmie to bed."

He closed the door and followed her into the kitchen. "That was one terrific meal you and your mom made today." He smiled and took a seat at the table.

Julie sat in the chair next to him. "Thanks, I love this time of year, the whole family together, the smell of turkey roasting and pumpkin pie baking. Does your family make a traditional Thanksgiving dinner?"

"Yeah, they do." Zach took her hand in his. "I'll . . . be home in a few days. But I'm sure the leftovers will be gone by then." His intense gaze met hers and Julie saw the conflict of emotions revealed in his eyes.

A few days. In only a few days, she

wouldn't have him sitting across from her. Her heart ached with the sudden sting of loss. She lowered her gaze, not wanting Zach to see her eyes brimming with tears.

Zach caressed her cheek. "I'm going to miss you, Julie. More than you know." Encircling her in his strong arms, he drew her close. Julie wanted nothing more than to spend every night of her life with Zach. This more mature Zach was even more appealing than the younger version from her memories.

Zach pulled her closer as she settled into his tender embrace. His silver-blue eyes darkened. "Julie," he whispered, nuzzling her neck, "I —"

"Hello?"

Abruptly, they pulled apart and Julie stood to see her daughter standing in the kitchen, rubbing her eyes.

"Emmie. Honey, you're supposed to be sleeping," she managed.

"I'm not tired, Mommy." Barefoot, Emmie made her way over to Zach, still clutching the white horse he'd given her for Thanksgiving. "Hi." She tilted her head up and waved a hand.

"Hello, Emmie." Zach smiled and ran a hand along his jaw. His heart broke. A *real*

Prince Charming wouldn't leave them behind the way he was planning to. He had to face the harsh reality that had revealed itself to him over Thanksgiving dinner.

He loved Julie too much to ask her to be his wife. He couldn't let her go through the heart-wrenching decision of leaving her family and her business behind, just to be with him. Especially since it affected her daughter, too.

She had made a wonderful life for herself in Washington. He couldn't take that from her. He knelt down to meet Emmie's gaze and lifted her onto his knee. She felt so warm and full of life. "Did you come up with a name for your horse yet?"

"I'm still thinking," she said, holding the animal close.

"Why aren't you asleep yet?" Julie asked, checking her daughter's forehead again. "It's late."

"I woked up." Emmie shrugged her shoulders and jumped from Zach's knee.

"Well, let me tuck you in again," Julie said softly.

"Okay." She took her mother's hand and turned to Zach. "Aren't you coming?"

Zach looked to Julie, who smiled and nodded her approval.

"Sure." He stood.

Handing him the horse, Emmie took his hand in hers. Once they reached her room, Emmie jumped into the bed.

"Come on, scoot under the covers," Zach offered. He reached for the sheets and the comforter and tucked them under her chin. "Listen, Emmie, I . . . have to go back home to Montana," he said, sitting on the side of the bed. "I have horses I have to take care of and . . . ranching stuff to do."

"You have *real* horses?" Her eyes lit with wonder.

"Yep." Zach chuckled.

"Can't someone else take care of them?"

"Well, my brothers have been watching them for me and feeding them, but now I have to help."

"I bet you have a white horse, too, huh."

"Uh, yeah, actually I do." He laughed softly.

"See, Mommy," she whispered, glancing to Julie who sat on the far corner of the bed. "He really *is* the Prince."

"Now, Emmie —"

"Well, I sort of like being the Prince, you know," Zach interrupted. He smiled at Julie and winked. Leaning over, he gave Emmie a kiss on the cheek. "I'll say goodbye to you now, okay?" He cleared his throat. "You be a good girl."

Emmie bit her lower lip. "Do you have to go?"

"Yes."

"But I'm going to miss you! I don't want you to leave us."

Zach drew in a deep breath. "I'll miss you, too, Emmie," he whispered. "Look. I have a deal for you. If you send me some of your drawings in the mail, I'll put them on my refrigerator, okay?"

She slowly nodded her head and sniffled. "Okay."

Miserable, his gaze went to Julie, who had suddenly gone quiet on him. "What do you think, Mom?"

"I'm sure Emmie would love to send you her pictures. Okay now, it really *is* time for bed." Julie kissed her, and brushed away the hair that had fallen across her forehead. "Good night, sweetheart."

" 'Night, Mommy." Emmie looked over at Zach. She waved one small hand. "Good-bye, Prince Charming."

"Good night, Emmie," Zach managed. Why had God allowed him to meet up with Julie again and her sweet little girl? Hadn't he had enough pain in his life?

Julie took his hand and shut the door to Emmie's room. She always knew he'd leave someday. But why did it have to be now? She couldn't stop a tear from slipping down her cheek. She wiped it away. "When are you leaving?" Her gaze searched his. She'd grown accustomed to looking into Zach's eyes, watching the blue-gray color change along with his moods — happiness, playfulness — the secretive nature that was still a mystery to her.

"Soon." He reached out for her hand.

"Your family will be happy to see you." She smiled, hoping to convince him that it was perfectly fine with her that he was going away for good.

Zach tugged her into his arms. "I don't want to leave you." He held her close. "I need you to understand," he whispered, his breath warm on her cheek. "I *have* to go."

"It's okay," she managed. "I'm just being silly." She took a deep, shaky breath. "You're a good friend, Zach. I'm glad our paths crossed again. Maybe we'll see each other again, someday." Julie pushed away from his tender embrace. Why had she allowed herself to fall in love with him a second time?

"Wait." Zach gently but firmly grabbed her wrist. "I haven't said goodbye yet."

"I . . . don't want to say goodbye." She broke free from his hold and hurried toward her room. "Not again."

Zach caught up with Julie and drew her into his arms. "Do you think I *want* to go?" he asked, his voice thick with emotion.

"You're going, aren't you?" she whispered.

"Yes," he answered lightly, nuzzling her neck. "I am. But it's the last thing in the world I want to do. Someday soon . . . you'll understand."

"I'll miss you, Zach, and all the fun we had getting lost together," she whispered, offering a smile.

"I don't want to leave you." He smoothed away the long strand of hair that had fallen across her face. "You have to believe that, no matter what happens." Gazing into her eyes, he brushed a tear from her cheek with the pad of his thumb. "Don't cry." He cleared his throat and drew a long breath. He kissed her again and Julie lingered in the sweet kiss, wishing with all her heart that things could have worked out differently for them.

"You'll be fine," he whispered, his breath warm against her cheek. "I'll call you," he said, his voice breaking. "I promise you." He kissed her again. "I . . . have to go." He turned and strode out of the room, quietly shutting the door behind him.

Julie's room, her house, her heart felt the

emptiness of his leaving. Why did God bring Zach into her life again? There had to be a reason.

What is it, Lord?

"What do you mean, we still haven't heard from Sarah?" Zach paced back and forth in his room at the lodge, staring hard at his boss. "We can't lose Sarah, too, John. What's going on?"

"We haven't heard from her since her tip that Ivanov was on his way up north. We have a couple of agents looking for them now." John drew in a tense breath. "Listen, Zach, we think we know where he's headed."

Zach turned from scanning the lake outside the window to face John. "He's coming here, isn't he," he stated.

"It's a sure bet. Look, the pinhole cameras and microphones are all installed. They'll send back the audio and video when he shows up. We're going to get this guy."

"We'd better make sure we have Julie covered. I hate having her in harm's way." Zach drew a deep breath and ran a hand along the back of his neck. How could he ever explain all this to her? She'd never forgive him. She would think he'd been using her. She'd be right. That was exactly what he had been doing, at least part of the time. "I have to tell her what's going down."

"We can't tell Julie anything. Not yet. It'll put her in even more danger if she knows." John drew a deep breath. "We can't make any assumptions about her innocence, either."

Zach turned to stare at him. "You still think she may be involved?"

"We have to keep that option open. You know that."

"Yeah." Deep inside, Zach knew John was right.

"You know the drill."

"Affirmative," Zach answered, glancing out the window again. "I know the drill all right," he mumbled. *Shoot to kill.*

"Zach, we need this slimeball alive. You got that?"

Zach forced himself to take a slow, deep breath. Great, now John could read his mind. Was he wearing his thoughts on his sleeve? That was a lethal legacy for any agent. "Affirmative."

"Good." John paced to the other side of the room. "We need a confession out of him, the works if we can get it. He's no good to us dead. Unfortunately. Our team has gone over a thousand details of every possible scenario. It'll go down just like we

252

planned."

"Right." Zach turned to meet John's gaze.

"Listen, Zach, keep a clear mind and watch your back." John looked more tired than Zach had ever seen him. "I'll keep watch inside the resort. You handle the grounds outside and Julie's house, as if I could ever keep you away."

"You got that right. Any news on Tommy?" Zach sat in one of the two upholstered chairs in his suite.

John sat in the other chair and leaned forward, resting his elbows on his knees. "No."

"Nothing?"

"No."

Surprised that John was so quiet on the subject of Agent Tomasino, Zach ran a few scenarios around in his mind. Was there something he didn't know? "What about Sarah. Tell me the details."

"She called to tell me she'd lost Viktor, but was following an *interesting* lead." John cursed.

"That's just like her to go off on her own." Zach ran a hand through his hair. "I told her not to do anything stupid."

"Yeah. That gal has to remember she has a life to live outside the Bureau. I just wish she'd realize that."

"Who do we have looking for her?" They were getting short on manpower. Zach turned to John for an answer.

"Agent Michaels is searching for her now." John stood. His weary gaze met Zach's. "We need to get as much info from Viktor as we can. The clock is ticking."

"I'm ready," Zach responded, rising to his feet.

"The team's on it, too. It could go down anytime now." John walked to the door and opened it. He checked the hallway outside Zach's room. He nodded to Zach, stepped out and closed the door behind him.

Zach turned to glance out the window again. Ivanov might be here already. Guilty or innocent, Julie was in danger. He closed his eyes for one brief moment and cleared his mind of all distractions that would get in the way of capturing Ivanov.

Zach visualized every detail inside Julie's house. The path he'd memorized, every tree or bush surrounding her home and the huge lake. The squeaky fourth step. He went over the hostage rescue scenarios the team had extensively practiced. He tossed his FBI raid gear into a duffel bag and quietly slipped out of his room. There was one more stop he had to make before checking his arsenal of weapons and hooking up with the other agents on the case.

If he were a praying man . . .

Okay, God, I'll give it a shot. You listening? Forget about me. It's Julie and her daughter I'm asking You to keep an eye on. Please, watch over them. In Jesus' name.

Carrying his duffel bag filled with full-dress black raid gear and weapons, Zach made his way to the attic for one last look.

He'd find the cardboard box.

Would its contents reveal Julie's guilt?

Or innocence?

Zach pulled up the old folding ladder and, without a sound, closed the small entryway behind him. Pulling the flashlight from the duffel bag he'd placed on the dusty floor, he aimed the beam of light across the walls and cobwebbed ceiling.

A small window near the top of the gabled roofline provided a touch of eerie moonlight to the old room. Surprisingly, the musty odor he'd anticipated was hardly noticeable.

He moved the beam of light across to the other side of the cramped space. He spotted the usual stuff someone might find in an attic: an old trunk, an antique-looking dresser in need of repair, an old dust-covered exercise bike.

Walking cautiously toward it, he observed

how out of place the heavy bicycle appeared standing alone against the wall. As he moved closer, a small, well-hidden doorway came into view. Zach aimed the light on the floor directly in front of the bike. Just as he suspected, there were fresh scratch marks on the old wooden floor. Someone had moved the exercise bicycle. Recently.

Grabbing a pair of black gloves from his bag, Zach slipped them on and moved the equipment away from the doorway. He'd have the team dust for prints later. He reached for his gun and slowly shouldered open the squeaky door. He let out a quick breath. A small, sophisticated-looking operations center revealed itself as the door opened.

His pulse kicked up several beats and his fingers flexed on the pistol. Computer, fax, all the latest technical devices had been stored up here. But who'd been using them? Julie? She'd never liked small spaces — always had a bit of claustrophobia. But she *had* been up here before. He knew that for a fact.

Using the flashlight, Zach checked his watch. He had only five minutes to meet with the team at the predesignated time. He pulled a digital camera from his supplies. Taking quick pictures of the evidence inside the makeshift office, he noticed a fax had been received. He quickly glossed over the letter then snapped a close-up. There was some kind of meeting. Information crossing hands. He noted the date on the fax. Something was going down *today.*

He snapped a few more shots and ducked back into the main room of the attic, closing the old door and making sure he left everything intact. One last glance to make sure things were all in place and then his gaze focused on something familiar. The thing he'd been searching for in the first place. The cardboard box Julie had been holding the day he'd let her run into him.

Zach checked his watch again. He had less than two minutes before he'd have to leave and meet with his team. Making his way to the box, he rushed for it and pulled back the flaps, knowing full well that Julie's guilt or innocence could be proven by the contents lying within the old carton.

Frowning, he paused as an old image stared back at him. A photograph from eight years ago — when he'd ridden that old Harley. He reached inside and found a couple more loose photos of him and Julie together. An album from their college days, love notes he'd written her, dried flowers. *This* was what she'd been hiding from him?

He had no time to think about the ramifications of the fact that she'd kept the pictures of them together. Other than the knowledge that all these years, she'd remembered him. Thought about him. Just as he'd thought about her. He focused his mind back on the case.

Someone else had been using this attic to support their terrorist organization. But who?

Viktor. As *Nick,* the man she'd been dating, he'd been using Julie and this attic as his operations center. She'd been in danger all this time. She was in danger now.

Zach placed everything back in its place. He grabbed his duffel bag and silently made his way down from the attic. As soon as his feet hit the ground of the hallway, his cell phone vibrated.

"Marshall," he answered, double-timing it down the hallway. His heart raced as his military instincts kicked in and all the pieces of the puzzle started to fall into place.

"Viktor's inside. Julie's in trouble."

"I'm on my way. Start implementing the plan." He checked his watch as he hurried. "Be there in . . . sixty seconds."

Would he have enough time to save the woman he loved?

THIRTEEN

"Hello, Julie."

Julie gasped and turned toward the chilling voice she knew too well. *Nick!* A shiver of fear crept up her spine. Doing housecleaning and laundry, she'd been too busy to set the security system. Gathering her courage, she placed the laundry basket on the counter and turned to face him. Her heart froze in fear but she refused to let him see it. "Nick. What are you doing . . . in my house? It's almost midnight."

He gave a quick laugh. His cold gaze roamed the length of her body. "I'm here to get something that belongs to me."

"You could've used the doorbell." She'd fought him off once at the hotel, but Julie doubted she'd be able to do it again. She'd had the element of surprise on her side that night. She tried to calm the overwhelming anxiety robbing her of her next breath. *God, help me.* She glanced to the wireless phone only a few feet away on the kitchen counter. She made a quick move toward it but Nick blocked her from reaching her only lifeline to help. Grabbing her by the shoulders, he pushed her against the wall, pulling her arms behind her. "You have something I need."

Julie's head hit the wall, hard. *Lord, please . . . keep Emmie safe. Help us, Jesus.* Swallowing hard, she forced herself to appear calm. "What are you talking about?" She tried to shrug off his hold but he increased the pressure on her arms until she cried out in pain.

God . . . please, don't let Emmie walk into this.

Lifting her chin, she forced herself to meet his gaze. "What do you want, Nick?"

He gave a quick laugh. "For starters, one of the gift items you took. The double-handle vase. Where is it?"

"What?" Was that all? Her thoughts raced to the many pieces of pottery she'd purchased the past year or so. "Which one are you talking about?"

"The gift you took at the warehouse the other day. The one inside the stockroom by my office."

"The . . . planter?"

"Yeah. Get it," he commanded, pulling

her roughly away from the wall, keeping a hold on one arm. "Now."

"Get it yourself." Filled with anger and pain from his roughness, she pushed him away and ran toward the door in an effort to escape. Maybe she could lead him away from her home, away from Emmie.

He caught up with her. With one arm tightly held around her waist, Nick plastered her against the wall. With his free hand he kept a stranglehold around her neck. "Don't mess with me, Julie. Where *is* it?" he demanded, tightening his grip so she could barely breathe.

Julie knew that giving him the pottery he wanted wouldn't be the end of the ordeal. Her heart filled with the image of Zach. She could see his deep blue-gray eyes, the same color as the ocean at Ruby Beach on a stormy day. Sincere eyes that spoke volumes of honesty, goodness and love.

If only he were here with her now. Zach Marshall was a man who could be trusted. Julie knew that in her heart. He was a good man, nothing like the evil one standing before her with a death grip around her throat.

Please, don't let Emmie come skipping down the stairs in her pajamas. Not now.

Struggling for air, she glanced past him to

the foyer and prayed that Emmie was still sleeping. In her peripheral vision, she saw a man crouched low just inside the foyer. Covered head to toe in some kind of military black commando gear, he put a black-gloved finger to his lips, indicating she should be quiet and not alert Nick to his presence.

He wore black boots, pants, shirt and a black ski mask. In his other hand, the man confidently held a semiautomatic rifle, his finger readied on the trigger.

A myriad of questions reeled in her mind and her knees buckled. Nick continued his grip on her neck, lifting her up along the wall. Julie thought about the recent unsolved murder on her property and the break-in. It all coincided with Nick's menacing presence in her life. Had *he* been the one who had ransacked her home? Had he murdered Paul?

"Where is it, Julie?" Nick demanded. "It wasn't here the last time I looked."

The last time? Ramifications of what he said hit Julie with a force to her heart, making her struggle for her next breath. Nick *had* broken into the house. He'd been looking for the giftware. But the vase hadn't been here at the house until after the break-in. He must mean something other than the vase. From the corner of her eye, the man in black encouraged her with a nod of his head. Apparently, he wanted her to lead Nick to it.

Swaying with dizziness, Julie closed her eyes for one brief moment. *Lord, please, send Your strongest angels to protect Emmie and keep her safe.* "It's in . . . my bedroom," she managed. "Upstairs."

"I know where your room is." Nick pulled Julie up the stairway until they reached her room. "Didn't have time to check it the last time I was here."

Nick held Julie with an arm wrapped tightly around her waist as his gaze roamed the room. Recognizing the pottery on the dresser, he grabbed the vase with his free hand and smashed it against the mirror she'd gotten from him the last time they'd done business. Potting soil and the poinsettia plant splattered everywhere along with sharp remnants of the vase.

Julie prayed that Emmie would sleep soundly as she sometimes did during some of the worse thunderstorms. How long would the man in the foyer wait before coming in? Until she was dead? *Think . . .*

Julie tried to pull away from the tight grip Nick had around her waist to no avail. After sifting through all the debris, he held something in his hands that looked like small CDs inside of plastic bags. A look of pure malice reflected in his wolflike eyes. Why hadn't she ever noticed the evil lurking there?

"You never should have taken this. It almost cost me my life," he growled hoarsely.

"You were stupid to leave it at the warehouse the way you did, where anyone could take it." She lifted her chin.

He pushed her onto the bed with such violence that she hit her head and shoulder on the hand-carved headboard.

"I can't have you identifying me." Nick unzipped the leather jacket he wore and placed the disc he'd retrieved from the planter in his shirt pocket. "You dug your own grave. Just like the groundskeeper you hired."

"Wh-what?" Blinking, Julie forced her eyes and then her mind to focus. Her head throbbed. Her shoulder ached.

"When I first came here he recognized me. He left Russia to start a new life and wanted no part of the past. Unfortunately for Paul, he knew I was working for the Russian mob. I had no choice. I eliminated him." He shrugged his shoulders. A look of pure hatred permeated from an evil place deep inside the man and settled in the warped, twisted smile on his face.

"*You* killed him?" Tears stung her eyes as Julie recalled the friendship everyone at the inn, guests as well as employees, had enjoyed with Paul. He'd taken such pride in his work.

"Of course I killed him, you fool." He wrapped a hand around her neck. "Just like I'm going to do away with you, now that I've got the vital information in my hands again. You've ruined my perfect cover. You were never supposed to see that vase. And you took the wrong mirror."

"Why not?" Julie wanted to keep him talking. "What information?"

Nick paused for a split second. Julie prayed he'd tell her everything. She needed to buy time for Emmie.

"Latest top secret military intelligence. Satellite positions, ground troops, weapons . . . everything. I'm selling the information and I don't care how many Americans die. As long as I get my money." He loosened his grip on her. With his free hand, he patted the pocket that held the disc. Taking advantage of her sudden freedom Julie pulled free, rolled off the bed and bolted toward the door.

Half a dozen law enforcement people

burst through the doorway and rushed past her. Who were they? FBI? Julie ducked for cover in the far corner of the room. One agent held an automatic rifle to Nick's head while the others barked commands, aiming a vast array of lethal weapons on him. Another agent removed a pistol and a knife from inside Nick's jacket.

Julie shuddered. He would have killed her. She could've ended up like Paul. Dead in a pool of her own blood.

Emmie. I have to get to Emmie. Please, God, let her be okay.

She made a move to stand.

One of the agents pushed her back into the corner. "Don't move!" he yelled, pointing a black-gloved finger at her. Frozen, trembling, Julie could only watch in horror as another masked agent cuffed Nick. He shoved him to the other agents who dragged him away, weapons aimed at point-blank range.

Only one agent remained — the one who'd been crouched in her doorway. The one who'd just shoved her into the corner and yelled for her to stay there. Slowly he walked toward her. What now? She wanted to get Emmie. Bending down before her on one knee, he slowly peeled the black knitted mask from his face.

Julie watched as inch after inch of the man's face was revealed — the square jaw, the familiar, kissable lips. She fought against the numbing blackness that threatened to overcome her senses and send her into oblivion. "Z-Zach?"

"Yeah. It's me, Jewels. I'm a special agent with the FBI. Are you all right?" he asked, his voice thick with emotion. "You did great." His fingers framed her face. "It's okay now. It's all over."

"I — I've got to find Emmie," she stammered, looking into the eyes of the man she loved.

"Emmie's safe with one of our agents," Zach said, tenderly pulling her close. "She's been asleep the whole time."

"Thank You, God," she whispered. Julie closed her eyes and carefully ran a shaky hand across the bump on the back of her head. "I want to see her for myself. Let me go to her."

Zach placed the strap of his automatic weapon over his shoulder and gently stroked her hair with his hand. "We'll get the medic on our team to take a look at that bruise on your head," he said with a frown. In spite of her shock at Zach's obvious identity, the sound of his familiar deep voice surrounded Julie with a sense of warmth and safety. "He won't hurt you anymore. I promise."

"But Emmie —"

"She's sleeping. We've had one of our female agents watching her the whole time."

Another agent stalked into her bedroom. "Hurry it up, Zach." His mask was off, his identity revealed.

"John?" Julie asked in disbelief, her voice barely audible.

"Hey, Julie," he said, giving her a nod. "You okay?"

She swallowed hard and nodded her head. "My head hurts." Her chef was an agent, too? But he was such a *good* chef.

"Let's move, Zach. I want to take a look in the attic before the chopper gets here. There's work to do." He shouldered his automatic weapon and left the room.

"Give me a minute." Zach turned to her. "We'll have the doc look at your head. Everything's going to be all right now," he whispered. "I promise."

Trembling, Julie settled into Zach's warm, strong arms. How could everything be all right? All this time he'd been on assignment as an FBI agent. Why hadn't he told her? A thousand other questions filled her mind. Did he really lose his wife and daughter in an accident? Or was that just a story he fabricated to use her? She felt nauseated at the thought.

Overwhelming feelings of fear and betrayal echoed in her heart. All this time, Zach had lied to her while she'd foolishly fallen in love with him all over again.

"Emmie," she whispered, her voice shaky. "I — I need to see her." Covering her face with her hands, Julie started to cry as the enormity of the situation hit her. "You're with . . . the FBI. Why didn't you tell me?"

Zach pulled her close. "I couldn't tell you, Julie." He drew in a quick breath. "I'll explain everything as soon as you're ready to hear it all." He gently held and rocked her in his strong arms. "Emmie's fine. You don't want her to see you like this, do you? Let me hold you a little longer." Sitting on the carpet of her bedroom, Zach stowed his weapon, removed his gloves and pulled Julie to him, holding her gently in his arms again. "Take as long as you need." With his thumb, Zach brushed away the tears that fell from her eyes. "It's okay now."

Julie didn't feel *okay.* But he was right. She couldn't let Emmie see her. Not like this. She drew a shaky breath and leaned into Zach's embrace. Overwhelming sadness, an ache of loss, hovered like a dark mist around her soul. The past few weeks had been nothing but one huge charade to Zach.

Though she was forever grateful for his heroism, Julie's heart broke into a million shattered pieces. He'd used her. How many lies had he lovingly whispered in her ear to solve the investigation? How could she believe *anything* Zach would ever say to her again?

"Tell me," she said, her voice barely audible. Her gaze met his. "Did you really lose your wife and baby daughter? Or . . . was that a ruse, too?"

"Julie," Zach said, his voice raw with emotion. "I would never lie to you about that. Yes . . . I lost them. Just like I said." He cupped her face in his hands. "Can you forgive me for the part I had to play? I was undercover. It's my job."

Julie looked into his eyes. She wanted to forgive him. He'd saved her life. And Emmie's. Her head ached. Her stomach felt nauseated. Trying to stand, she realized the extent of her dizziness and had to sit down again.

"I need a medic," Zach said into the microphone on his vest. "Now." He turned to Julie. "You're going to be all right."

"Yes, as soon as I see Emmie." Julie felt Zach's strong arms around her and knew she loved him with all her heart. But did he feel the same now that his job was done?

He's been using me. Emmie, too. The whole time.

Zach held her close. "Looks like you might have a slight concussion." The anger reflected in his eyes was obvious. "That snake won't ever touch you again," he whispered, his breath warm against her cheek.

"Zach . . . bring me to Emmie. I need to see her."

"Sure." Lifting her from the carpet, he walked her into Emmie's room. Julie forced her eyes to focus. A female agent dressed in raid gear sat in one of the little chairs.

Sarah? Zach's buddy? A fellow FBI agent?

"Hi, Julie," Sarah whispered. She smiled and touched Julie's arm. "Look, she's fine," she said, turning to Emmie.

Emmie lay with the blankets kicked off as usual, in her flannel pink pajamas, her little hand tightly wrapped around the white horse Zach had given her. She was sleeping peacefully.

"Thank you for watching her," Julie whispered, wondering again about Sarah's relationship with Zach.

"Best assignment I ever had," Sarah answered quietly. She placed her weapon over a shoulder and left the room.

"Thank you, Zach." Julie turned her face into his chest. She shed quiet tears of sadness for their pretend relationship and happy tears of relief that Emmie was okay. *Thank You, Jesus, for keeping us safe.*

Zach paced from one end of his kitchen in Silver Lake, Montana to the other. Had it been only a week since he'd held Julie in his arms? It seemed more like a year.

Sipping a cup of coffee and leaning against the granite countertop, he looked out toward the dining room at the front of the house. Through the window, he watched Luke's black truck make its way up the long, snow-covered driveway. Jake sat in the passenger seat. His brothers were probably on a mission to cheer him up. They might as well head back home.

Doors slammed as they emerged from the four-wheel-drive vehicle. Zach walked to the front entrance and opened the door, bracing himself for the bitter cold that swirled around him. Leaning against the doorjamb, he took another sip of coffee. "What are you two doing here?"

Luke pulled on a heavy pair of work gloves and strode over to the back of the vehicle. "Just following orders, Zach," he said, grinning over his shoulder.

"Oh, yeah? From who?" Zach took another swallow of the hot, bitter coffee.

"Mom." Jake, his younger brother, gave a quick laugh. "She insisted we cut down a tree for you. Said you needed some Christmas spirit."

Great. "You're kiddin', right?" They pulled a huge blue spruce from the back of the truck. Zach hurried toward them, his hiking boots making footprints in the six inches of fresh snow that had fallen overnight. "Put it back."

Luke pulled down the tailgate. "Listen, Zach, this tree is *your* problem," he said, pointing a gloved finger at him. "You know how long it took to cut this down and haul it onto the truck? I'm exhausted. *And* freezing my backside off."

"Give us a hand," Jake said, pulling up the collar of the brown leather jacket he wore. "You know Mom around Christmas. She won't take no for an answer and we're not taking this tree back."

His mother was a hopeless romantic when it came to Christmas. And she was already on his case about going back to church. Fine. He'd set the thing in a bucket of water and place it in the great room at the front of the house. But he wouldn't decorate it. He didn't want to be reminded of God and "joy to the world" when his own life was constantly being ripped apart. Their breaths came in white puffs as his brothers stood in the cold morning air, staring at him. Zach placed his mug of coffee on the front porch railing. "Let me give you a hand."

"It's about time," Luke mumbled.

Once they'd settled the tree inside, his brothers sat at the kitchen table.

"You look a wreck, Zach. You growing a beard?" Jake grinned. "Not exactly the FBI look you've been sporting all these years."

"Knock it off. I just didn't feel like shaving the past week, that's all." Zach poured two more mugs of coffee and handed them to his brothers. He took a seat and joined them at the table.

"What's going on with the investigation?" Luke asked, exchanging glances with Jake. "All the loose ends tied up?"

Zach glared at him. "Nothing I want to talk about."

Luke chuckled. "It's obvious that something's gnawing away at your gut. I don't want to have to treat you for ulcers. Talk."

Jake folded his arms across his chest. "Let's have it."

"You two are a real pain in the —"

"Never mind that. Just tell us and we'll be

on our way," Luke interrupted. "I have work to do."

After swallowing another gulp of coffee, Zach told them how he and Julie had met again, and how he had to keep his cover and investigate her even though they'd fallen in love. "Julie's a smart, beautiful woman. I don't think she'll ever forgive me for keeping the truth from her. But, she was a major suspect. I couldn't —"

"Blow your cover," Luke finished for him.

Zach cleared his throat. "Exactly."

"Did you explain everything?" Jake asked. "I mean, you had no choice."

"Yeah. She understood how I had to do my job. But, I think deep down she feels like . . . I used her."

"You did." Jake leaned back in his seat. "She knows that."

"Yeah," Zach admitted.

Luke placed his mug on the table. "What happened exactly? Can you talk about some of the details?"

Zach cupped the warm mug in his hands. "Every time I thought she was innocent, she did something that made her look even guiltier."

"What happened?" Jake asked.

"I did what I had to." Zach managed a smile. "Turned on the charm and got everything I wanted."

Raising an eyebrow, Luke chuckled. "No wonder she won't talk to you."

"It's not what you're thinking. *Information.* That's what I got." *And some of the sweetest kisses on the planet.*

"Right, if you say so."

"It's not like that with Julie," Zach answered, a little more abruptly than he'd intended.

Luke laughed richly. "Relax, Zach. I'm not one of the bad guys." He raked a hand through his light brown hair and exchanged glances with Jake.

"What's so funny?" Zach challenged.

"Nothing." Jake cleared his throat. "Nothing at all. What else can you tell us about the case? You've been pretty close-mouthed about it. Even more than usual."

Zach toyed with the empty mug in his hand. "Turns out a guy Julie did business with and dated a couple of times was one of our most wanted suspects. We've been hunting him for a while." Zach straightened in his chair. "He'd slip into the lodge from time to time and hunker down in her attic. Hid the latest in electronic devices up there. Smuggled top level military secrets in some of the items Julie purchased from him."

"Was she ever in real danger?" Luke asked.

"More than she ever realized." He thought about all the times Julie had gone up into that attic. How many times had Ivanov been up there while she was, without her knowing it? His blood chilled at the thought. Zach knew the horrendous crimes that Ivanov was capable of executing. He stood and walked to the coffeemaker on the counter to refill his mug. "Anyway, in the process of getting to know her for the sake of the investigation, I fell in love with Julie all over again." Zach leaned against the counter and stared at his mug. He missed her more than ever.

"Why don't you ask her out here for the holidays?" Luke asked, shooting a quick glance at Jake. "Since you're working on the case from home."

"I've already asked her," Zach admitted.

"What did she say?" Luke asked.

"She said she'd think about it," Zach answered, looking up from the mug in his hand.

"You *do* need cheering up," Jake acknowledged.

"Yeah." Zach joined them at the table. "I need more than that, little brother."

"You love her?" Luke asked, taking another swallow of coffee.

"Yeah." Zach almost groaned. He missed

her more than he thought was possible. "I love her."

"You told her that, right?" Jake asked.

Zach glared at him. His youngest brother considered himself an expert when it came to women. "I haven't had the chance to tell her." He might never have the chance.

Jake sat back in his chair. "No wonder you're as ornery as an overloaded pack mule."

"Knock it off. I hurt her, even though it was the last thing I wanted to do." Zach drew a deep breath. "There's something else."

Luke sat forward in his chair. *"Something else?"*

"Yeah. Julie has a daughter. She's the same age as Ashley would've been. . . ."

"How'd you handle *that?*" Luke asked, running a hand across his jaw.

"It was tough, at first. The Bureau never filled me in on that minor detail. They just let me find out for myself." He shook his head. "The kid kept calling me 'misty man.' I still have no idea why, but I'd like to find out someday. Then she insisted I was Prince Charming."

"You've lost it over this woman," Luke said.

Zach shook his head. "Yeah, I know."

"You're going to ask her to marry you, right?" Jake was never one to beat around the bush.

"I want to, but —"

"But what?" Jake asked, tilting back in his chair.

"But . . . I won't do that to her," Zach admitted.

"Why not?" Luke asked in disbelief. "She loves you, doesn't she?"

"Yeah, I think so. But that was before she found out I was with the Bureau." He dragged in a deep breath. "She has the inn. She's put her whole heart into running the place." Zach glanced at his brothers. "How can I ask her to give up everything for me?"

"So, you just *left?*" Jake asked, looking astonished.

"What else was I supposed to do?"

"You *have* called her since you got back, right?" Luke asked.

"Yeah." Zach cleared his throat and took another swallow of coffee. "I called her from the cell phone on the ride home."

"That's it? *One time?*" Jake shook his head in disbelief. "Call her again."

"Look," Zach replied. "Julie likes things *planned out.* I could never offer her that kind of life. I might always live on the edge. That kind of life is the last thing Julie wants."

"Listen, Zach, Julie's the only one who can make that decision." Luke leaned forward on the edge of his chair. "You can't make that choice for her."

"Luke's right," Jake agreed.

"If you don't ask, you'll never know. You ready to live with that?" Luke's serious gaze met his.

No. Zach realized they were right. Julie was a strong woman, more than capable of making her own decisions. His heart filled with hope. Did she care enough for him to drop everything she'd built over the past several years? Could she leave the family who had been a lifeline to her — and spend her life on the Marshall Ranch — with no safety net but him?

Julie helped herself to a cup of hot coffee. After a restless night, she needed all the caffeine she could get to stay awake. A few days ago, Zach had called to apologize again and ask her to come to his ranch in Montana for Christmas. She'd slept fitfully every night since, thinking about him.

She'd managed to get Emmie off to school on time this morning, and now Julie found herself amidst the decorations the employees were placing throughout the inn. For some reason, most of the boxes had found their way into her office. She cleared a path to her desk and sat in the soft brown leather chair to enjoy her first cup of coffee. Staff members decked with balsam garlands and wreaths worn around their necks, peeked in her office from time to time, making silly faces at her and "ho-ho-ho-ing" until she had to laugh.

"I need your signature on the shipment we just received," Beatrice said, walking into the office, clipboard in hand. "Oh, my! Let me get these boxes out of here. You hardly have a place to stand."

"Don't worry about it." Totally recovered from her mild concussion, Julie finally felt like herself again. Physically, that is. Her emotions were another matter.

"Your office is usually so neat and tidy, I can't stand to see it this way." Beatrice poked her head out the door and grabbed the first person she saw. "Gary, get some of these boxes out of here right away, okay? Place them over by the far end of the lobby, by the tree."

"Sure thing," he said, grabbing a couple.

"And get someone to help you with the heavier ones."

In a few minutes, Julie's office was back to normal and Beatrice shut the door behind her. "Okay." She sighed. "Now why did I come in here again?" She pushed a strand of curly gray hair away from her eyes. "Oh, yes. Your signature. Here's today's mail." She placed the clipboard and a pile of mail and catalogs into Julie's hands. "The parcels are in the back room."

"Thanks." Julie noticed from the shipping manifest that the gifts she'd ordered online for Emmie had finally arrived. "Good, Emmie's presents are here." She signed the form.

Beatrice took the clipboard and studied Julie for a moment. "I'll be right back."

Julie took another sip of the hot drink, cradling the cup in her hands. Her thoughts returned to Zach. She understood the difficult position he'd been in, not being able to blow his cover. He'd proven her innocence when it looked as though she was directly involved and guilty.

Despite her initial anger, she realized that Zach had a job to do. Because of his discipline and high standards, he'd saved her life and Emmie's, too. She'd always be grateful for that.

Julie sorted through the mail until she got to a large manila envelope. Checking the return address, she knew what its contents contained. Photographs of her and Zach in the Western attire they'd dressed in at the

Old Tyme Photography Studio in Port Townsend.

Flipping through various-sized photos, she came to the one that had been unrehearsed — Zach with his strong arms around her, kissing her under the brim of that black Stetson.

She focused her attention on the lobby outside her office. The Christmas tree, a beautiful, giant Douglas fir, was already placed in its stand in the far corner of the lobby by one of the floor-to-ceiling windows facing Shadow Lake. Its distinct, sweet aroma filled the lobby with the balsam scent of a freshly cut tree. In a few minutes, Julie would join in the fun and help to decorate the grand tree.

"May I join you for coffee?" Beatrice poked her head in the door and smiled.

"Sure. I'll pour you a cup." Julie stood and walked to the Capresso coffeemaker.

Beatrice sank into the chair across from Julie's desk. She checked her watch. "It's only nine-thirty? I feel as if it's past noon."

"I know what you mean. I didn't get much sleep last night. But the house is spotless." She smiled and handed Beatrice a mug filled with coffee.

"Has he called yet?" Beatrice asked. She sipped her drink.

"Who?"

"Oh, please." Beatrice rolled her eyes.

"Okay, okay. Yes, that one time on his way home from the airport, and then again the other night." Julie shook her head. "I miss him."

"Of course you do. I've never seen two people more in love. I'm thoroughly convinced that handsome young man of yours is deeply and irrevocably in love with you, Julie. And you love him just as much. As for Emmie —" Beatrice waved her hand "— she adores him."

"I know." Julie had been praying hard the last few days, asking God for direction. God was, apparently, letting her make the decision on her own.

"I still can't believe he and John are with the Federal Bureau of Investigation. They certainly had us fooled."

Julie smiled. "They actually thought *we* were spies."

Beatrice started to laugh. "Can you imagine?"

Julie chuckled. "I wonder if we'll ever know all the details."

"I doubt it," Beatrice answered, getting comfortable in the seat. "Some nights, it's a wonder I get any sleep at all, with the nightmares."

"You, too?" Julie sighed. "I thought it was just me."

"Oh, for goodness' sake. Next time you can't sleep, give me a jingle, will you? At least we can talk to each other instead of staring at the ceiling."

"I will." Julie imagined many long, sleepless nights pining over Zach. She took in a quick breath and sat up in her chair. Suddenly everything seemed clear. She couldn't live that way.

"Beatrice, I have a huge favor to ask."

Was she too late?

FOURTEEN

Two more hours.

Julie gripped the steering wheel with one hand and checked the wrinkled road map she had spread out across her lap. She'd made the turn onto Route 200 toward Great Lakes, Montana, several hours ago. Hopefully, she hadn't missed the next exit. Battling a fierce wind and light snow for the past hour, driving had become a challenge.

"How are you doing, Emmie?" she asked, glancing into the rearview mirror at Emmie who sat in the backseat.

"I drawed a picture for Prince Charming."

"Mr. Marshall," Julie answered, smiling. "You need to remember his real name."

"I like Prince Charming better." Emmie giggled.

Her daughter had been thrilled about the spur-of-the-moment trip. Julie, on the other hand, was filled with conflicting emotions. Was she doing the right thing surprising

Zach? It had seemed like a good idea the day before yesterday. Now, she wasn't so sure. "Do you want some juice?"

"No . . . thank you very much. Are we there yet?"

Julie smiled. They'd gone over the subject of good manners all day yesterday in the car. Emmie was a quick learner. "You remembered your manners. I'm proud of you."

"Thank you very much," Emmie said with a giggle.

Julie planned to call Zach from the car phone in another hour and get specific directions to his ranch. The wind tried to wrestle her car into the narrow shoulder along the road. Regaining control of the small vehicle, Julie checked her watch. They should be in Silver Lake by four this afternoon, if the weather cooperated. She rubbed the back of her neck and turned on the radio to search for a local station.

An angry gray sky on the eastern horizon revealed itself as she rounded a turn on the interstate. They headed straight toward it. "Better check the forecast," she said quietly to herself. They'd had such good weather for most of the trip. Surely, the approaching weather front was nothing to worry about.

■ ■ ■ ■

"What do you mean she's not there?" Zach paced the floor of the huge family room, his gaze resting briefly on the massive Christmas tree in the corner. "Maybe Julie's at her parents' house? Where's Beatrice?"

"I don't know where Beatrice is." The girl sighed. "I can see you're upset . . . so I guess it's okay if I tell you. Julie and her daughter left yesterday morning for their road trip to Montana. She called this morning and said they'd be there around four this afternoon."

Zach swore his heart stopped beating. "She's *driving?*"

"Yes. Is . . . something wrong?"

"There's a blizzard bearing down on us. She's heading right into it." Why hadn't Julie told him? There was no way he wanted her making this trip by herself in that old car of hers. Not in this storm.

"Are you still there?" the clerk asked.

"Yeah." He raked a hand through his hair. "Why isn't Beatrice at the inn?"

"I don't know. She never came in today . . . and there's no answer at her house."

His pulse kicked up several notches. This bit of news sat heavily in his gut. Zach glanced outside to the accumulating snowfall. The wind howled and numerous pine trees swayed violently in the noisy gusts. "You know if she took her cell phone?"

"Yes. Do you need her number?"

"No, I've got it."

"I hope they'll be all right. Please . . . ask Julie to call the lodge when she's settled in, okay?" the receptionist asked, obviously worried.

Zach couldn't come up with any words to comfort her. Not when he saw the weather conditions outside. Not when another wind gust almost shook the shutters off his house. "I'll make sure she gives you a call. Thanks for filling me in." As soon as he hung up the phone, he punched in Julie's cell phone number. No luck. Maybe she was in a dead zone.

If she planned to be here by four, Zach figured she was still on Route 200 just before she needed to make the turn onto 83 at Clearwater Junction. Not the best place to be in a blizzard.

He'd offered to drive there and pick them up himself since all the flights were already booked. Why hadn't she let him? Did she know what to do if she found herself stranded in subzero weather? Would her compact car get enough traction on the icy, snow-covered roads? There were bound to be huge trucks out there skidding and jack-knifing.

God, don't do this to me again. Watch over them.

Zach headed for his bedroom and threw two blankets into a duffel bag. He stepped into a pair of heavy hiking boots. Lacing them up, Zach ached to hold Julie in his arms again. They had already wasted too much time as it was. His love for Julie ran deep. To lose her now . . .

He hurried down the stairs to grab a first aid kit from the pantry. He microwaved a quart of apple cider and poured it into a thermos, and then he dialed John Castle-rock's mobile number. He filled him in on what was happening. "I'll be somewhere between U.S. 83 and County Road Seven. I have the phone with me, but I'm not sure it'll work in this storm."

"Be careful and watch your back," John warned.

"Affirmative."

"I'm sending a couple of agents to Bea-trice's place." John paused. "Listen, Mar-shall, I don't like the way this is playing out. I'm ordering the team to your ranch ASAP."

"You think the terrorists are headed here?"

"Yeah. I'm going to check another hunch now."

"I don't like the idea of bringing Julie back here if something's going down."

"Don't blame you. But it can't be helped. Just get her off the road. She'll be better off with you than being stranded like a sitting duck out on the highway."

"Right." Zach snapped his phone shut. Julie was unfamiliar with the winding Montana roads. She couldn't even find her way to that restaurant for breakfast in her *own* state. Now, there was the added danger of an ambush.

He unlocked the gun cabinet and grabbed a high-powered rifle and enough ammo to take out a full squad of Yuri's bad guys. Locking the cabinet, he realized the very real possibility that there might be a shooter already out there, tailing Julie and Emmie. He shoved a fully loaded pistol into his shoulder holster. Would he reach them in time?

Julie gripped the steering wheel so hard, her arms ached. The ice-encrusted wipers weren't working. The last partially snow-covered sign she'd passed indicated the road she needed to turn on was coming up in one mile. Had she missed the turnoff? A violent wind gust shook the little car, pushing it close to the edge of the road. She had no idea if she headed toward an embankment or the mountain's edge.

One thing she did know was that she couldn't keep driving in this sudden, savage snowstorm. She had to pull over, and soon. She could hardly see more than a few feet ahead of her. Spying a small area where she could pull the car over, Julie thanked God and headed toward it.

Skidding and fishtailing, she guided the compact sedan over to the pull-off. The car stopped abruptly when it ran into a four-foot drift. The engine died. The wind howled and whistled. She'd never felt so alone.

God, show me what to do. Julie thought about Zach and decided to pray for him to turn his heart to God again. She wanted him to find the faith of his childhood. Faith in Christ would be the only way to ease his loss. Julie knew that.

Lord, speak to Zach's heart. Heal the pain he hides so well. Show him the way home . . . to You. Help Emmie and me to get to his house safely today. Amen.

Julie turned the key in the ignition and tried to restart the car. The engine refused to start. How would they keep warm in this treacherous blizzard without any heat? She undid her seat belt and turned to check on her daughter.

Emmie rubbed her eyes. "Are we there yet?"

"We're . . . going to rest a while, okay?"

"Okay. But we've been driving for . . . two months!"

"Two *days*, sweetheart. But it has been a long time, I know. Do you want to come and sit up here with me?" Julie asked.

Emmie nodded her head. "I'm cold."

"Bring some of your books up here, too. We'll share a blanket." Julie reached into the backseat and helped her daughter to undo her seat belt. "Come on, I'll help you climb over."

Julie held her arms out to her daughter and lifted her into the front seat. Another violent wind gust shook the small car. Julie glanced out the passenger's side window. There was a guardrail several feet from the car, but it was the only thing between them and a hundred-foot drop. Was the howling wind strong enough to blow the car right off the mountain with them inside? Taking a deep breath, Julie forced herself to remain calm and think.

She settled Emmie into the passenger seat and covered her with a heavy blanket. After reading two books, Emmie drifted off to sleep. The snow fell steadily. It wouldn't take long for her little car to be covered in the drifting snow. Julie adjusted the blanket over her daughter and prayed they'd be all right.

Julie opened her planner and flipped through the pages to find Zach's home phone number. She shouldn't have waited so long to call. Pressing in his number, she waited for him to answer. A recorded message informed her that all circuits were busy.

"Mommy?"

"Yes, sweetheart?" She tucked in Emmie's blanket.

"We're stuck, huh."

"Yes." Julie busied herself by making sure Emmie was snug in her makeshift bed. "We're going to wait out the storm."

"We'll be okay, Mommy. You'll see. Prince Charming will find us." Emmie smiled then closed her eyes and fell asleep once again.

Julie ran her hand along Emmie's forehead, smoothing away the hair that had fallen across it. "I hope you're right, Emmie," she whispered, her voice almost giving out on her.

But Prince Charming didn't even know they were coming.

For the next two hours, Julie prayed that the storm would stop and the car would start again. She tried the engine several times with no luck. She also ventured out to check the exhaust pipe and prayed for wisdom.

God, there must be something I can do. Show me.

Trying to clear out the huge amounts of drifted snow around the vehicle, she had to get back in the car before she froze to death. She knew she shouldn't start the car again even if the engine *did* turn over. The carbon monoxide fumes would come into the car and asphyxiate them in a matter of moments, even if they opened the windows a bit.

Julie couldn't remember ever feeling so cold. She removed her jacket and placed it over herself and Emmie as an additional blanket. Her daughter, just getting over her cold, needed the warmth more than she did.

Cuddling with Emmie, Julie shivered and thought about going for help, but there was no way she'd leave Emmie alone. She remembered hearing somewhere that the worst possible thing to do in a winter storm was leave your car. But if the snow kept falling as it had the past few hours, it might be days before someone found them.

She had to do something. Soon. God would show her what to do. But first she would sleep. Just for a few minutes. Maybe an idea would come to her after a little nap.

■ ■ ■ ■

Zach drove his truck a mere fifteen miles an hour through the snow-packed roads. He'd wasted twenty minutes convincing the locals who had closed the road to let him pass. Once he'd flashed his badge, they'd reluctantly opened the gate onto the highway for him, as soon as he'd put the chains they provided on his tires.

Making the turn onto the county road, there was still no sign of Julie's car. Would he even be able to spot her vehicle in the whiteout conditions he faced? On the other hand, he hoped they weren't too visible. If someone had followed them, what kind of a lead time did Julie have? One hour? Maybe two? Surely, he would've passed them by now if she'd been able to keep driving in the blizzard. Zach had plenty of time to think as he maneuvered his vehicle through the snow. He remembered a loving God from when he was just a kid. Did that loving God really exist anymore?

He recalled Sunday school and Bible verses, and the peace and comfort he used to find in his faith. Suddenly, Zach knew in his heart that the God of his childhood *was* real. Words of friends and family members who'd assured him of God's love came back like a flood. Swallowing his pride, Zach prayed out loud.

"Jesus, keep Julie and her little girl safe. I'll recommit my life to You. I believe You sent Your only Son to die for the sins of the world. And for my sins, too. I receive this gift, my salvation in Jesus' name. Forgive my anger and let me start a new life in Your will. I'll be the Christian I used to be. Just . . . help me find them before it's too late."

After an agonizing thirty minutes in the brutal storm, Zach made another turn south on U.S. 83 and headed for Clearwater Junction. Moments later, through a break in the icy white haze of blowing ice and snow, Zach spotted something red far off in the distance. What *was* it? With every second his truck approached a little closer to the red whatever-it-was waving frantically in the high wind gusts, Zach tried to identify the object.

A nightgown? A red-plaid nightgown?

Focusing on it from a distance, Zach saw the outline of a car. *Julie's car.* Drifting snow had almost buried the small white vehicle. His gut tightened with apprehension. Would they still be inside?

He parked his truck behind the lonely

vehicle. Shoving his driver's door open, a fierce wind fought against his efforts and bombarded him with icy snow pellets. He adjusted his Stetson and trudged through snowdrifts to the driver's side of Julie's car. Zach brushed his gloved hand on the frosted, driver's side window to see Julie and Emmie in the front seat. They weren't moving.

The first thing he thought of was carbon monoxide poisoning. If Julie had tried to keep the car running for heat, if the tailpipe had been covered with snow they could be —

No. Please, God, not again!

Zach refused to let the negative thought settle into his mind. He couldn't get this close only to lose them. He tried the door. It didn't budge. It had been frozen shut and locked from the inside. He pounded his fist on the window.

"Julie," he shouted over the bitter, howling wind. "Julie, wake up!"

FIFTEEN

Zach broke the driver's side window in the backseat and reached in to unlock the front door. The frozen lock wouldn't budge.

Using his Swiss Army knife, he pried up the plastic button. After two attempts, he pulled open the heavy, iced-over door of her car. Taking the corner of the red flannel nightgown that had been jammed in the door, he reached for Julie and drew her close. She was cold. He bent his head to gently kiss her cold lips. Her eyelids fluttered and opened to reveal the most beautiful blue eyes he'd ever seen.

"Julie," he whispered hoarsely. He drew a deep breath and held her close. "Thank God I didn't lose you."

"Zach?" She sighed and seemed disoriented. "Oh, Zach. How . . . did you know where to find us?"

"It was an answer to a prayer. Come on. We're going home." He helped her into her coat and wrapped the blanket tighter around Emmie. Zach carried the sleeping child in his arms and they trudged back to his truck in knee-high snowdrifts. Julie struggled and he placed an arm around her waist. "Hold on to me," he shouted over a powerful wind gust.

Zach helped Julie into the passenger seat. He secured Emmie in the back, fastened her seat belt and placed an extra blanket over her. Once the doors were shut against the storm, he turned to Julie and pulled her to him. "Are you all right?" he asked, running a gloved hand through her hair.

"I — I'm just so . . . cold." She leaned into his embrace.

"I'll get you back to my place. You'll be fine in no time." He turned to Emmie, who was stirring in the backseat.

"Hi." She lifted her little hand in a wave. "I knew you would save us."

"You did, huh?"

She coughed and nodded her head.

Zach smiled. "We're going home to my house, okay?"

"Uh-huh." Emmie rubbed her eyes. "Can I see your horses?"

"Of course." His heart filled with fatherly love — an emotion Zach thought he'd never experience again. In seconds, the little girl was sound asleep.

Looking closely at Julie, seeing how pale and cold she was, Zach realized she might be suffering from hypothermia. He cranked the heat up in the truck and pulled Julie into his embrace in an effort to warm her. "I thought I'd lost you," he said, his voice barely above a whisper. Pulling off his gloves, he ran a hand along her cheek. His gaze met hers and silently he thanked God that she was all right. He'd prayed more the past few hours than he'd done in a dozen years. It felt good. Like a heavy burden had been lifted. He'd been a stubborn fool to keep God at bay.

"I — I should have told you we were coming," Julie whispered, her breath warm against his ear. "I wanted to surprise you." She shrugged and smiled ruefully. "Surprise."

Zach kissed her on the forehead and breathed another silent prayer of thanks. "Let me get your things out of the car. I'll be right back." He shut the door behind him and made his way back to Julie's vehicle. Returning a couple of minutes later, he hurriedly stowed her gear — a purse, three suitcases, two shopping bags filled with gifts — and a frozen, red flannel, lifesaver of a nightgown.

Once he was back in the relative safety of his four-wheel-drive truck, he shut the door behind him and pulled Julie close, holding her again for one more minute. "Thank God you're all right," he whispered. "Do you know what it did to me, knowing you were out in this storm? To see you passed out like that in the car. I . . . thought the worst."

Wrapping her fingers around the collar of his leather jacket, Julie leaned her head against his chest. "Thank you," she said, her voice shaky. "I . . . can't believe you found us. Emmie had more faith than I did."

"Come on." He drew a long breath. "Let's go home."

Julie nodded. "How did you know where we were?" she asked after a moment. "I tried calling . . . I never got through."

"I called the inn. The girl at the front desk told me you were on your way to Montana."

"Wasn't Beatrice there?"

"No. Is she supposed to be there today?" He didn't want to voice his suspicions to Julie. Not yet.

"Yes, she is. Especially with me not being there." Julie closed her eyes for a few seconds before opening them again. "That's not like Beatrice. I hope nothing's wrong."

A rush of adrenaline pulsed through Zach.

They hadn't received the full report on the Brit yet. Was she out in this storm now, looking for Julie? For him? He reached inside the duffel bag for the thermos. "We'll call her later. Try to rest and take a few sips of hot cider."

"Thanks." Julie's hands shook as she reached for the container. "I thought we'd die out there," she whispered, making sure Emmie couldn't hear her words.

"You're safe now. I'll call my brother Luke." He took her hand in his and gently gave it a squeeze. "He's a doctor, remember? I want him to take a look at you."

"I'm fine . . . really," Julie responded, trying to twist off the top of the thermos with trembling, gloved hands.

"Let me do that." Zach easily opened the lid, poured the cider and stowed the thermos in the space between them. He shifted into gear and eased out of the snow-entrenched pull-off. Flipping open his FBI-issued cell phone, he punched the speed dial key for his brother's number.

Once he explained Julie's condition, Luke agreed to meet them at Zach's place. "I'll take the snowmobile in from the wilderness area. I'll probably get there before you."

"Thanks," Zach answered.

The windshield wipers worked furiously

303

to clear the icy snow, their noisy protestations growing louder with every swipe across the glass. Visibility worsened. Zach needed all his concentration on getting them home in one piece.

Home. It *would* be a home now that Julie was with him. Glancing over at her, he noted her slow, even breathing. She was sleeping. She'd been through so much these last few weeks. And now, someone was taking Viktor's arrest personally. His instincts told him they were gunning for *him.* At his home.

A deep sense of foreboding filled him. And maybe this time, it was God's voice warning him, too. Either way, something evil was brewing.

Julie woke and glanced at the digital clock on the dashboard. An hour had passed. Still numb with cold even though she felt the warmth from the car's heater, she undid her seat belt and checked on Emmie in the backseat.

Julie reached back and tucked the blanket in around her sleepy little girl. Buckling her seat belt again, Julie settled back in her seat. The vehicle slowly made its way through deeply packed snow and high drifts. An eerie, whistling wind relentlessly buffeted the large 4×4.

"Here we are," Zach said about half an hour later. He drew a deep breath. "Home."

He made a right-hand turn into a long, tree-lined driveway completely covered in blowing and drifting snow. After a couple more minutes, a massive two-story log home came into view. Porch lights had been turned on, and in the descending twilight the sight of the well-lit house filled Julie with a strong sense of homecoming.

Massive windows and a gabled rooftop lent a sense of strength to the house. Snow-capped pine trees around the perimeter of the house conveyed a sense of safety to the winter-wonderland, picture-postcard image.

Zach pressed the button on the automatic garage door opener and drove the truck into the garage. "Good. Power's on. Let's get you and Emmie inside." He shut the garage door behind them.

A door leading to the house opened and a tall man with hair a little lighter than Zach's greeted them. Julie immediately saw the strong resemblance between the brothers.

"Glad you made it." Luke glanced from Zach to Julie. "You okay?" he asked.

"I — I'm fine," Julie answered trembling.

"You'd better take a look at her, Luke. She's still way too cold." Zach walked around the car to get Emmie. "Come on, sleepyhead," he said, gently waking her.

Julie hurried to follow him and her knees buckled. Before she fell, Zach reached an arm around her waist. "Come on, Jewels, let's get you inside."

Surprised at how weak she felt, she nodded her head and leaned against him. There was no place she felt safer than in his arms.

Zach led them inside and gently lowered Emmie onto a comfortable-looking leather chair by the fireplace in a huge family room. "Sit here," he suggested, guiding Julie into another chair by the fire. Leaning over her, Zach promised, "Everything will be all right. Don't worry, okay?" He placed the heavy cotton throw that had been lying on the back of the chair over her. "You need to warm up."

"I — I know." Julie nodded and shivered. "Thanks."

Zach turned to his brother. "Luke, this is Julie and her daughter, Emmie."

"Hi, Julie. Good to meet you. Feeling any warmer?" he asked.

"Yes, a little. But I'm . . . still shivering."

"Good, that means your body's compensating. Trying to get your temperature back to normal." His attention turned to Emmie, who was still sleeping. "Your daughter looks

306

fine. You did a good job keeping her warm. At your expense?" he asked knowingly.

Julie nodded and tried to control her trembling. "I had to keep her warm, so I put my coat over her."

"Was that before or after you stuck your red flannel nightgown in the door?" Zach asked quietly.

"Before," she admitted. Julie turned to Zach. His loving, concern-filled gaze met hers. How could she live without seeing him every day, without his strong arms around her? "I was only outside a few minutes to get the suitcase out of the trunk. The idea to use something colorful . . . just came to me. The brightest thing I had was my new Christmas flannel nightgown." Looking back, it was only by God's grace she'd made it.

"No wonder you're in such bad shape. It was more than thirty below out there." Zach gently ran his fingers along her jaw. "I might've missed you if I hadn't seen that red thing whipping around in the wind gusts."

Tenderly, he kissed her. Julie knew she'd be all right. She shivered again and reached for Zach's hand. "Thank you for coming to get us."

He drew a quick breath and smiled. "Any

time, Jewels."

Luke cleared his throat. "Okay, I hate to break this up, but let me take a quick look at your daughter first." He turned his attention to Emmie. "By the way, there's a roast in the oven, compliments of Mom. I placed everything in there about an hour ago." He opened his medical bag and took out a stethoscope.

"Great. I wondered what smelled so good." Zach tucked the comforter up to Julie's chin. He turned to Luke. "Thanks for building the fire," he said, nodding toward the fireplace.

"No problem. Listen, Zach, get something hot for Julie to drink. Tea with some kind of natural sweetener, like honey."

Before she could protest, Zach nodded in agreement. "Sure. I need to make some calls while I'm in there. Be back in a few minutes."

Luke nodded. "Take your time."

Zach knelt by Julie's side. "I'll be right back," he whispered. He kissed her on her forehead, stood and then hurried into the kitchen.

Julie ran a hand along her left temple. The throbbing headache wasn't helping her sense of concentration. Finding it difficult to focus, another deep wave of chills took hold even as she gathered the blanket up to her chin.

She turned toward the welcoming heat of the fireplace. The flames cracked and popped, warming the room and casting a golden glow over the floor-to-ceiling stone hearth.

"She'll be fine in a couple of days," Luke said, pulling a couple of items from his bag. "It's just a bad cold. You just rest a while, okay, young lady?" he said, turning to Emmie.

"Okay." She crossed her arms over her chest. "But I'm not getting no shot."

"You're not getting *any* shot." Julie tried not to laugh as her gaze met Luke's.

"No shot for you, kiddo." He pulled a red lollipop from his bag. "You deserve a little treat, okay?"

"Yes." She coughed then nodded and took the candy from his outstretched hand. "Thank you very much."

Luke smiled. "You're very welcome."

Zach returned with a mug of hot tea. "Here." He handed the cup and saucer carefully to Julie. "I put in some honey."

"Thank you, Zach." She stopped the tears that threatened to spill from her eyes. "For everything."

A few minutes later, Julie settled Emmie into a comfortable bed in a cozy guest room. Julie sat on the edge of the bed while Zach stood behind her.

"I drawed you a picture," Emmie said, looking up at Zach. "But . . . I think it's in the car." Her eyes filled with tears. "Now you can't put it on . . . your fridgerator. Like you promised."

Zach ran a hand along his jaw. "We'll find it when the weather gets better, and then you can give it to me, okay?"

Emmie coughed again. "All right."

"You just sleep now." Julie helped her take a sip of juice. "You're going to be just fine." Julie smoothed a strand of hair from her daughter's forehead and smiled. "Sweet dreams."

Zach took Julie by the hand and guided her into the hallway. "Okay . . . now it's your turn."

"What?" Julie asked.

"Come on." He guided her toward Luke who stood at the far end of the hallway. "You're still too cold."

"Let's check your pulse." Luke reached for her wrist. "We need to warm you up, Julie, and get your heart rate up."

"Wh-what?"

"You've got a mild case of hypothermia.

Did the tea warm you a little?"

"I — I guess so," she said, shivering. "What should I do now?"

"First, get into some warm clothes. The stuff in your suitcase is still too cold to wear."

"Done." Zach placed an arm around Julie's shoulder and guided her to his room. "Let's go."

"What about Emmie?"

"It's quiet in there." Luke nodded toward the guest room. "I'll check on her, but it sounds like she's asleep already. She's had quite a day. Zach," he added, "get Julie to wear a hat. Maybe one of your knitted caps. That'll help."

"A knitted cap? Inside the house?" Julie asked.

"Doctor's orders," Zach replied, grinning. "Come on, Jewels, you'll look cute in raid gear."

Zach reached into a drawer for a freshly laundered pair of black FBI sweatpants and a sweatshirt along with a clean pair of thick socks. And a black FBI-issued knitted cap. Walking to his bed, he placed them by Julie and sat next to her on the bed. "You sure you're all right?"

"Yes." She ran a hand along his jaw. Her

311

hand was ice-cold. "I'll be out in a minute."

"Right." Zach slowly backed out of the room. "Call if you need anything, okay? I'll . . . be just outside the door. Don't forget the hat."

"Oh, right."

Zach left the door ajar a few inches so he'd hear her if she needed any help. He walked down the long, wide hall to another guest room where he found his brother closing up his medical bag. "You should head back to the main house before it snows even more."

"Yeah," Luke answered. "I think we've seen the worst of it, though. But is something else on your mind?"

"It's possible," Zach admitted. According to his latest conversation with John, a couple of agents were on their way to check out Beatrice's place. "Listen," Zach said, running a hand across the back of his neck. "Tell Mom thanks for the meal in case things get hectic here tonight and I don't get a chance. I really appreciate it. And . . . watch your back, okay?"

"Sure thing. You, too. Call if you need any help. I'm only ten minutes away with the snowmobile if you need me." Luke finished getting his stuff together and closed his medical bag. He cleared his throat. "I like her."

"Who? Mom?" Zach laughed.

"Very funny," Luke answered, chuckling lightly. "You know I meant Julie."

"Yeah. What's not to like." Zach smiled.

"It'll work out, I'm sure of it. Here's more cough medicine for Emmie," he said, handing him a small plastic bottle from his medical bag. "It'll probably make her sleepy. Try to get Julie to rest a little, too. She's going to be tired for the next few days. She'll need to take it slow."

"Thanks." Zach placed the medicine on the night table. No kid should be sick at Christmas. An image from long ago raced through his mind and he drew a quick breath. "Can you watch Emmie for a minute? There's something I want to get before you leave."

"Sure."

Tonight he would confront the past and get a box of his *own* down from the attic.

Sixteen

Julie changed into the warm, black, FBI sweats Zach had placed on the bed, standing after she pulled on a thick pair of socks. A bay sitting area with floor-to-ceiling windows revealed the blinding snowfall outside in the reflection from the numerous lights posted on the roof.

She glanced into the large, gold-framed mirror that hung over a dresser and reached for the knitted cap. She fitted it on her head as fashionably as possible and made her way to Emmie's room.

Zach's baritone voice drifted through the hallway as he spoke in quiet conversation with her daughter. Pausing at the corner of the doorway, she stood unnoticed.

"How are you feeling, Cindi Rella," Zach asked.

"I have a . . . a throat ache," Emmie replied.

"A throat ache, huh. Don't you worry.

You'll feel better soon. We're going to take good care of you."

Julie touched a shaky hand to her lips. For so long, she'd raised Emmie on her own. She'd had to be there for her daughter, and wanted to be there for her, one hundred percent of the time. Now with Zach caring for Emmie, even for this one instant in time, her heart filled with overwhelming happiness.

This is what she'd hoped and prayed for — a good man who would be a real father to her little girl. Deep in her soul, Julie knew Zach was that man. But there were too many loose ends in their renewed relationship. Too many questions remained unanswered. Did he love her? Was he ready to commit to the kind of relationship for which she yearned? Had he made his peace with God? Julie leaned against the wall in the hallway, still hidden from their view.

"I'm sleepy." Emmie sighed and rubbed her eyes.

"Well, that's to be expected. Tomorrow, I'll show you my horses just like I promised. Would you like that?"

"You have a white horse . . . right?"

Zach chuckled. "Yep."

"Can Mommy come, too?"

"Yes, Mommy, too." Zach pulled the covers up to her chin. He drew a deep breath and cleared his throat. "I have a gift for you."

"A present?" Her eyes widened in anticipation.

"Yeah." Zach smiled. "You want to see it?"

"You mean *now?*" She clapped her hands together.

"Right now," Zach answered, chuckling.

"What is it?" she asked, sitting up in the bed.

"Here, see for yourself." Zach reached down and brought up a box from the carpet, placing it carefully next to her on the bed.

"Oh, goodie!" Emmie coughed and stood on her knees.

Helping her to open the huge box, Zach pulled out the doll with long, blond hair tied into braids with blue calico ribbons. The doll wore a matching blue dress and red apron. A special collector's book was also enclosed.

"Oh!" Emmie gasped with joy and clapped her hands together again in delight. She looked at Zach with pure adoration. Like any daughter might look at her daddy. "For *me?*"

"For you." He placed it into her outstretched arms. "She's a special doll, Emmie. She'll help you to get better in time for

Christmas."

"She will?" Emmie looked up into Zach's eyes and smiled.

"Yes." Zach's breath caught.

"Thank you." A moment passed as Emmie turned her attention to the new doll. "She's so pretty." She smoothed the dress and held her close. Pressing the doll's face to her cheek, Emmie briefly closed her eyes. She held the doll up to study her face, and then turned to Zach. "I love you, Prince Charming."

"I . . . love you, too, Cindi Rella." He playfully touched a finger to her nose.

Julie's knees gave out on her. Sliding down against the wall, she sat on the floor of the beige carpeted hallway and covered her mouth to stifle a quiet sob.

This was the kind of life she wanted for her little girl, a good man to be Emmie's daddy — to love her and tuck her into bed at night. Julie's heart filled with an everlasting love for Zach Marshall. He was the man she wanted to grow old with. If she could just have one more wish for Christmas . . .

Zach pulled up the covers for Emmie and her doll. "Your mom and I will be in to check on you. You get some sleep now, okay?"

"Where's Mommy?"

"She's changing into some warm clothes. She'll be in to see you in just a few minutes. Okay?"

Emmie nodded and sighed in relief. "Okay." She lovingly held the doll in the crook of her arm. "Thank you very much . . . for my new dolly."

Zach smiled. "You're very welcome." He walked to the bedroom door and started to close it behind him, but left it open a few inches so they could hear her in case she started coughing again. He worried about Julie. She would need all her strength if the night played out the way he thought it would. And it had nothing to do with Emmie's cough.

In the hallway, he turned and found her sitting on the carpet. "Julie? Honey, what's the matter?" He helped her to her feet and pulled her close. "You all right?" She was still cold.

She nodded her head and sniffled. "I'm . . . fine."

In his Bureau-issued sweats, she looked like an agent who'd had a rough night. Even in the black knitted cap, she was the most adorable woman he'd ever known. "You need to lie down."

"But Emmie needs —"

"You can see her in a minute. You need to warm up first." Lifting her into his arms, he carried her through the hall and back into the family room, in front of the fire. Pulling back the down comforter he'd taken from his room, Zach lowered Julie onto clean, plaid flannel blankets, grateful that his housekeeper had been by early in the day before the storm. He tucked all the blankets around her, then sat next to her to keep her warm. Holding her close, Zach felt her body trembling from the hypothermia. Gently he stroked her hair. "Why are you crying?" He kissed her temple. She shivered in his arms. Julie was much weaker than she'd been letting on.

"The doll you gave Emmie," she said, wiping away a tear on her cheek, "was it meant for . . . Ashley?"

"Yeah. I planned to give it to her when she got a little older." He cleared his throat and rested his chin on her forehead. "That day . . . never came," he said, his voice breaking.

"Oh, Zach."

"I know." He pulled her close. "I want Emmie to have it."

Julie's teary gaze met his. Her gaze softened and she leaned in to kiss him. Zach returned her kiss knowing he never wanted

Julie to disappear from his life again. She was meant to be with him. God must have reunited them for a reason. Was it so they could spend a lifetime together?

Only Julie could make this place into the home of his dreams, filled with happiness and more children to love. He knew that in his heart. She'd already brought a glimmer of hope and joy back into his life. Reluctantly breaking the kiss, Zach gazed into her blue eyes. Holding her close like this, he wanted her with him forever. Zach rested his chin in her thick, silky hair. He drew a deep, ragged breath. There was trouble brewing. Trouble more severe than the storm that continued to rage outside.

He had to scan the property again for possible intruders as he'd been doing every twenty minutes. The team hadn't arrived yet. He and Julie might have to handle things on their own. Was she up to it?

"You warmer now?" he asked.

Julie smiled. "Yes," she whispered.

His heart broke with a sudden revelation. Julie would never marry him. Not with the life he'd made for himself. He might always be a target of some cowardly, disgruntled criminal.

He wouldn't place Julie in harm's way. That wasn't the kind of life she deserved.

After Christmas, he'd drive her back to Washington where she'd be happy and safe. He'd keep his love for her bottled up inside, just as he did the first time.

"Come on, let's go check on Emmie." Holding her close, Zach checked his watch. He needed to check the perimeter around the house again and call John. It was also time for an update from Quantico. "You okay now?"

"Yes," she answered, smiling up at him. "I'm always better . . . when I'm in your arms, Zach."

His heart broke as he steeled his emotions. She needed to be stronger than ever. When he broke things off with her, they would both need their strength.

Julie woke from a light sleep. The shivering that recurred every few hours made sleeping difficult. Zach had insisted she eat at least a few bites of the pot roast, carrots and potatoes his mother had made for them. The warm meal had given her the energy she needed and she'd finally fallen asleep. Julie glanced at the black digital clock Zach had on his night table. She pulled the blankets to her chin. Three o'clock.

The sound of a hacking cough made her

forget the blankets and rush to her daughter's room. "Are you all right?" she whispered, trying not to alarm Emmie. It was hard to imagine that such a deep, heavy cough could emerge from such a little girl. "Here, sweetheart, this will help." Julie reached for the glass of water on the end table. Her hand visibly shook and a good amount of water spilled onto the carpet.

Zach walked into the room dressed in black FBI gear. Looking as if he was ready to take on the world, she remembered his heroism and bravery back at her home in Washington. But why was he dressed this way now? Was something happening?

Zach turned his gaze to Julie and raised an eyebrow. "Is everything okay?" he asked quietly.

"Just a minute, sweetheart," Julie whispered as she faced her daughter. "I'll be right back." Grabbing Zach's wrist she led him into the hallway. "I'm worried about her cough."

"Did you give her more cough medicine?" Zach asked, raking a hand through his dark hair. In his other hand, he held the FBI cell phone. He had no right looking this good. Not now.

"No, but since we're all awake, I think I will."

He pulled Julie close and gave her a quick hug. "She'll be all right," he whispered. He lifted her chin and his gaze met hers. "Let's give the medicine time to work, okay?"

Julie nodded and took a deep breath. "You're right."

"It's in the kitchen. I'll get it and be right back."

She loved his levelheaded, calm approach to life. His assurance was just what she needed. She walked back into the room and sat on the edge of the bed. Julie adjusted the covers for Emmie and the doll Zach had given her.

"She's beautiful." Julie smiled and touched the doll's hand.

Emmie coughed again. "Prince Charming gave her to me." She smiled, her eyes filled with undeniable joy.

"I know," Julie whispered, caressing Emmie's hair. "That's what makes her . . . so special."

Zach returned to the room holding the bottle of cough medicine. The phone was clipped snugly against the loose waistband of his sweats. "Here," he said, nodding to Julie.

Before Emmie could protest, Julie slipped the cough syrup into her mouth.

"Ew!" Emmie grimaced.

"I'm sorry, but you need the cough medicine."

Emmie sighed dramatically before coughing again. "I'm cold."

"Here, let's pull the blankets up a little higher." Julie arranged the comforter around her daughter and gave her a hug. "That should help you feel warmer." Julie listened as Emmie said her prayers. "Now get some rest. Good night, Emmie."

" 'Night, Mommy."

Zach helped Julie to her feet. "Come on," he said quietly as he led her into the hallway. "No sense in going back to bed. Let's go downstairs." He raked a hand through his hair. "I need to fill you in on a *situation,*" he said quietly.

"Oh?" Her heart skipped a beat. Julie knew that look in his eyes. Something was wrong.

Guiding Julie down the stairway before him, Zach said a quick silent prayer. He needed God's hand to be in the mix tonight, more than ever before.

Julie stopped on a step and turned to face him. "What is it, Zach?"

"I have to fill you in on some new information." He'd been running surveillance every twenty minutes. A gnawing premonition sat heavily in his gut. "Come on, let's get downstairs."

When they got to the bottom of the stairs, he gazed into her blue eyes and drew a deep breath. He needed to tell her how much he loved her, before it was too late. "Julie —"

An ominous click echoed through the house as the few lights that had been on went off, throwing the home into total darkness.

"Julie, we have to move. Now."

"What? Why?"

"Trust me." He led her down the darkened hallway to the kitchen.

"Wh-what's wrong?" she whispered.

He reached for his infrared binoculars. "The investigation isn't over yet like we thought." He scanned the area outside. Taking Julie's hand, he led her away from standing directly in front of the floor-to-ceiling windows.

"But, I thought you arrested Nick. Is . . . is he back?" The sound of her shaky voice broke his heart.

"Hold on, Julie," Zach said quietly. He adjusted the focus on the binoculars and pulled the cell phone from his waistband. He hit a speed dial key. "Marshall here," he said when he heard Castlerock's out-of-breath greeting.

"What's up, Zach?" John's voice drifted in and out of the static-filled connection. "You in trouble?"

"Affirmative. I've got two, maybe three operatives moving in on the ranch. They've cut the power to the house." He held his arm out to Julie and brought her to him. She moved into his embrace. Zach was struck by the natural instinct to hold her close. "When's your ETA?"

"This storm's slowing us down." John gave the word for the team to double-time it. "Half an hour. Will that be soon enough?"

"Negative. I'll have to handle this on my own until you get here. They're at the east end of the property and my guess is they won't wait thirty minutes. Copy?"

"Roger that. Listen, Zach, we have new evidence —"

Silence. The garbled connection ended. Zach turned to Julie, who stared wide-eyed at him.

"What's happening?" she asked. "Is it Nick?"

"No, but a couple of his associates out for revenge, I'd guess." Zach retrieved a key hidden in a drawer. He opened a locked cabinet high on the wall in a little room off the kitchen. "You ever handle a gun?" he asked, pulling a couple of fully loaded

326

firearms from the rack.

"A gun?"

"Yeah. Ever handle one?" he repeated, praying she'd say yes.

"For a couple of semesters . . . in college. I took a course at the police station during my freshman year. Tiff insisted I come along with her —"

"You did?" Zach drew a deep breath of relief and pressed a compact .40 millimeter automatic into Julie's hand. She swallowed and stared down at the weapon. He gently tipped her head up until their eyes met. He needed Julie to realize the seriousness of what was happening. "It's got a full clip, and the safety's on. Understand?"

"Yes." She swallowed. "I know how it works."

Zach took a moment to study the beautiful, sweet woman at his side. She was a sight to behold. A beautiful blonde — holding a loaded weapon and wearing FBI gear.

"Come on." He hated having to place her in harm's way. "I'll give you a quick refresher course." He took one more look out the window with his night-vision binoculars. "We have to move. Now, Julie. My guess is . . . we have ten minutes at the most."

"Okay. We have to get Emmie." Julie swallowed and gathered all her strength. She said a silent prayer. "Tell me what to do."

"Follow me and stay low. Keep away from the windows." He guided her with a steady hand on the small of her back.

"Where are we going?"

"We'll get Emmie first. Then I'm taking you both to the safest room in the house — the basement. I had a room built specifically just in case something like this went down."

Within three minutes, Zach had a soundly sleeping Emmie wrapped in warm blankets and placed on a mattress in a makeshift, fortified bedroom in the basement. She still held the doll in her arms. Apparently, the cough medicine had knocked her out. Maybe the kid wouldn't remember any of this. If they were lucky.

Raking a hand through his hair, he knelt next to Julie and checked his watch again. A couple of minutes was all he could spare. He hoped he had even *that* long. For the next two minutes, Zach gave Julie another quick refresher course on how to fire and reload her weapon. He stowed a few more clips of ammo in her hands praying she'd never have to use them.

Taking off the safety on her gun and hoping she'd remember everything he told her, he met her gaze in the unlit basement. "I've got to go," he whispered. "If anyone but me comes through this door . . . shoot to kill. No questions. If you don't, if you hesitate for even one second . . . they'll kill you both. You got that?"

"I . . . understand." She nodded her head. "Do your job, Zach. End this evil. And come back to us." Julie surprised him with a quick, tender kiss.

He noted the look of determination in her blue eyes. Did she have any clue as to what a strong, courageous woman she'd become? She was as brave as any person he'd ever known. If Julie *did* have to use the gun, he wouldn't be around to know it. He'd put himself in the line of fire before he'd let *anyone* get to them.

"Any questions?" he asked, knowing they had no time to spare.

"No. I'll be waiting for you." She ran a hand along his jaw.

"I'm sorry I have to put you and Emmie through this. I'd do anything to change things . . . if I could." Cupping his hand on her face, he took one last look. Would he live to tell her how much he loved her, how he always had? How he loved the strong woman she'd become.

"Remember everything I said." He cleared his throat and prepared himself for the battle ahead.

He walked out of the concrete bunker inside the basement and shut the heavy door behind him. The cold metallic sound of the metal bolt reverberated through the cellar. Zach steeled his emotions in preparation for what lay ahead. Would Julie be able to handle the gun? Would she be okay in the confined space? He prayed her need to protect Emmie would keep her claustrophobia at bay.

Zach raced up the stairs and implemented the plan he'd rehearsed over and over in his mind in case a scenario like this presented itself. Two agents were missing. He would trust no one. As far as he was concerned — he was on his own. But this time, he *knew* he had God with him.

Jesus, be with Julie and her little girl. Protect them from what's going down tonight.

And . . . if You have an extra minute, watch my back.

SEVENTEEN

Tracking his prey soundlessly in the night was what Zach Marshall did best. Could his luck hold out one more time? He turned to the right and spotted two figures standing by a pine tree.

Zach took cover behind one of the larger trees. Adrenaline pulsed through every cell in his body as he confirmed one of the men as his former best friend and partner in SEAL Team Six, and the Bureau. *Tomasino.*

His gut knotted in anguish over the traitorous posture of someone who'd once been a close, trusted friend. As if sensing his presence, the former agent scanned the area where Zach crouched behind the cover of a tree.

"What is it?" the other man asked in a thick Russian accent. Zach recognized Yuri's unmistakable voice. If the man in charge was here, who else was out there hiding?

As Zach watched from his hidden vantage

point, Tommy held his hand up to silence Yuri. Soundlessly, Zach moved to a wider tree. Not the *world's largest spruce tree,* but it would do.

Focus, Marshall.

He would use the element of surprise and make them come to him. It would only take thirty seconds for Tomasino to find him. Maybe less. Zach would do anything to divert them away from the house. Away from Julie and her daughter. Glancing at his watch his gut tightened with the realization that it would be a full fifteen minutes before the team arrived.

The cold, steel barrel of a semiautomatic weapon pressed hard against the back of his head. Zach froze and swallowed hard. Good. His plan had worked. They'd come to him. *Now what?*

"Drop the rifle, Marshall, and get out in the open so we can both see you."

Zach slowly let go of the firearm and let it drop a few feet from where he stood. Holding his hands up in mock defeat, Zach turned to face Tomasino. The man who'd trained with him at Coronado, bunked in the same room. His former partner, the Christian buddy who'd told him more than once to start praying again and get right with God. Where had his friend gone wrong?

Tomasino grinned and trained his weapon higher, pressing it against Zach's temple. "How you doing, buddy?"

Zach gave a quick laugh. "I've been better."

"Yeah." Tommy chuckled. "I'm sure you have."

"Enough talk. Toss the pistol out of your shoulder holster," Yuri commanded from several feet away, waving his rifle at Zach.

Zach feigned a smile and cautiously made a move to lose the Glock. That would leave him with only one weapon. The .38 snub nose with the trigger filed down so it wouldn't catch when he pulled it out of the holster in his back waistband.

Should he risk losing the gun he held in his hand, or make a move now? The rifle was still close enough on the ground to reach for if there should be a distraction. He visualized a couple of scenarios to execute a method of escape. If there could be one in this mess.

"Careful, Zach," Tommy cautioned. "Lose the gun."

He knows me too well. Got to think of something different.

Reluctantly, Zach tossed the gun to the ground. He calculated the time it would take to reach for the .38 still hidden in his waistband. Fewer than ten seconds to grab it and fire with any accuracy. He had to stretch this situation out to buy some time. A few more minutes and the team would be in place.

Tommy took a step closer and kicked the discarded weapon several more feet away. He stood directly in the path between Zach and Yuri. Something a former SEAL or agent would never do.

You must be slipping, buddy. That's a no-no. Or have you forgotten?

Tommy gave Zach a *look.* In less than an instant, Zach knew what would go down. His senses heightened. Tommy turned and fired his weapon at Yuri, hitting him twice. One shot in the arm, forcing him to drop his weapon and another in his leg, making sure he couldn't escape.

Pulling the snub nose from his back waist holster, Zach trained it on Yuri and then on Tommy. He could trust no one.

Yuri wasn't dead. Not yet anyway.

Tommy had some major explaining to do before Zach would lower his weapon.

"Hey, Zach, calm down, buddy. It's *me.* I'm one of the good guys, remember? You don't think I'd actually be a part of that," he said, quietly indicating with a nod of his head the terrorist bleeding on the white snow. "Do you?"

"Drop your rifle, Tommy," Zach ordered. "And quit calling me *buddy.*"

"Okay. Whatever you say." He tossed his weapon to the other side of the clearing and raised his hands. "But I think you might regret —"

"Don't make a move . . . or you both die." A woman's voice reverberated through the small clearing. "Looks like I hit the jackpot. Drop your weapon," she added, nodding to Zach.

Her distinct accent made Zach's gut tighten. He exchanged glances with Tomasino then slowly dropped his gun, his last hope for survival, to the ground.

But he hadn't trained at Coronado for nothing. Hand-to-hand combat, the element of strength over his opponent, was still an option. If he went down, it wouldn't be without a good fight.

His thoughts filled with the image of Julie. Scenes from the past few weeks played in his mind sending a wave of deep love for her through his heart.

Moving closer, the female shooter trained her weapon on Zach. He noted the curly gray hair peeking out from under the ski mask that fully covered her face.

"Who wants to go first?" she asked. The

sound of a twig snapping filled the cold night air. The woman glanced toward the almost indiscernible noise.

The moment gave Zach the opportunity he needed to retrieve his weapon. In a split second, he rolled across the snow for his gun and fired with deadly accuracy at the gray-haired woman. In a matter of seconds, she lay dead.

The team arrived a moment later as Zach stood with his weapon still drawn. He kept his gun trained on Tomasino while the team surrounded the two fallen criminals.

"I've been undercover, Zach," Agent Tomasino said, holding his hands up in front of him.

"It's true, Zach. Believe it." Agent Sarah Robbins silently moved past him holding her arm. Blood trickled down her wrist. She grimaced in pain. "I've been briefed. You will be, too." She leaned against the tree, still clutching her arm.

"Sarah?" Zach kept his eyes on Tomasino. "You've been shot."

"It's nothing," she managed.

John Castlerock and other members of the team joined them. "Agent Tomasino's been undercover, Zach," John said, heading toward Sarah. "It's over."

"Anything else I need to know?" Zach asked.

"Negative. But we'll all be debriefed," John answered.

Taking another glance in Tommy's direction, Zach dragged in a deep breath and lowered his gun. Muttering under his breath, he pulled out his cell phone and made a quick call to Luke, who answered on the first ring.

Sarah had passed out sitting against the tree. "John, I've got my brother on the line. He's a doctor and can help until the chopper arrives." He handed the phone to John.

John Castlerock nodded and took the phone. "Good." He knelt at Sarah's side. "As soon as she comes to . . . I'm going to read her the riot act."

"You'll have to stand in line," Tomasino muttered. "She almost got us both killed back in Seattle. I was undercover with Yuri when she almost ran into us."

"Is she going to be all right?" Zach asked, nodding in Sarah's direction.

John nodded. "Think so." He examined her arm. "Looks like a flesh wound. But there's a lot of blood."

"Who's the woman?" Zach asked, nodding to the female who'd tried to execute him.

"Time to find out." John nodded to Zach. "Go ahead."

Zach slowly pulled off the woman's ski mask. His heartbeat nearly tripled. He turned to John. "*Yuri's wife.* Katya. I thought she was still in Russia."

Katya Kostoff had headed up the biological warfare plans, often testing her formulas of death on the country's citizens, killing tens of thousands of innocent people and children. Zach stood. In disgust he tossed her cap to the ground.

He couldn't remember a time, even in this horrendous investigation, when he was *glad* that someone was dead. But he was. God help him. The world was a better place without the likes of that sick woman.

Tomasino muttered under his breath. "Yuri never mentioned she was in the country. You think *she* was the woman in the van? The one who shot up your windshield?"

"Probably," Zach answered, annoyed that Tomasino had known his every move. She fit the size of the woman he'd seen in the van. Zach retrieved his rifle then turned to Tomasino. "If *you* were with Yuri the day she was in the van . . . who was the guy driving?"

They both turned to John, who'd been

listening to the conversation. "We still have a loose cannon out there," John muttered from Sarah's side. He ordered the team into position. "Listen, Zach, I've sent two agents inside your place to go over the interior for explosives. We're not taking any chances. We'll find this guy."

"I'm going in." Not waiting for a reply, Zach double-timed it back to the house, scanning the grounds and the entrances to his home — the wide front porch and double-door entry, the side door, the doorway to the kitchen at the back of the house. He rushed inside his home to be with Julie.

Jesus, please keep Julie and her daughter safe.

Keeping in the shadows as he ran into the house, Zach prayed again.

What do you say, God. You still have my back?

Julie held the gun in the palm of her hand, staring as if it would go off at the slightest move.

Swallowing hard, she took in the details of the bunker-like walls inside the room. Small drops of perspiration beaded lightly on her forehead.

She felt as if she'd been transported back in time to her grandparents' farm when she was six years old. It was the summer her dad had been away in Europe. She'd wandered away from the farmhouse and walked into an old shed she'd never seen before. Closing her eyes, Julie saw in full detail the walls of the old shed and the large door that had somehow locked her inside.

She remembered with vivid clarity how scared she'd been. She remembered wishing somehow, that her daddy would come to get her. Then the sinking realization that he wouldn't come. Couldn't come. In her desperation to get out, Julie had found a rake and managed to lift the high latch from its locked position.

Pushing the door open, she'd run as fast as she could back to the farmhouse, telling no one about what had happened. When her mom, frantic with worry, had questioned her she said only that she'd been lost. Ever since, she'd been claustrophobic.

Julie opened her eyes and turned to her daughter. It seemed like an hour since Zach left, warning her to shoot first and ask questions later.

"If anyone but me comes through this door, shoot to kill. No questions. If you don't, if you hesitate for even one second . . . they'll kill you both."

The sound of muffled gunfire filtered its

way into her tiny prison, and filled every cell in her body with the absolute knowledge that she would do whatever it took to protect Emmie.

Maybe she should take Emmie out of the small room. Maybe the intruders Zach had referred to knew she'd be hiding in the damp, dark little space. What if something had happened to Zach? How would she know? Julie forced herself to breathe slowly before a panic attack took hold.

"God, please . . . let him be okay. Put Your hand on his back and guide him, Father. Protect him from evil. In Jesus' name."

Standing, she held the gun low against her thigh. With her back to Emmie, Julie walked to the door and leaned her head against it, straining to hear something. Anything.

Silence.

How long should I wait? What if Zach needs me?

If it were just her, she would've been outside where she could help. Taking a step back from the door, she took in the gray concrete of the walls, the pipes and wiring above her in the ceiling. Okay she reasoned, her pantry at home was much smaller than this room. And she'd spent an hour in there organizing canned goods.

But you're not hiding inside the pantry.

Her hands grew clammy and she started to tremble. Wiping the back of her free hand across her brow, Julie shook off the suffocating feeling that surrounded her and drew another quick breath. God would get her through this somehow.

"Mommy?"

Startled, Julie bit her lip to stifle a scream and almost dropped the gun. Turning, she hid the weapon behind her back and walked the few yards to her daughter.

"Emmie." She sat on the edge of the makeshift bed, placing the gun safely and quietly on the floor. "How do you feel, sweetheart?"

"Oh, Mommy." Emmie smiled sleepily. "This is . . . the funnest day *ever!*"

Did her daughter just say this was *fun?* Maybe she had a fever and was delirious.

Julie cleared her throat. "Fun?"

Emmie nodded. "I'm so glad we came here. Thank you, Mommy." Emmie sighed, turned to hug her doll, and then drifted off peacefully as if she were sleeping in the bed of a princess.

Tucking the blankets around her daughter, Julie was thankful for Emmie's optimism. It was just what she needed to get through this ordeal. Julie silently thanked God for using her daughter to calm her own fears.

Suddenly the walls didn't feel as if they were closing in on her. With God's help, she'd make it out of the small space and any other situations she might face in her life.

A noise from directly outside the room had her adrenaline rushing in a heartbeat. *Someone's out there.* Turning briefly to make sure Emmie was still sleeping, Julie gripped the gun in both hands as if she were on the firing range. A light knock on the door made her want to scream.

"Julie . . . it's me. Open up."

Zach? She swallowed hard. What if he was being forced to get her to open the door? What if opening the door . . . was the *last* thing he wanted her to do?

Oh, we should've come up with some kind of code or something.

"It's over. Everything's secured." He knocked again. "Julie? Open up. It's okay."

Could she believe him?

"We got all three of them, Jewels." She heard his low chuckle through the thick door. "I just heard on my earpiece that everyone has been neutralized. Now . . . let me in so I can kiss you senseless."

Julie shook her head from side to side. "How do I know someone's not . . . making you say that?"

"What? That I want to kiss you?"

343

"You know what I mean." How could he joke at a time like this?

"Julie." Even through the heavy door, Zach sounded tired. Or was it something else. Maybe someone had a gun to his head.

"I'm serious, Zach." Her fingers shook as they clasped the gun. Her arm ached from the death grip she maintained on the weapon.

"Okay, Julie. Ask me something only I would know. When I give you the answer, you'll know it's all right." A second passed before he spoke again. "Listen, Jewels, the team's here. They've surrounded the property. We've taken down the bad guys."

Julie turned to make sure that Emmie was still asleep. "What were you wearing when we had those . . . photos taken, you know, when I almost got us lost? And what was I wearing? And what was the name of the town?" she added for assurance.

Zach chuckled and she pictured his slow, crooked grin and the gleam of mischief in his deep blue eyes. "A Stetson, a shotgun . . . and a smile," he answered, his husky voice almost turning her into a pile of mush on the floor.

Julie closed her eyes and leaned against the door. Just thinking of how good he'd looked that day, wearing a Stetson, a shotgun and a smile . . .

Shaking off the image, she cleared her throat. "Okay, now answer the other questions."

"Will there be . . . a reward if I get 'em all right?" Zach teased.

Julie smiled. "There could be."

"Anyone ever tell you . . . you'd make a great agent?"

Julie laughed lightly. "Just answer my question."

"You were wearing . . . a cute little outfit with a pink feather boa. Oh, and a killer smile, too." He chuckled deep and low. "And that city we finally made it to was Port Townsend. Now . . . let me in, woman, or I'll break down the door."

"Julie?" Zach leaned his palms against the steel door and waited. For someone who suffered from claustrophobia, she sure was taking her time. "Are you letting me in or what?"

Didn't she know he'd never compromise her location?

Tonight he'd hold her in his arms as if they had a real future. Tomorrow, he would have to say goodbye. She'd never consider marrying into this lifestlye. Especially after the night they'd just experienced.

The door slowly creaked open. Zach wanted to push it in and pull her into his arms. But he didn't want to frighten her. She probably still had the Glock in her hand. Was she all right or was there someone else in there, too? Beatrice? Zach steeled himself as a sense of apprehension filled his gut. The Brit was still missing.

He dropped his hands to his side and waited. Julie stood before him, gun drawn firmly in both hands, feet spread in the classic firing position. "Are you sure you're alone?" She peeked into the hallway then lowered the weapon.

"Yeah, the place is secure." He scanned the interior of the bunker. Except for Emmie, who was asleep on the bed, they were the only ones there. "It's just me." He couldn't help the instant smile that spread across his face.

"Please, take this." She carefully put the safety back on the weapon, and handed the gun to him. Zach checked the gun then stowed it in a jacket pocket.

"My pleasure." He pulled Julie to him and held her close. If only they could be together forever. As husband and wife, living a life together on the ranch he loved.

But she'd never want the life he led. Plans had already been put in place to start an undercover operation with the ranch as a working cover. His brothers would be part of the covert operation, too. Zach would have the best of both worlds — the excitement of the Special Ops life, and the peaceful life of horse ranching that he loved. But he wouldn't have Julie.

God, I felt Your presence with me tonight. Thanks for renewing my faith, and bringing me back to You. Especially at Christmas. Thank You for keeping Julie and her daughter safe, and for helping me to be there for them. If You could just grant me one more favor . . . make Julie my wife.

Zach slowly released her from his embrace. His gaze rested on her face. She looked remarkably calm. Peaceful. *Are you all right?* Familiar blue eyes responded to his silent question. *Yes.* He reached out and pulled the black knitted cap from her head. Silky, long blond hair cascaded past her shoulders.

Fisting his hand in her hair, Zach pulled Julie to him. The kiss they shared left no doubt of the deep love they felt for each other.

Would they go their separate ways . . . again?

Or would God give them one *more* gift for Christmas?

■ ■ ■ ■

"You warm enough?" Zach asked, holding
the leather reins on the horses and turning
to Julie. The blizzard had finally ended while
she and Emmie had recuperated. It was
snowing lightly, and he didn't want either
of them catching a chill.

"Yes, I'm perfect." Julie smiled and
squeezed his arm.

Zach whistled the two horses to a trot.
The jingle bells on the old-fashioned sleigh
rang as they sped along the snow on one of
Silver Lake, Montana's most beautiful white
Christmases in recent history. In a few
minutes, they'd arrive at the main house of
Marshall Ranch, where the whole family
gathered every year for Christmas.

Zach had many reasons this year to cel-
ebrate the birth of Christ. He was amazed
at the joy that filled his heart, as if he were
a child again at Christmastime. His faith
had been restored. Zach's heart was light
and carefree. The peace that surpassed all
understanding filled him with a sweetness
he hadn't known since childhood.

His family couldn't wait to meet Julie and
her little girl. Zach knew his mom would
adore the child. He turned to Emmie who

sat between him and Julie. She held her new doll protectively in her arms. If the happy smile on her face was any indication, the hooded, red wool coat she wore appeared to be warm enough even in the cold night air.

Zach turned his gaze to Julie. She wore a black wool coat and a plaid Christmas shawl that she'd draped over her head and shoulders. When she'd walked down the spiral stairs of his home in a long, black velvet dress with a red ribbon belt, his heart filled with love. He'd never seen her looking more beautiful. He wanted to see her coming down those stairs in his home always, for every Christmas to come.

Long blond hair, in contrast to the dress, fell in soft waves around her face and across her back. He'd remember the image of Julie forever over the years as he lived his life and she lived hers. Zach had already resigned himself to the fact that after the holidays, Julie would head back to the rain forest of Washington and the Inn at Shadow Lake.

"Is that the house, around the bend?" Julie nodded toward the well-lit log home in the distance. "The white Christmas lights are lovely."

"Yeah, we're almost there."

"I can't wait to see the home you grew up

in, Zach." She turned to him and smiled. "It's beautiful."

Seeing the smile that lit her soft, beautiful face warmed him. He bent his head to give her a quick kiss under the brim of his black Stetson.

A few minutes later, he guided the horses into the long driveway and wrapped the reins around a fence post by the front entrance of the log home which his parents had affectionately named *The Ponderosa,* after the ranch on the old television show. "Come on, Emmie, I'll help you down first," he said, jumping off the sleigh. He lifted the little girl from the seat just as his mother opened the front door.

"You made it," she said, standing in the doorway. "I'm so glad." She smiled and turned to Zach's dad, who placed an arm around her shoulder.

"Are you . . . Grandma and Grandpa Marshall?" Holding the doll in her arms, Emmie ran the several feet to Zach's parents and gave them a hug.

"Yes. Yes, we are." His mom held Emmie close. "Oh, you sweet child." She wiped a tear from her eye. "Merry Christmas," she whispered. Zach knew the emotions his mother experienced at the sight of Emmie and the feel of a warm hug from a sweet little girl. His heart filled with happiness, knowing how God would bless his family with Emmie's presence this Christmas. If only it could be forever.

"Merry Christmas," Emmie responded.

"Merry Christmas, Emmie," his mother managed, tears brimming in her eyes.

"We're so glad you're feeling better, Emmie." His father knelt down to be at eye level with her. He patted her on the head and smiled.

"Thank you very much," Emmie said with a smile.

His mother reached out and gently took Emmie's outstretched hand in hers. "Come in and have some Christmas cookies with us."

Zach walked over to the other side of the sleigh and helped Julie down. Hand in hand, they walked to the front door. "Mom, Dad . . . I'd like you to meet Julie."

"Merry Christmas." Julie smiled. "It's so good to meet you."

"Nice to meet you, too," his dad answered, a big smile on his face. He affectionately slapped Zach on the back.

"Come on in, and get out of the cold. It's so good to have you here." His mom motioned for them to step inside.

After a few minutes, they removed their

coats and settled in the great room by a roaring fire. His mom served hot chocolate in designer Christmas mugs. A vast array of his mom's traditional homemade holiday cookies filled a couple of platters on the coffee table.

Half an hour later, Luke walked into the room from the foyer and greeted everyone. Concerned, Zach walked over, wanting to check on Agent Sarah Robbins's condition. She'd looked a little pale when he and Julie had visited her at the hospital.

Luke strode over to Emmie. "Hi." He knelt down next to her while he unbuttoned his overcoat. "You look like you're feeling better. Still taking that cough medicine I gave you?"

"Yes." She nodded her head. "But I don't like it."

"Good job." Luke chuckled then stood. He gave his mother a hug, shook hands with his father and gave Julie a hug.

"How is Sarah?" Zach asked when they were alone.

"Fine. But I thought seriously about sedating her so she'd sit still a few minutes. I wanted to check her incision. See how it's healing and whether the sutures were still intact." Luke placed his coat in the closet then turned to Zach. "I never met a more stubborn woman." He ran a hand along the back of his neck. "I called her folks. They insisted on coming out to stay with her for Christmas. Understandable." He shook his head. "She was furious. Didn't want them to worry. I thought she was going to cuff me." He chuckled. "Fat chance of that."

Zach studied his brother. "Sounds just like her."

"Her parents seem like real nice folks. How'd they ever manage to produce a daughter that feisty?"

Zach laughed. "Beats me."

Julie cuddled closer to Zach. She couldn't have imagined a more perfect Christmas, sitting close to the man she loved, under the Christmas star, riding in a horse-drawn sleigh over the most pristine snow she'd ever seen. He'd asked his mother to keep an eye on Emmie as she slept and had whisked Julie away on the sleigh.

"Okay." She smiled. "Where are we going?"

"You'll see." A few minutes later, they were sitting outside in the sleigh, riding toward the eastern sky where the moon rose over the horizon and glistened across the freshly fallen snow.

The moon lit what looked like hundreds

of miles of snow-covered terrain. "It's so beautiful here." Julie turned to him and smiled. Her heart filled with joy. "No wonder you wanted to come back."

She understood a lot about Zach since meeting his family. He resembled his father. They had the same deep blue-gray eyes. Zach and his brothers were tall, with broad-shouldered builds similar to their father's.

Both Luke and Jake had their mother's lighter coloring. A touch of blond along with the brown, and their eyes were a lighter shade of blue. Still, the resemblance was uncanny.

His mom was a beautiful woman, honey-blond hair, trim, and about five foot six inches tall. She'd welcomed Julie and Emmie with open arms. Emmie had taken to her immediately.

Julie couldn't have asked for a more blessed Christmas. She thanked God again for his saving grace and for the many blessings He'd given to her, her family and to Zach's family, too.

"Happy?" Zach placed an arm around her shoulders.

"Yes." She snuggled against him. "I can't remember ever being this peaceful, Zach." She brushed a tear away and smiled.

"What? You crying *again?*" he teased, easing the horses to a stop by a cluster of tall pine trees at the top of a hill.

"It's the cold air," she answered with a laugh.

Zach turned around in his seat and took both her ungloved hands in his, warming them for a moment. With his thumb, he tipped back the black Stetson he wore. His eyes glistened in the moonlight of the starry Christmas night. Julie's heart skipped a beat as he bent to kiss her. She welcomed his touch with pure joy.

Reluctantly, Zach slowly broke away. "Julie, I love you." He took a deep, shaky breath. "I want you in my life. Every day. Every night." He kissed her again and gently nuzzled her neck, running his hands through her hair.

"Zach, I love you, too." Julie had to remind herself to breathe. The only sound she heard was the beating of her heart and Zach's sweet words.

"Does this look familiar?"

He took a tiny jeweler's box from his coat pocket. It was the ring he'd proposed with so long ago. "Marry me, Julie. Come to Montana and live with me as husband and wife. We'll fill our home with happiness and . . . a brother and sister or two for Emmie." He chuckled and cupped her face in his hands. "I promise to love you forever and take you on the greatest adventures of your life." He smiled a slow crooked grin, yet his eyes filled with a hint of sadness.

Julie felt as if her heart had stopped beating. Taking a deep breath, she placed a hand to her lips. She wanted to wake up next to Zach Marshall every morning and live a lifetime of adventures. "Yes, Zach, I'll marry you and live here with you on the ranch." She ran a hand along his strong, chiseled jaw. "I love you. I always have. I don't think I ever stopped loving you."

"Julie." He pulled her to him and kissed her gently, possessively. It was a kiss filled with promises for a lifetime of love. "What about your family and the life you've built back in Washington?" he asked. "Can you leave all that behind? And you have to know . . . I'm involved with Special Ops now, more than ever. I can't tell you the details yet. Is that the life you want? Are you sure?"

Julie nodded. "Yes, Zach. With you by my side, I *am* sure."

He ran a hand through her hair. "What about the inn? I think you should keep it. You love it so much, I'd hate to see you lose it."

"Zach." She laughed easily. "Mom and

Dad want to buy a partnership in the resort. Dad's bored with early retirement, and Mom can't wait to run the gift shop. Between the two of them and Beatrice, I'm certain that everything will run smoothly."

She smiled, thinking of Beatrice's outrage that the Bureau thought she was a spy. Her broken leg was mending nicely. If it hadn't been for the agents who'd gone to *visit* Beatrice, she might not be in such good shape. They'd driven her to the hospital, interrogating her all the way, after they heard her calling for help from the kitchen floor on which she'd slipped. Julie almost laughed out loud remembering the way Beatrice had told the story.

"What about Emmie?" he asked, holding her face in his hands.

Julie smiled and took his hands in hers. "Haven't you noticed?" She felt her eyes fill with tears of happiness.

"What?" he whispered, feathering kisses along her jaw.

"Emmie loves you just as much as I do," she whispered.

"I love you, too, Julie." Zach chuckled. "You've made me the happiest man on earth. You, and God . . . and Emmie."

They kissed again and Zach gently placed the jeweler's box in her hands. Opening it,

Julie gasped. An exquisite round solitaire diamond set in platinum sparkled in the moonlight. "Zach, it's beautiful!"

"Let me put it on your finger." He removed it from the box and placed it on the ring finger of her left hand. His gaze met hers. "It looks perfect. I remembered this ring was still up in the attic and I've been thinking about it since Thanksgiving."

"Thanksgiving?" Julie felt her eyes misting over yet again.

"Yeah. I wanted to ask you then," Zach admitted.

"You did?" Julie's heart reeled at the sweet nature of what Zach had just revealed.

"I decided I couldn't ask you. Not then. You still didn't know the truth yet about why I was really at the inn." He drew a deep breath. "Looking back, I guess God really knew what He was doing." He gave her a wink and a smile.

"Yes, Zach. He surprised us both on our journey back to each other." She laughed lightly. "I guess He had a different road map than we did."

"A map, huh?" Zach laughed. "I guess He did." With one arm, he held her close and kissed her. With his free hand, he grabbed the reins and cracked the horses into motion. The quarter horses broke into a gallop and the sleigh sped down the snow-covered hill.

"I love you, Zach."

"I love you, too, Julie. Always have . . . always will."

Julie was thankful for all she had. With God to guide her path, she'd grown into a strong woman who no longer wanted or needed to live in a misty cocoon of comfort.

Zach had returned to the faith of his childhood, and the old happiness she'd seen in his eyes was back.

Emmie's prayers for a "Prince Charming for Mommy" had been answered. Julie's prayers had been answered, too.

Zach was the loving husband she yearned for, and the good father to her little girl she'd prayed for all these years. Turning to her new fiancé, Julie's heart filled with happiness.

She couldn't wait to begin a lifetime of adventures with Zach Marshall — her first love.

Dear Reader,

While on a business trip to Seattle, my husband, Richard, and I decided to take a drive along the Pacific Coast and visit the port towns along the way. To our delight, we found the beauty of the Olympic National Park and "The World's Largest Spruce Tree."

At that moment in the beautiful misty rainforest setting of the Pacific Northwest, the romantic suspense reunion story of Zach Marshall and Julie Anderson was born.

I hope you have enjoyed reading *The Inn at Shadow Lake* as much as I enjoyed writing it. For me, Julie and Zach will always live on in my heart.

It is also my hope that their story has blessed and encouraged you, and that their message of faith and love will live on in your hearts, too.

Best regards and blessings,
Janet Edgar

Dear Reader,

I was honored to be the one who made "the call" and bought Janet Edgar's first book, and was very thankful that she waited until *after* we were off the phone before the celebratory screaming began. We were both thrilled when she joined the Steeple Hill family, and looked forward to working together on *The Inn at Shadow Lake* and many other books. Sadly, Janet passed away on May 17, 2005, after a valiant battle with cancer.

Janet was the kind of person who would send cards "just because" — even using seasonal e-mail stationery and images to make people smile. Her delight in her colleagues within the writing community and her dedication to her own writing were amazing. Janet will be greatly missed, but her loving spirit will always be remembered.

Diane Diety

QUESTIONS FOR DISCUSSION

1. What first made you pick up this book? Was it the title? The author? The cover image? The copy on the back of the book?

2. Zach's faith was shattered when he lost his wife and young daughter in a tragic accident. It's through Julie's loving example that he slowly begins rebuilding his faith. Is his faith journey believable? Why or why not?

3. Julie has to forgive Zach for several reasons and she does so, without hesitation. Would you forgive Zach? Why or why not?

4. Julie and Zach's past relationship ended when Zach proposed, but Julie turned him down. However, Zach didn't wait for her explanation and rode out of her life, regretting his hasty actions for years. Have

365

you ever acted rashly and later regretted it? What was the situation? What was the impact on your relationship?

5. Several people are under suspicion in this story — Julie, Nick, the housekeeper, the missing FBI agent — and Zach doesn't know whom to trust. Did *you* know who Zach should trust during the course of the story?

6. Emmie isn't a replacement for Zach's lost daughter, but a welcome addition into his life. And Emmie, like her mother, helps Zach heal and move on. Do you have someone in your life who came along in a time of need and helped you through? Did you ever thank that person for the blessing they are in your life?

7. Everyone in this story has someone to confide in: Julie has Beatrice, Zach has John. Who do you confide in? How long have you known this person? Where did you meet?

8. Were the secondary characters necessary to the story? Were the villains realistic?

9. What will be your most vivid memories

of this book? What lessons about life, love and faith did you learn from this story?

10. Both Julie and Zach came from close-knit families. In what ways do you think their upbringing may have been similar? In what ways do you think it might have been different?

ABOUT THE AUTHOR

Her love for writing started in elementary school, when **Janet Edgar** saw her book report published in the school newsletter. The experience of seeing her written words in print made a powerful impact on her life. She is thankful to God that even when she was a child, He was directing her paths.

The Inn at Shadow Lake is Janet's debut book. She is thrilled to be a member of the Steeple Hill family.

Married for over thirty years to her high school sweetheart, Janet has two grown children. Prior to working full time on her writing career, she worked as a marketing coordinator, radio talk show host, "extra" on a popular daytime television series (soap opera) and elementary school teacher.

Janet served as secretary of Faith, Hope and Love, the inspirational chapter of Romance Writers of America. She has also served as newsletter editor of a local RWA chapter and is a member of several more RWA chapters throughout the United States. She is also a member of the American Christian Fiction Writers.

Janet and her husband, Richard, live in a Southern-style house in Central Ohio with two adorable little dogs, Buddy and Molly.